SILENT COURT

A Selection of Recent Titles by M. J. Trow

SILENT COURT

M. J. Trow

CRÈME de la CRIME

This first world edition published 2012
in Great Britain and the USA by
Crème de la Crime, an imprint of
SEVERN HOUSE PUBLISHERS LTD of
9–15 High Street, Sutton, Surrey, England, SM1 1DF.
Trade paperback edition first published
in Great Britain and the USA 2012.

British Library Cataloguing in Publication Data

Trow, M. J.
  Silent court. – (A Kit Marlowe historical mystery)
  1. Marlowe, Christopher, 1564-1593–Fiction. 2. Dee, John,
  1527-1608–Fiction. 3. Walsingham, Francis, Sir,
  1530?-1590–Fiction. 4. William I, Prince of Orange,
  1533-1584–Fiction. 5. Great Britain–History–
  Elizabeth, 1558-1603–Fiction. 6. Netherlands–History–
  Wars of Independence, 1556-1648–Fiction. 7. Detective and
  mystery stories.
  I. Title II. Series
  823.9'2-dc23

ISBN-13: 978-1-78029-019-5 (cased)
ISBN-13: 978-1-78029-522-0 (trade paper)

All Severn House titles are printed on acid-free paper.

Severn House Publishers support The Forest Stewardship Council [FSC],
the leading international forest certification organisation. All our titles that
are printed on Greenpeace-approved FSC-certified paper carry the FSC logo.

Typeset by Palimpsest Book Production Ltd.,
Falkirk, Stirlingshire, Scotland.
Printed and bound in Great Britain by
MPG Books Ltd., Bodmin, Cornwall.

ONE

He remembered to pull the hood over his head as the boat glided under the archway. The drips from the green-slimed stones stung like hail and the soft fingers of hanging weed stroked his face. He shivered again. All the way along the river, past Limehouse and Ratcliffe, he'd felt the raw cold of that November morning. The gilded turrets of Placentia were white with hoar frost and winter, he knew, would come early this year.

Beyond the archway, the boatmen busied themselves. The oars came upright, clear of the sluggish water and pointing to the leaden sky. He could hear the clang and thump of the shipwrights working in the yards and along the wharfs at Petty Wales. Her Majesty's yeomen in their scarlet livery saluted and escorted him, with their halberds at the slope through the barbican and up the hill.

He had always hated this place, its noise and smell. His Uncle Ned had been Lieutenant of the Tower in the reign of Good King Harry and it had left its mark. The rankness of the river gate had left his nostrils now, only to be replaced by the stink of shit from the animal pens. All very colourful of Her Majesty to own a menagerie, but she didn't have to smell the place day after day. He wondered what they were feeding the poor creatures; some of them were clearly far from well.

'Sir William's expecting you, sir,' a yeoman told him, clanking with keys and looking grim under his helmet rim.

He nodded in response, too cold to make his jaw work yet. The river's wind had bitten through his cloak, doublet and shirt into the marrow of his bones and he felt his knee click as he climbed the turn of the stair. The grey morning lit this part of the passageway and he was soon padding along the rush-strewn floor, past the oak panels that William Waad had put in to make his nest that little bit cosier. When you're Lieutenant of the Tower, you need the odd perk. It was a dour old building, with walls that sweated out the dank smell of fear. No amount of oak panelling would make it feel like home, but the man was doing his best.

'Mulled wine, Francis?' William Waad was a solid, square-shaped man, with a florid face and a curious grey curl which he combed carefully forward to hide from the world that his hairline, like the river at ebb tide, had long receded. He had the twinkling eyes and roguish smile of a favourite uncle, except that men like Francis Walsingham didn't have a favourite uncle. Not even Uncle Ned.

'I thought you'd never offer, William.' Walsingham smiled, taking the warm cup gratefully. 'Bitter on the river this morning.'

'You've come from Placentia?' Waad ushered his guest to a chair near the fire, dismissing the guard with a nod.

'I have. And I swear it gets further away every time I make the blessed journey.'

William Waad had been waiting for Walsingham for three days. He knew you couldn't hurry men like him without running the risk of calling the white-hot beam of his attention on to places perhaps it would be better kept from. After all, oak panelling didn't come cheap and it might be better if the power that was Francis Walsingham did not think about that too much. Mr Secretary Walsingham kept his own counsel and moved at a pace not used by other men. In his more poetic moments, Waad imagined Walsingham as a spider, sitting at the centre of a web that shimmered like gossamer in the morning sun but which would hold you fast in a deadly and final embrace.

Mr Secretary leaned back in the chair, letting the feeling flow back into his frozen feet as the fire cracked and whispered in the grate. He closed his eyes and let the warmth of the wine do its work. Then his eyes flashed open again and he was himself, dazzling, mercurial, a man with a job to do. 'What says Master Topcliffe?' he asked.

'You know Richard.' Waad chuckled, pouring himself a warmed goblet too. 'He always gets his man.'

Walsingham looked at the Lieutenant of the Tower. 'Oh, I have no doubt of that,' he said, 'but these are dangerous times, my dear William, and speed is of the essence. What's been tried?'

William Waad was a meticulous keeper of records, but he didn't need to consult the ledger lying on his desk. He knew Topcliffe's methods, as did Walsingham, but the man was endlessly inventive in the world of pain. Subtle methods were all very well but they were usually slow and, in this case, timing was everything. 'Beating, of course,' he said, quaffing his wine. 'The screws. Not strappado, however. You know Richard doesn't like it.'

'Too . . . Spanish?' Walsingham asked. He couldn't imagine Topcliffe objecting to a man hanging by his wrists for any other reason.

'It smacks of the Inquisition, yes.' Waad nodded. 'But I think it's a mechanical thing with him. Too many ropes and pulleys, I imagine. He believes in art, not science.'

Walsingham smiled. 'What about the rack?'

Waad shrugged. 'Waiting for you,' he said. 'Er . . . you have the warrant?' The Lieutenant of the Tower was a careful man. For years he had sat at the back of the Privy Council meetings, scratching with his quill and dipping into his ink pot. He carried nearly as many secrets in his head as Walsingham and one thing he had learned very early on was never stick your head over the parapet or somebody will blow it off. Only the Queen could give permission for the rack.

Walsingham fumbled inside his coat and produced the vellum, with its wax seal and the royal cipher. '"*Ad immo*",' he quoted from the document. Then, as an afterthought, he doubted the level of Waad's scholarship and he added, 'To the utmost.'

Waad chose to ignore the man's condescending air. Had it not come from the lips of Francis Walsingham, he would have thought it kindly meant, but with the Queen's spymaster, it was never possible to be sure how *anything* was meant. 'Shall I have a guard take you down?' he asked.

Walsingham stood up and drained his cup. 'No, no

need. I know my way. Good morning to you, William.'
He shook the man's hand and turned in the doorway. 'You
know, I like what you've done in here.' He waved to the
panelling and the tapestries. 'Very . . . homely.' And he
was gone.

'We're pretty proud of this,' Richard Topcliffe grunted in his
hoarse Derbyshire vowels. He ran his hands lovingly along
the wooden frame, letting his stubby fingers play lightly over the
gear mechanism, easing the levers. 'Francis Throckmorton,'
he said with a leer, 'allow me to introduce the Duke of Exeter's
daughter. I'm sure you two are going to get on.'

Francis Throckmorton wasn't sure how much more he could
take. His nose was broken, he was sure of that and speaking
was difficult because of his swollen lips. His right hand was
crushed, the fingers black and bloody from Topcliffe's screws
and he had no feeling at all in his right arm. He had heard
of the rack, of course, whispered of in hushed tones behind
the locked doors that had become part of his nightmare world.
The recusant priests on the road had worse tales to tell, from
high Germany where they broke men on the wheel and spurred
on their wild dogs to rape women of the true faith. And Spain,
where they strangled men with wire to the delight of the
crowd.

'This is how it works,' Topcliffe said, beaming with satisfaction. 'We're going to tie you down, the lads and I, one wrist
here –' he pointed to a corner of the frame – 'the other here.
Your ankles –' he pointed to the opposite end – 'and then . . .
and this is the beauty of it. I can operate this by myself.' And
he cranked the lever so that the planks jarred down and the
ropes creaked taut.

Throckmorton gulped, saliva and blood filling his mouth.

'Of course,' Topcliffe said, 'something's got to give. You'd
think the ropes would snap first, wouldn't you? But no, that'll
be your joints, laddie, first your arms, then your legs. By then,
of course, I think you'll be ready to have that little conversation we talked about.'

'Mother of God,' whispered Throckmorton.

'Now!' Topcliffe suddenly barked and his men dragged

Throckmorton upright, dragging him across the floor slippery with blood and lashing the ropes around his wrists.

'Stop that!' a voice thundered from the doorway overhead. Topcliffe clicked his fingers and the men let Throckmorton drop, sprawling on the rack in pain and fear. They all looked up as a black-robed figure padded down the half twist of the stone staircase and stood in front of them.

'Sir Francis.' Topcliffe half bowed and the guards did likewise.

'Mother of God, indeed.' Walsingham knelt by the rack, looking in horror at what he saw. His cold eyes flashed again on Topcliffe. 'You, rackmaster, you've gone too far this time. Does Sir William Waad know of this?'

'I . . . er . . .'

Walsingham stood up. 'You've beaten your last victim,' he snarled. 'Get out. You, man,' he snarled at Topcliffe's assistant, 'bring me butter and honey. And get this man some water and some brandy.' They all dithered. 'Now!' Walsingham roared and they scampered into the shadows to do his bidding.

Walsingham was on his knees on the cold stone. 'Francis, Francis,' he soothed. 'I had no idea. What on earth happened?'

The man's shoulders slumped and Walsingham helped him to sit up. 'Can I . . . get off this thing, Sir Francis?'

'My dear boy.' Walsingham took the lad's weight and half carried him to the chair. This wasn't much better; Topcliffe's fetters were still clamped to the arms. Walsingham unhooked his cloak and draped it over them for sensibility's sake.

Throckmorton looked at the older man. 'But you know, surely?' he said with as much clarity as his swollen lips would allow. 'You had me arrested.'

'Me?' Walsingham looked puzzled. 'Francis, I assure you . . .'

'Trumped up charges. Letters to the Queen of Scots. Mendoza. It's all nonsense.'

'Well of course it is.' Walsingham patted Throckmorton's good hand. 'No, no, that wasn't me, dear boy.' He sighed and looked furtively around him. 'Lord Burghley, I'm afraid. You know what he's like.'

'No,' Throckmorton mumbled, tears welling in his eyes.

'No, I don't. I've never met Lord Burghley. I know nothing of those charges. Topcliffe said—'

'Topcliffe!' Walsingham snorted. 'You'd never think the man came of a good family from Derbyshire, would you? Such an oaf.'

'Oaf?' mouthed Throckmorton. 'That's putting it mildly, Sir Francis.'

'Well,' Walsingham said firmly, 'he's unleashed his bestiality for the last time. It's positively barbaric.' He looked around him, the dank walls, green with mould, the corners of impenetrable black. 'I had absolutely no idea, Francis.'

'Where are we, sir?' Throckmorton asked, gripping the man's sleeve. 'Are we near the river? I keep getting a smell . . .'

'No, no,' Walsingham explained. 'This is the White Tower, dear boy. The river's . . . er . . . that way.' It took him a while to get his own bearings.

'It's just . . . the rats,' Throckmorton whispered, his eyes wild. 'I've never seen so many rats.'

Walsingham nodded, his face a mask of sympathy. He looked at Throckmorton's crushed hand. 'We'll get that looked at,' he promised. 'Honey works wonders, I'm told. And the Queen of Scots?'

Throckmorton blinked back the tears. Then he sat upright, as far as the pain would allow him. 'I am not a traitor, Sir Francis,' he said solemnly.

'My dear boy,' Walsingham patronized. 'Whoever said you were?'

Throckmorton tried to chuckle, but it was just a gargle in his parched throat. 'Topcliffe, for one. Lord Burghley, apparently, for another.'

'They just misunderstood,' Walsingham assured him. 'The letters they claim you wrote . . .'

'I just felt sorry for the Queen, that was all.'

'The Queen of Scots?' Walsingham needed to be clear. There could, after all, only be one queen.

'She's in prison, Sir Francis,' Throckmorton explained, as though to a village idiot. 'I know how that feels.'

'Indeed,' nodded Walsingham. 'So there was no mention of the Spanish ambassador?'

'Who?'

'Mendoza.'

'Um . . . there may have been. I don't remember.'

'And nothing about . . . what was it again, that ridiculous notion, an invasion by the French under the Duke of Guise, linking up with English Papists?' Walsingham was chuckling at the patent absurdity of the idea.

'That was William Shelley's rubbish. I warned them . . .' His voice tailed away to silence.

Walsingham smiled and patted the man's shoulder, the one that had come so close to being dislocated. 'I must go, Francis,' he said. 'I'll see that the brandy is brought to you. Get a doctor down here. Then I'll see William Waad about your release.' He shook his head. 'It's an outrage that an Englishman can be treated like this in Elizabeth's England.'

'Thank you, Sir Francis.' Throckmorton was still swallowing blood.

'Think nothing of it.' Walsingham smiled and swung his cloak over his shoulder on his way to the steps.

Beyond the door, he accepted the goblet of brandy from Richard Topcliffe and the men drank together. 'Your very good health, Richard.'

'And yours, Sir Francis.' The rackmaster grinned. 'Any joy?'

'Oh, yes, indeed. Never fails, does it? Nasty torturer, nice torturer routine. Good job, by the way.'

'We like to please.' He smiled. His assistants appeared at that moment with butter and water. 'You won't need those, lads. Get 'em back to the kitchens.'

'Could I trouble you for quill and parchment, Richard?'

'Of course.' Topcliffe rummaged in his desk, sliding the heavy manacles and collar to one side.

'Mrs Topcliffe well?' Walsingham asked. 'And the little Topcliffes?'

'Never better, sir. Little Dickie had a touch of the croup last month.'

'Hmm,' Walsingham sympathized. 'It's this damned weather. If we had a summer this year, I don't remember it.' He dipped the quill and scratched a quick note on the parchment before binding it and dripping the red, molten wax from Topcliffe's candle on to the ribbon. 'Right,' he sighed, hauling on the cloak. 'I think I've got what I came for. Love to Mrs Topcliffe.'

'Sir.' The rackmaster beamed.

'Oh, Richard, I don't want to tell you your job; gammers and egg-sucking and so on. But work on the other hand now, there's a good fellow. It disorients them.'

'Very good,' Topcliffe said, always happy to improve on his work. 'And the rack?'

'Er . . . yes, why not? Have your dinner first, dear boy. We've got Guise. I just need times and places for the planned invasion now. Oh and strength of the enemy, if you can. There's a bonus in it for you.'

'Oh, sir.' Topcliffe was hurt. 'I don't do it for the money, you know that.'

'Yes.' Walsingham nodded, frowning into the man's bright blue eyes. 'Yes, I know.'

Under the grey sky, the one that Francis Throckmorton would not see again until the day the axeman sliced off his head on Tower Hill, Francis Walsingham stood by his messenger's horse, stroking the animal's muzzle and nose.

'You can take this letter to Master Christopher Marlowe, fellow.' He threw the horseman a purse. 'Michelgrove, near Arundel. You will find him at the house of William Shelley. He'll know what to do.'

'Very good, sir.' And the horseman wheeled away to clatter through the barbican, making for the Bridge.

The mist curled along the Arun that Sunday morning as the bell of St Nicholas called the faithful to church. Christopher Marlowe reached the packhorse bridge that crossed the river and looked up at the great, grey castle towering over the town. Through the frost of the morning, the good folk of Arundel were making their way in twos and threes up the hill to the church. Marlowe had received Walsingham's letter by galloper that morning and he had it in his hand now. He looked across to where the carriage rocked to a standstill and the footmen busied themselves helping the family down.

Catherine Shelley was a beautiful woman, tall and stately, with soft, fluttering hands and a musical voice. She nodded to Marlowe as she reached the ground and started clucking around her daughters. Jane, at twelve was already beginning to look like her mother, with a finely drawn, nervous face and slender body.

She stood looking down at the ground, feeling gawky and awkward in a dress which was stiff and unyielding. She had begged her mother for a more grown-up dress and was regretting it already. The stiff lace collar dug into her neck and made it sore. The layers of petticoats weighed heavily on her bony hips and made her stomach ache. She felt that every move had to be planned, that to walk at all needed a momentum that she just didn't seem to be able to gather together. And still Master Marlowe seemed not to be aware of her existence, only speaking to her to correct her Latin or Greek. She would flounce in and out of the dining hall so that he would notice her, slamming doors and dropping things, get her Cicero wrong so that he had to spend more time with her while correcting it. He filled her dreams. She was in Hell.

Her sister Bessie, on the other hand, had no such pretensions. She loved Kit Marlowe with the undying passion of a little girl who had been ignored by everyone for most of her life, who suddenly is the recipient of smiles and hugs, no matter how absent-minded, from a man who seemed to make her mother, her sister and all of the maids blush and go weak at the knees. That both Bessie and Marlowe were equally unaware of why this should be was to their credit. He encouraged her in her pirouetting and posturing, her turning cartwheels, even if he had to constantly disentangle her from her petticoats and help her find which way was up. She declaimed what she could remember from the simplified verses he set her to learn and never walked when she could skip, never skipped when she could jump. She danced to his lute playing and sang with his songs. In spite of her constant motion, she was still a plump little thing and held hidden in her padded cheeks the secret of the greatest beauty of all the Shelley women, still to come.

'Good morning, Master Marlowe.' William Shelley was wearing his best today, his ruff well starched, his beard trimmed.

'Master Shelley.' Marlowe half bowed. He had known this man for three months and had lived in the attic room of his house for two. They had even fished the Arun together, vying with each other for the best catch of mullet. He had come to know him as well as any casual tutor could – that had been his brief from Walsingham. What Walsingham had not told Marlowe to do was to get too close to these people. It was not safe. Nor to get too close to their home life. But here he was, ravelled in the apron strings of the women, grudgingly admiring the man and beginning to regret the last two months' work.

'Bad news?' William Shelley nodded to the parchment in Marlowe's hand.

'I may have to go back to Cambridge,' the tutor told him, 'sooner than I expected.'

Shelley frowned. 'The girls will miss you, Kit,' he said. 'We all will.'

Marlowe nodded. Arundel was cold this morning, with everyone's breath streaming out in front of them. Bessie of course was blowing on purpose, steam coming from her mouth as if she were a horse. She was stamping and prancing to complete the picture. But although it was cold, and noses were red and pinched with it, Marlowe knew it was nothing, in this soft and southern place, to the cold that would already have Cambridge in its grip. There, the wind would be a lazy wind, lazy because it bit straight through flesh and bone, rather than go round a person. No matter how many layers of clothes and piles of blankets, in winter he always went to bed cold, woke up colder still and then it just got worse all day. Here, his attic room was warm with the risen heat of many fires. He had the run of the house and it was his greatest pleasure to go down to the library at night and read by the light and the warmth of a log fire, mumbling comfortably to itself in the enormous grate. Sometimes, Catherine Shelley would join him, and would sit on the other side of the fireplace with her candle in its mirrored candlestick, stabbing at her embroidery and making polite conversation. It was a comfortable life and he realized, standing there on the packhorse bridge, that it had become too comfortable by half. Shelley's voice broke into his thoughts.

'On your way to church?'

Marlowe half smiled in that mercurial way of his. 'Not this morning, William. I just thought I'd wander the river for a while. Helps me think. You?' He turned to face his employer, never forgetting for a moment why he was really here.

'We've been invited to his Lordship's again.' Shelley smiled with all the bonhomie at his disposal. 'No doubt we'll attend divine service in the castle.'

'No doubt you will.' Marlowe smiled back and he watched them go, walking in line abreast up the hill, little Bessie leaping and pirouetting on her pattens, Jane glancing back at the black-cloaked figure at the bridge head. The church bell was still clashing and clanging and the bright cross-crosslet flag of the Howards snapped in the stiff breeze overhead.

'You're quiet tonight, Kit.' Catherine Shelley looked up from her embroidery at the tutor. For a moment, he didn't react, but then he raised his head and smiled gently at her.

'I'm sorry. I'm thinking.' He sat himself up and rubbed his hands together. 'What were you saying?' He looked at her in the firelight, her candle throwing its light on to the handiwork on her lap. She tipped her head to one side and tutted softly. 'What?' The laugh in his voice turned her heart to water. She had been aware all day that she should store images of Master Marlowe, the tutor, the poet, away against the day. If she could only keep one, that would be it. The eyebrow raised, the mouth smiling uncertainly, the laughing word held on the air.

'I hadn't said anything,' she said, smiling back at him, 'except to say you are quiet tonight.'

'I'm sorry,' he said. 'I hadn't meant to be a curmudgeon. I

just have a lot of planning to do, with . . . with the journey and other things.'

'Back to Cambridge? You'll take a horse, won't you? William has offered you a horse?'

He shook his head. 'That is too much. And anyway, how could I get it back to you?'

'There would be no need,' she said. 'Let it be a gift from the girls. They will miss you so much, Kit.' She paused and a blush crept up her neck. 'I will miss you. You are company for me in the evenings. William is . . .'

'Your husband is a busy man,' Marlowe finished the sentence for her. 'Often away, I know.'

She looked at him, her head cocked on one side. 'He is here and there, Kit, here and there.' She looked down at her lap and twisted her hands together. 'I want to ask you something.'

'Well, I'll answer you if I can.' His heart beat so that he thought she must surely be able to hear it. In his life of ducking and weaving, of fantasy and half truth, he had never had to lie to someone so innocent before. His usual dealings were with men who would kill a queen for the sake of a pope, kill thousands for the sake of an ideal. This was different. He waited.

'Can I have a portrait of you?' The words came out in a rush. 'The girls would like it.'

'I have no portrait to give you,' he said. He hoped the relief didn't show on his face. Although he could dissemble with words, he was still working on keeping his emotions from view and wasn't sure he always succeeded.

'I have been . . . well, as you know, I like to sketch. I had lessons when I still lived at my father's house, before I married William and the girls were born. My teacher is quite famous now, at Court; my Uncle George – George Gower, I don't know whether you have heard of him . . .' Catherine Shelley knew she was babbling, but couldn't seem to stop.

'I have heard of him, yes,' he said. 'You sound as though your childhood was very happy.'

'Oh, it was.' Her eyes lit up. 'The girls and I still go some-times back to my parents' house. My brother has it now, of course, but we still have a suite of rooms there.' She smiled at the recollection. 'It's in Yorkshire. It's good for the girls to run free sometimes. Life is very . . .'

'Confined.' He watched her carefully. A question he had wanted to ask her had been answered. When the time came for her husband to be scooped up by Walsingham's men, she would have a roof over her head and the girls would have somewhere to run free.

She nodded her head once. 'Yes. You know us so well, Kit.' She turned as she heard the door of her husband's study open. He called for his steward and the man's hurrying footsteps echoed through the hall. 'He will have finished his business soon,' she said, leaning forward and making Marlowe a conspirator in her plan. 'So, quickly, Kit, can I send my sketches to Uncle George, to have a portrait made of you? For the girls?'

He smiled at her and leaned back in his chair, with his legs spread out to the fire. 'On one condition, Mistress Shelley,' he said.

'Of course.' She knew it would not be the condition she hoped for, but she hoped for it just the same.

'That I can have a copy. It doesn't matter who paints it, if it is a student, not the master, but I would like one. For my rooms, you know; in Cambridge.'

She forced a smile; it was for his sweetheart, she feared. But she was a polite woman, well brought up by yeomen in Yorkshire. 'It would be our pleasure, Kit,' she said.

William Shelley jerked upright at the click from his study door.

'Kit.' He hurriedly slid the parchment he was writing on under a pile of others and propped the quill into the inkwell. 'It's late.'

Marlowe closed the door behind him and sat down uninvited. Shelley had never seen the man look so grim, so focused. There was an indefinable fire in his eyes.

'What's the matter?' he asked.

'I had a letter today,' Marlowe told him.

'Yes, I know. From Cambridge. You have to go back.'

'No,' the tutor said. 'Not from Cambridge.'

Shelley frowned. 'I don't understand,' he said.

'I had two letters today – the one you know about. It just had two words.' Marlowe looked grimly at Shelley. 'Francis Throckmorton.'

'Who?'

'The second letter came hard on the heels of the first. You were still at the castle; in the private chapel, no doubt. It talked of five thousand Horse, twelve thousand Foot. Pikemen, arque-busiers. I'm still in the dark about the field pieces.'

Shelley blinked, his lips dry, his heart thumping. His smile told a different story. 'You've lost me,' he said.

'Of course –' Marlowe stretched out his booted feet and crossed them at the ankles – 'these are just the projected figures.'

'Projected?' Shelley repeated.

Suddenly, Marlowe slammed his fist down on the carved arm of the chair. He was sitting bolt upright. 'The Duke of Guise will bring that army, those seventeen thousand men, to a landing place somewhere on the Essex coast. No doubt when the third letter arrives, it will tell me exactly where. Somewhere on the Crouch would be my guess. How many transports Guise will need, I don't know. And it doesn't matter.'

'Kit . . .' Shelley was blinking again, his hands outstretched in confusion.

'Those Englishmen loyal to the Bishop of Rome will rally to Guise's standard, march to wherever they're holding Mary of Scots and overthrow the Queen. The Thames will run red.'

'Stop!' Shelley bellowed. 'These are the ravings of a madman, sir.'

'Indeed they are.' Marlowe nodded. He was almost whispering.

'And what has any of this nonsense to do with me?'

'In the county of Sussex,' Marlowe continued, as though reading a litany for the dead, 'those Englishmen loyal to the Bishop of Rome include Charles Paget, Esquire, His Grace the Earl of Arundel, Sir Aymer Middleton, Roger Bantry . . . and William Shelley, gentleman. Husband, father.'

'Employer of Christopher Marlowe,' Shelley added in a low growl. 'Spy and traitor.'

Marlowe stood up sharply. Shelley knew the man carried a dagger in the sheath in the small of his back. His eyes flickered across to his own broadsword propped in the corner. Marlowe was younger, fitter, faster. He had already given up any thought of silencing the man when the door crashed back and half a dozen armed men burst in, their swords drawn, their faces grim.

'No,' said Marlowe levelly. 'Not traitor. That label belongs nearer to home.'

'William Shelley,' the sergeant-at-arms barked. 'Under the powers vested in me by their Lordships of the Privy Council, I am placing you under arrest on a charge of High Treason.'

'I trusted you with my children,' Shelley hissed at Marlowe as they hauled him round and bound his wrists behind his back.

Marlowe closed to him. 'And I trusted you with my country,' he said.

'Take him away,' the sergeant ordered. 'And get the women.'

'No!' Marlowe blocked the doorway.

'Walsingham's writ says the whole family,' the sergeant snapped at him. 'Wife, Catherine; daughters, Jane and Charlotte.'

'Show me,' Marlowe insisted.

The sergeant fumbled in his purse and dragged out the tatty scroll with Walsingham's seal. Marlowe read the contents briefly by the flickering candles; then he tore it up and threw the pieces in the sergeant's face.

'I don't give a rat catcher's arse for Walsingham's writ,' he said. 'Does the Privy Council make war on women and children now?'

The sergeant hesitated. He hadn't expected this. Whose side was this man on? Judas Iscariot with a conscience? Well, yes, it made some sense. He had four men at his back and Marlowe was alone. Even so, the sergeant was a man with an infinitely flexible spine. They didn't pay him enough to take on one of Walsingham's men. And there was something in Marlowe's face he didn't like.

'Just him, then,' the sergeant grunted. 'But there'll be questions asked,' he warned Marlowe. They bundled William Shelley along the corridor to where their horses waited in the darkness of the courtyard.

Marlowe watched them go. He saw Catherine rushing across the stones in the dim light from the hall, her servants tussling with the guards. He knew there was no point in going down himself. It was all over in seconds. No one was hurt, just two ladies, consoling their weeping mistress and baffled serving men watching the knot of horsemen cantering into the darkness of the night.

TWO

Robert Greene stood at the corner of Lion Yard that Thursday evening. The curfew hour for the University scholars had come and gone, yet they were still there, whispering and sniggering together in the shadows, scurrying from The Swan to the Brazen George and always to the Devil. It had been the same in his day, when the most exciting thing in the world was a roll in the hay with some girl and beating the proctors at their own game, shinning over college walls and sliding down roof ledges.

It was damned cold there on the edge of the marketplace, the stalls silent and deserted now, cloaked in the November dark. He stamped his feet like a sizar without money for his coal and blew on his hands. Where *was* the man? He'd said half past ten of the clock. Quite distinctly. Now it was nearly eleven and Greene decided to call it a night; he clearly wasn't coming. He threw his cloak over his shoulder and strode over the already-frosting cobbles. Then he saw him, shoulders back, spine straight, striding over the pavements as if he owned the place.

'Dr Harvey,' he hissed as they met at the corner.

'Is that you, Greene?' Gabriel Harvey knew perfectly well who it was, but he wouldn't give the guttersnipe the satisfaction.

'Good evening to you, Doctor.' Greene nodded.

'There's nothing conceivably good about it, Greene,' Harvey snapped, poking his nose out to squint up at the blue-black of the Cambridge sky. 'I left a warm fire and a hot toddy to come here. And every step I took I wondered why I did. Your note said it was urgent.'

'It is,' Greene assured him. 'Er . . . The Bell?' Both men looked up at the iron inn sign creaking and cracking in the wind. The clapper had long gone, spirited away by some drunken scholar on a spree, so the empty bell just clanked dully against a thick arm of withered ivy which hung from the wall. It sounded like the ghost of a dead bell, still marking the hours with no one to hear it ring.

Harvey peered in through the thick, warped panes. 'And sit drinking with half the scholars of my college? Are you utterly out of your mind?'

'It's Marlowe.' Greene blew on his frozen fingers again, hopping from foot to foot.

Greene stood upright, turning slowly to him. In the light from the inn, his face was a mask of fury. 'Where?'

'In Petty Cury,' Greene whispered. 'I saw him myself. Not two hours since. I can show you the very spot.'

'Why?' Harvey asked. 'Will Machiavel have burned his cloven hoof into the cobbles? Mother of God, give me some respite from all this.' He looked the man squarely in the face, then gripped his shoulders, shaking him. 'You're sure, man? The last I heard of Marlowe, he was going south with those strolling players. He let everyone know he'd done with Cambridge. Of course –' Harvey released the man as a thought occurred to him – 'we all know what that was about. He couldn't cut it, the scholarship, I mean; the cut and thrust of debate. No, his Dialectic was sloppy, his Greek only so-so. I wasn't impressed.'

Greene hardly liked to argue with Harvey in full spate, but facts were, after all, facts. 'He's back.'

'Damn!' Harvey thumped the door frame of The Bell.

'I thought you should know.'

Harvey sneered at the informant. Ordinarily, he'd wipe things like Robert Greene off his patten soles, but in a way the St John's graduate was a kindred spirit. They both hated Marlowe; that gave them a certain bond.

'What will you do?' Greene asked.

'Do?' Harvey pulled himself up to his full height. 'Perhaps it's best you don't know.' He half turned, then he half turned back. 'Watch yourself, Dominus Greene,' he said. 'If the Devil is loose in Cambridge, then none of us is safe.'

There were just shadows in the Court at Corpus Christi college that night. The last roisterers had crept home under the fitful moon and the proctors had missed them again. Under the eaves in the cramped attic rooms, the sizars snored softly in their hard, narrow beds, dreaming of the Aristotle, the Plato, the Cicero and the Horace crammed into their heads day after day. The frost drew its silent pictures on the inside of their grimy windows and brought a kind of beauty to the room which the meagre belongings of the sizars could never bring. A mouse crept out, without much hope of finding anything and then froze as its ears, triangulating madly for the smallest sound, heard the soft padding of Old Tiberius, the college cat, as he made his way up the staircase at the far corner where the path wound its way into the silent churchyard of St Bene't's.

A hand reached out and stroked the animal, who arched his back and purred, his tail curling upwards and his chin lifting for a tickle. Kit Marlowe crouched alongside the cat. 'Oh, Tiberius,' he whispered, 'I'll wager you say that to all the returning graduates.' He straightened and turned to the stairway, on up past his old room, the one he had shared with the lads from Canterbury, his home for three long years.

On the landing he fancied he heard something, but it was probably just the creak of the stair, old dry wood shifting against the ancient stone. He felt for the panelled tracery of his door and pushed gently. He couldn't see the two men waiting for him inside. One, a taut, lean scholar, stood with his back against the wall, a dagger glinting in his right hand. The other crouched on the opposite side of the door frame, a lead-weighted cosh in his fist. There were three men by that doorway and nobody seemed to be breathing.

'Hello, Tom,' said Marlowe. 'Hello, Matt. Aren't we all a little old for tricks like this?'

The other two spun into his vision, laughing and roaring, hugging him and slapping his back. 'Kit, you whoreson zed, it really is you!' Matthew Parker was jumping around as if his pattens were on fire. Tom Colwell held Marlowe's shoulders squarely and peered into his face in the gloom of the unlit room. He shook his head. 'The years have not been kind,' he said and Marlowe threw him backwards so that he bounced off the bed.

'It's not four months since I saw you two bastards last,' he laughed. 'Light a candle there, Matt. Let's see if you've been able to grow a beard yet.'

They all laughed, babbling about this and that as the room glowed with candles. What old Norgate was doing with the College, how furious the proctors Lomas and Darryl were now they had no powers to punish the boys, the girl that the old Puritan, Tom Colwell, had fallen for. It all came out in a rush and tumble, washed down by the wine Tom had been saving for this occasion. He knew it would happen, that Kit Marlowe would be back; he just hadn't known when.

'How's home?' Matthew Parker wanted to know. 'Does Canterbury still stand?'

'Home?' Marlowe had almost forgotten the word, the smell of the tanneries where he was born, the beer of The Star where he had carried pots and held gentlemen's horses, the sound of his father's hammer tapping the studs into clients' boots. But in the one letter he'd written to these lads in the past weeks, that was where he told them he was, resting before he came back to Cambridge. He was ever a dissembler; now he had to keep his skills up to the mark, even when the boys who were boys when he was a boy were sitting and drinking with him. He smiled. 'Home is still there. Canterbury still stands.'

'Kit.' Colwell stood up, his goblet in his hand. 'Here's to us, eh? The Parker Scholars back together again.' And he drained the cup. 'The Parker Scholars!' Parker and Marlowe chorused and did the same.

'Is Cambridge ready for us, do you think?' Parker laughed. And they drank into the night.

There was a time when the trio in front of him would have reminded Marlowe of the three wise men, sitting on their camels in the star-led watches of the night. But that was then, when he was a carefree scholar who knew so little of the world. Now, it was different. Now, the three men in front of him that Friday morning looked more like a Court of the Inquisition.

In the centre, looking greyer and more cobweb-wisped than he remembered him, sat Dr Robert Norgate, the Master of Corpus Christi. He was feeling his age now that November had come and he didn't care to stray too far from the fire that crackled and spat in his study. To Norgate's right sat Michael Johns, as good a man as ever put on a scholar's cap and tried to din into dimmer heads the weight of his scholarship. He had never thought to see Marlowe again and was glad he had come back to the fold. There had been talk of strolling players and the London theatre. He was quietly glad that that had all been nonsense. On the Master's left, as on the left hand of God, sat Gabriel Harvey, looking like a man staring at a dose of the plague.

'I say no, Master,' he snapped.

Norgate turned to him, as well as his rheumatism would allow. 'I know you do, Gabriel. Just as I know that Michael here has said yes.' He couldn't turn to Johns as well, so the teacher of Rhetoric had to make do with a cursory wave. 'I –' Norgate placed his fingers together near his pursed lips – 'must perforce play Solomon. Again.'

He looked at the scholar in front of him. He had heard that Marlowe was back. He had heard he had left Cambridge in a travelling player's cart bound for London. He had heard that men called him Machiavel. He had heard he was not as other scholars. He had heard . . . but what had he not heard about Christopher Marlowe? The man had caused a riot, single-handed, in Cambridge in the summer that had just passed. He had brought the sweating sickness to the town with a single sneeze. No doubt he had kissed Christ in the garden at Gethsemane and given the apple to Eve in another garden long ago. Given time the rumours would grow to include his giving advice to God when he created the camelopard, surely a joke of creation of which only Marlowe was capable.

But in front of him stood a graduate like any other. But not quite like any other. The man had his hair cropped short like a sizar. Norgate had heard he was a roisterer, swaggering about the town in a velvet doublet with a dagger at his back. Yet, here he was, in the drab fustian of Corpus Christi with the badge of the pelicans and lilies. Good God, he even had a book in his hand.

'There have been unfortunate incidents,' Norgate said, 'Dominus Morley, concerning you.'

Marlowe did not move. He had long ago given up reminding the old boy what his name really was.

'You have enemies in this town, sir.' Norgate was sure the scholar knew that already, but he would be failing in his duty should he not mention it.

'What man does not, Master?' Marlowe flashed a smile at Harvey.

'If I remember right, you did not actually take your degree ceremony.'

'I did not, Master. Events conspired.'

'Yes.' Norgate sighed. 'Yes, they do tend to do that, don't they?' he tapped his finger ends together, sucking his teeth and wrestling with his decision. He felt Harvey tensing beside him, Johns calm and quiet at his other elbow. 'Let me make sure I understand you, Dominus Marley,' he went on. 'You wish to be entered for your Master of Arts degree at Corpus Christi College in the University of Cambridge?'

'I do, Master.'

There was a silence which rang all over Corpus Christi, all over Cambridge. Only the fire spat its contempt, desperately trying to influence Norgate at this crucial juncture in the old man's life.

'And if I allow you back, you will abide by the precepts of this College and the laws of Her Majesty and of God?'

'I will, Master,' Marlowe answered.

Another eternity passed and a log shifted ominously in the grate.

'Very well.' Norgate cleared his throat. '$Γενεσθ$,' he said, in classical Greek. '*Genestho*, let it be so.'

Both men alongside Norgate let out the breaths they had been holding for what seemed like hours. They stood up at the Master's instigation, Johns turning to give Norgate a hand in rising from his chair. Harvey stood staring forward, wrong footed in not giving the old man a hand and in having Marlowe, reinstated, standing in front of him with an unreadable expression on his even features beneath his cropped hair. The three bowed to Marlowe, who bowed back. Johns' bow was garnished with a smile, Norgate's with a wince of pain. Harvey inclined his head so little it was touch and go whether it could be called a bow at all, but Marlowe was minded to be generous; his own bow was lavish and would have looked better with the velvet doublet and the colleyweston cloak, but the fustian had carried the day with Norgate, so it would serve.

'Welcome back, Marley.' Norgate extended a hand.

'Thank you, sir,' he said, and he took it. Would the man *never* remember his name from one sentence to the next?

The Master shuffled out of his study with a furious Harvey in his wake. 'Wait.' The man suddenly spun round. 'What's that book, Marlowe?' He pointed to the leather volume in the graduate's hand.

'This?' Marlowe held it up. 'A little something I picked up in Canterbury over the summer,' he said. 'Cassius Dio's *Historia Augusta*. Quite a find, don't you think? Especially in a backwater like Canterbury.'

Harvey snorted and left the room.

'What is it really?' Johns asked.

Marlowe smiled and passed the slim volume to him. Johns flipped the covers open and read aloud, '"What arms and shoulders did I touch and see, How apt her breasts were to be press'd by me! How smooth a belly under her waist saw I! How large a leg and what a lusty thigh! To leave the rest, all lik'd me passing well; I cling'd her naked body, down she fell; Judge you the rest; being tir'd she bade me kiss; Jove send me more such afternoons as this."' He looked at Marlowe. 'Doesn't sound much like Cassius Dio to me,' he said.

'Does it sound like Ovid?' Marlowe asked.

'The works of Ovid are banned by this university. They corrupt young minds.'

'Needs work, then?' Marlowe winked at him.

'It does.' Johns smiled. 'Welcome back, Kit.'

'Trumpy Joe' Fludd should have been at his lathe that Saturday morning. They'd elected him Constable again and again he had said yes, much to his Allys's disgust, so here he was, standing like an ox in the furrow in the centre of the road that ran south to London. Behind him the smoky city of Cambridge was beginning to stir and the farmers from the neighbourhood were already on their way to market, driving their flocks of sheep and their gaggles of geese. One by one the drovers in their smocks nodded to Constable Fludd. He was a good man, they knew, straight and fair. He would count them into the town, make sure all was right at the colourful stalls, then count them back out again.

But Fludd's mind was not quite on his work this morning. He barely acknowledged the drovers, most of whom he'd known all his life; they had swum together in the dykes of the fens and had played football up and down the village streets. But now they were dour men driving their stock to market and he was the Constable, looking out for the children of the moon. He'd heard a whisper of their coming from old Ben the farrier who'd shod their horses at Stocking Pelham. A chapman from the south had seen their scarves fluttering along the Harcamulow Way. Yet another had heard their bells tinkling as they took the old high road to Barbraham. That was why they'd elected Fludd Constable again; he was damned good at his job and he cared.

There had been no moon men in Cambridge since before the Queen came calling and that was when Joe Fludd was still in his hanging sleeves, stumbling his way around his father's furniture. But he knew their reputation and he knew the law. He heard them before he saw them in the mists of the cold November morning, a tinkling of bells and a rattle of drums on the road, the singing, chanting almost, rumbling deep and low in an alien tongue he couldn't understand. There was the groaning of wagon axles and now and then the shrill of a pipe or a girl's voice, he couldn't tell which, would rise sweetly above the rumble, cutting through the muffling mist. The two men with him tightened their grip on their staves as the bobbing heads came in to view, some on foot, some astride piebald ponies.

'Four children on one horse,' Nathaniel Hawkins muttered. 'Aye, that's them all right. Children of the moon.' He looked at Jabez Hazel, his opposite number. 'They say they can look into a man's soul. Best not stare into their eyes, Jabez.'

'No more will I,' Hazel mumbled back. 'What'll we do, Joe?'

Fludd flashed furious glances at them both. 'We'll remember

we are the Cambridge Watch, gentlemen,' he told them.
'And while we're not looking into their eyes, we'll keep a
very close watch on our purses, eh?' And he smiled, raising
a hand to halt the column on the road.

The Constable counted sixteen, but half of these were children, all of them with tattered clothes and patches, streaming
with bright ribbons of taffeta and silk. They wore broad-
brimmed hats heavy with feathers stolen from countless farm-
yards to the south – goose quills and pheasant's plumes nodded
there with the downy fluff of chickens and ducks. The leading
traveller hauled on his rein and signalled the column to halt.
He barked something incomprehensible to the man at his elbow
and slid out of the saddle. At that signal all the riders
dismounted and the children scuttled forward to scamper in
their rags around Jabez Hazel, laughing and holding out their
grimy hands.

'I am Constable Fludd of the Cambridge Watch,' Fludd told
the men. 'Who are you and what brings you to this town?'

'We are the travelling people.' The leader doffed his hat,
bowing low. 'The offspring of Ptolemy, lately come from the
lands of the East.'

'Egyptians!' Hawkins spat, narrowly missing a child who
poked his tongue out at him.

'What is your name?' Fludd asked the leader.

'Men call me Hern,' he answered, replacing his hat.

'The hunter?' Fludd frowned.

'I hunt if I must,' Hern told him. 'But not with gentry riding
to hounds with their hawks and boarspears. I hunt in the courts
and alleyways.'

'You are counterfeiters –' Fludd stood his ground – 'using
great subtle and crafty means to deceive people.'

Hern threw his head back and roared with laughter. 'You
know your law, Master Constable,' he said. 'But so do I. Can
you do no better than quote the Act of the late King Henry,
God rest his soul? Tut, tut, sir, you are behind the times. Your
charge is to drive us out of your town, take us roped and tarred
to the nearest ship and if we go not, you are to hang us, sir.'

Fludd blinked and licked his lips. He hadn't expected this.
This Egyptian, with his hard, flinty eyes, his twisted mouth

and curious patterns of speech knew the law all right and was inviting Fludd to move against him. Behind him the children were pulling his men's breeches and tugging at their doublet points. 'Stand fast!' he bellowed at the constables, knowing how rattled they were.

As Fludd stood there, undecided as to what to do, Hern stepped forward and with the speed and smoothness of a snake, took Fludd's right hand in his. 'You are a carpenter,' he said. 'And you have two children; a daughter and a son. The girl is well grown and a joy to you. The boy is but a baby yet; what is he now, two months, three?'

Fludd's mouth popped open.

'It's a trick, Joe,' Hawkins growled.

'Our Lord was a carpenter,' Hern said, still looking Fludd in the face, as if into his soul.

'Egyptians aren't Christians!' Hazel blurted out. 'You worship the Devil.'

Hern's eyes flashed to him. 'You have two children, Master Fludd,' he said softly. 'A boy and girl. Beware your wife is not brought to childbed again. She will not survive it.'

Fludd felt the muscles in his jaw flexing, his heart pounding, but Hawkins wasn't going to let any of it go. 'How many children have I got, Egyptian?' he asked.

Hern let Fludd's hand go and turned to his horse. He patted the animal's soft muzzle and whispered in its ear. The horse snorted, shaking its ears free and began pawing the hard, rutted ground. Once, twice, three times the hoof clashed on the furrow.

'Your wife has had three children,' Hern said, then he turned to Hawkins, 'and not one of them is yours.'

The travellers roared with laughter and Hawkins yelled at the children who scampered away.

'It is market day, Master Constable,' Hern said. 'All we ask is that you let us set up a stall in your town square that we may sell our wares.' He clicked his fingers and the scampering children stood stock still, their faces solemn, their eyes staring. 'Then I may feed my children.'

Fludd stood blinking again, trying to take in the bizarre and motley crew in front of him, the painted wagons and the swarthy men, the dappled horses and the fluttering flags. And above all, the suddenly silent children, like sentinels in the morning.

'One day,' he said, as though waking from a spell. 'One stall. My men and I will be watching. And if you're not gone by cock-shut time, Hern the Egyptian, I'll hang you myself, while your children look on.'

It didn't quite work out that way. Henry Whetstone usually liked being Mayor of Cambridge. It gave him a chance to line his fur-edged pockets, distribute largesse to his friends and relatives, acquiring more friends and relatives in the process and it was pleasant to hear the vicar of St Mary's ask the Lord to watch over his soul every Sunday. But that Monday morning was not usual. For three hours before he arrived at the Courthouse in St Mary's Square, a queue of angry petitioners had been assembling in the pouring rain, getting angrier by the minute as the water splashed off their hat brims and trickled down their necks. He had their complaints in front of him now, dashed off quickly in a scribble by his harassed clerks who had borne the full wrath of the good townsfolk. Others, angrier still, were not content to leave their complaints with a clerk. They wanted to see the Mayor in person: it was disgraceful; there ought to be a law against it; there *was* a law against it; they hadn't voted for the man in the first place.

'"Disgraceful",' the Mayor read from piled papers in front of him. '"There ought to be a law against it".' He threw the documents down, gnawing his lip with fury as he glared at Joe Fludd. 'What do we pay you, Fludd, to guard this town?'

Not enough, was the man's silent answer, but he remembered what his Allys had told him and behaved himself. 'My constabulary allowance is . . .'

'I know what it is!' Whetstone thundered. The jovial, red-faced merchant was anything but jovial this morning and if his face got much redder, he was liable to explode. Purple tinges were beginning to mottle his cheeks. His gout always played him up in wet weather and now this. 'You are aware of the law regarding Egyptians?' he asked.

'Yes, sir.'

'Tell me,' Whetstone snapped, 'just so that we are both sure.'

'They are to be escorted from the town or county and taken to the nearest port.'

'And if they refuse to go?'

'They are to be hanged, sir, without the benefit of trial.'

'Did you hang them?'

'No, sir.'

'Did you escort them to the nearest port?'

'No, sir.'

'Did you even escort them from the town?'

'No sir.'

'No,' Whetstone growled. 'No, you let them in, gave them a stall out there.' He pointed to the square beyond his leaded window panes. 'You allowed them to tell fortunes, read palms, carry out conjuring tricks.' He held up a piece of paper. 'Margaret Walker of Cherry Hinton is convinced she will not see another summer as a result of their auguries.' He rummaged and found another one. 'Nicholas Coke was told he will be hanged, drawn and quartered before Lady Day. These people are worried, Fludd. Worried. *And* they had to pay for the privilege. Then, there's the stealing. Apples. Eggs. Four geese. How can they lift four live geese without anybody noticing?'

Fludd had no answer.

'Why did you let them in?'

'I don't know, sir,' the Constable told him. 'It seemed like a good idea at the time.'

'Where are they now?'

'Making for a port, sir.' Fludd could at least be positive about that. 'King's Lynn.'

'Get yourself a good horse and follow them. I want to know exactly where these *travelling people* are.' The mayor managed to make the two words sound like a particularly virulent curse and Fludd almost felt his skin crackle under the heat of it.

'And if I catch them, sir? I have no jurisdiction outside Cambridge.'

'That is entirely your problem, sir,' Whetstone snapped.

'You created this mess, you can clean it up. Oh, and, Fludd . . .'

'Yes, sir?' The Constable was already halfway to the door.

'How's the carpentry business these days?'

'It's doing quite well, sir, thank you.'

'That's good, Joseph, I'm glad. Because I think your constabulary days are over.'

Fludd closed the door carefully behind him, afraid that if he slammed it now, he would never stop slamming it, imagining the Mayor's stupid head between the planks and the jamb. Then he squared his shoulders and went in search of a good horse.

Nicholas Faunt was waiting for Christopher Marlowe at the bottom of his staircase the next morning as the scholar spun round the final turn of the spiral, late as always, his grey fustian flying in the breeze of his passing. He nearly trod on him and brought himself up short. Faunt's nose was blue with cold and he slouched in a huddle against the hard stone of Corpus Christi. He had ridden hard and long through the night and was not in the best of moods.

Marlowe didn't know the man, but months at William Shelley's house had sharpened his wits and made him circumspect.

'Dominus Marlowe?' Faunt stood upright.

The university form of address. An insider? It seemed possible, but Faunt did not have the look of a scholar, the parchment grey skin and the fussy abstraction. He was wearing spurred boots and carried a sword.

Marlowe stepped back up two risers and his hand went automatically to the small of his back for his knife, to meet only shirt over skin; he was a scholar right at this moment and his knife was back in his room, hidden in the mattress. 'I am Marlowe,' he answered.

'Nicholas Faunt.' The man extended a gloved hand.

Marlowe took it. 'Sir Francis Walsingham's secretary,' he said, with a half smile.

'Among other things.' Faunt looked about him. 'Is there somewhere we can talk?'

Marlowe motioned up the twisting wooden stairs and led
the way. He unlocked his study door and let the man in. 'I'm
sorry there's no fire. I can offer you wine, at least.'

Faunt nodded. He crossed to the window with its thick and
twisted glass and looked out on to the Court below where
scholars hotfooted it from one lecture to the next. 'Some things
never change,' he said.

'You know this college?' Marlowe paused in mid-pour.

'Man and boy,' Faunt said. 'Old Norgate must be in his
grave by now, I suppose.'

'Possibly –' Marlowe passed the cup to him – 'but he was
fit as a fiddle yesterday. When were you up?'

'I took my Master's degree in the year of Grace 1579. You
were still at the King's School in Canterbury.'

'And doubtless you can tell me a great deal more about
myself.' Marlowe looked into the man's blue-grey eyes.

'Of course.' Faunt began to run those eyes over Marlowe's
books, their leather spines cracked and fading. 'Your father
is John, he is a tanner and cobbler. Your mother is Katherine,
of the Arthur family from Dover. You have an older sister,
Mary . . .'

'Had,' Marlowe corrected him. 'She died.'

Faunt stood corrected, but as Walsingham's secretary he had
learned to have no sympathy and so offered no condolences.
'You were christened in the church of St George the Martyr,
Christopher, the carrier of Christ.'

'I am flattered, Master Faunt, that you should have bothered
to learn so much about me . . .'

'Don't be,' Faunt told him flatly, sipping the wine. 'Despite
appearances, this isn't a social call.'

'Walsingham sent you,' Marlowe said, guessing. 'About
William Shelley.'

'Shelley's in the Tower and singing like a lark. He isn't the
problem.'

'So who is?' Marlowe knew it wasn't him, or he would
be dead by now, knifed silently from behind in any dark
entry you cared to name.

Faunt put the goblet down. 'You are, Dominus Marlowe.
You still have uses left in you, or you would be dead by now.'

Marlowe stepped back, grimly satisfied to hear his thoughts come back to him. He had room for manoeuvre, should this secretary prove to be as slick with a blade as he was with words; the poet could recognize the type from a thousand paces, or whenever he looked in the mirror. 'I assume this is about the women,' he said.

'This . . .' Faunt bellowed, then checked himself. 'This is about tearing up Sir Francis Walsingham's warrant and taking it upon yourself to disobey orders.'

'Is that what I did?' Marlowe had honed his expression of hurt innocence on the grindstone of nurses, teachers and lecturers until it was well nigh perfect, big eyes peering out from behind tumbled curls and a pouting lip. Many a tab grown too big for comfort had been covertly disposed of by barmaids the length and breadth of Cambridge who could not bear to see Master Marlowe in distress. But he knew it was pointless trying it on the implacable secretary and so kept his face poker straight.

'You know very well it is,' Faunt snapped. 'Sir Francis is very displeased.'

'And so he sent you to . . . what? Smack my wrist? Slit my throat?'

Faunt hesitated for a moment, looking as if he would like to do both, one after the other and in that order.

'Neither,' he said. 'Do you by any chance speak Flemish, Dominus Marlowe?'

'As a matter of fact, I do. I may be a little rusty, but back in Canterbury, some of my best friends were the Huguenot weavers along the Stour. But, Master Faunt, you know that already or you would not have ridden so far and so hard to find me.'

Faunt looked sternly at the man, then guffawed, slapping Marlowe's shoulder. 'I like you, Kit,' he said. 'And Sir Francis has a little job for you.'

'Indeed?'

Faunt crossed from the window, mechanically checking the door. He leant his back against the studded wood, arms folded. 'What do you know about the Prince of Nassau?' he asked.

Marlowe poured more wine for them both and passed the

goblet to Faunt. 'Statholder of the Netherlands,' he said, 'leader of the rebels against the overlordship of Philip of Spain. They say he has outlandish ideas. Every Jack's as good as his master, that sort of thing. Men call him William the Silent.'

'He's a marked man.' Faunt sipped his wine.

'A Protestant leader in a Catholic country? Of course he is.'

'But it's more imminent than that. He'd been relying on the Duke of Alençon to front his cause, but that's fallen apart now, largely because Alençon is an utter shit. That leaves the Statholder somewhat exposed. There have been attempts on his life already. He's had to move his court to Delft.'

'I don't see . . .'

'Walsingham wants a man to watch Nassau's back.' Faunt finished the draught. 'You.'

'Me?' Marlowe laughed and shook his head. 'You've read me wrongly, Master Faunt. I am a scholar . . .'

What happened next was a blur of velvet, leather and steel. There was a dagger in Faunt's right hand and it sliced in a vicious arc towards Marlowe's throat, but the scholar was faster and he hurled his wine in Faunt's face and kicked the blade aside. The next thing the secretary knew he was biting the wood of the door with his arm rammed painfully up behind his back.

'Scholar, my arse!' he mumbled against the oak and slowly Marlowe released his grip.

Faunt tugged down his doublet and straightened his ruff, realizing only now that his lip was bleeding where Marlowe had banged his head on the door. 'I believe I've made my point,' he said, clearing his throat and looking for his hat. 'Yes, you,' he repeated, 'and next time I won't give you any leeway at all.'

Marlowe recovered the man's dagger from where it had bounced under the table and, tossing it in the air, handed it to Faunt hilt first.

'How will you get there?' the secretary asked.

'By ship to the Hook,' Marlowe told him. 'Thereafter we shall see.'

'You can't just turn up at William the Silent's court,' Faunt said. 'There'll be watchers on the roads. The whole place from Antwerp to the Zuyder Zee will be crawling with Spaniards. How's your Spanish?'

'Non-existent,' said Marlowe.

'You can't go as a tutor. It worked with Shelley, but Nassau has his own people. An Englishman would stick out like a sore thumb.'

'If he has his own people, why am I going at all?' Marlowe asked.

'I didn't say they were any good.' Faunt wobbled his goblet for a refill, still dabbing at his swollen lip. 'In fact, I'm appalled how lax Nassau's court is. People coming and going all over the place. His headquarters is in some bloody converted nunnery so it's about as safe as a snake pit. You're some sort of playmaker, aren't you? Mummer or something?'

'Something.' Marlowe nodded.

'There's a troupe of Egyptians recently passed through this town of yours, making for the coast.'

'Are they?'

'They are. Find them, Dominus Marlowe. Join them. And get to Delft before Hell opens up.'

THREE

Allys Fludd knew better than to try to talk her husband out of doing his constabulary duties, but that didn't stop her. She stood at the stirrup of his hired horse and held on with one hand, her baby cradled in the crook of her elbow and little Kate hanging on to her skirts.

'Joe,' she said. 'If you would only tell me where you are going. When you'll be back. You have that cabinet half finished in your workshop and it will be me who has to explain when it isn't ready.'

Fludd was not a natural horseman and having someone hanging on to one stirrup didn't make him feel any more secure in his seat. He had asked at Hobson's stables in Trinity Lane for their fastest horse and he was already feeling that may have been a serious mistake, as the stupid animal caracoled round and round as soon as it felt his grip on the rein tighten even slightly. Fludd was afraid that the animal's flicking hooves would kick his daughter into the middle of next week, but he was also afraid that he would fall off and look as much of an idiot as he felt.

'Allys,' he begged. 'Please let go and let me get on. The sooner I'm gone, the sooner I'm back and the cabinet can be finished and this mad animal can be back in the stables and all will be back to normal.'

'Normal, Joseph Fludd, normal? And what is normal here, may I ask?' Before he could even part his lips, she answered her own question. 'I'll tell you what's normal. You, chasing off after all and sundry, players, murderers, scholars. When you became Constable for the *first* time,' she said, with heavy emphasis, 'you promised me it was just for a while. You promised me it would only be once. You promised me that it was just a matter of gathering up the drunken men of the town and putting them in the castle to sober up. You said there would be no mixing with the Colleges, no . . .' With every new thought, she shook the stirrup from side to side and it was obvious to Fludd that she was wishing it was his neck. The effect might be the same; the skittish, highly bred horse was on a knife edge and one more shake would break the fragile bond of her final wit and she would be off possibly never to come back to earth.

'Please, Allys,' he said, jogging and jigging in the saddle and hopelessly grabbing the reins. 'Please, stop that or I will be thrown. If you want me dead, then carry on; if you want me alive, and I assume you do, then please, step away from the horse.'

Allys Fludd came out of the tunnel of her own temper and looked up, to find herself staring into the rolling eye of the half-mad mare. She let go of the stirrup and stood back. Slowly, the animal calmed down and Fludd began to half enjoy the feeling of being astride so much elegant horseflesh. He sat high above his family, and waited for his wife to be as calm as his ride. When the hectic spots of anger had faded from her cheek, he began to explain. He had only got as far as his dressing down by the Mayor when a sudden commotion down the road set the horse off again and before he could say another word, he was flat on his back on the verge, one foot still in a stirrup and, by some miracle, the reins still in his hand.

'Constable Fludd, Constable Fludd, come quick.'

The voice was quite clear, although its owner was nowhere in sight. Allys rushed into the house to put the baby in its crib and set its little sister to watch over it, then came back out to disentangle her fallen husband, who was twisting on the ground like a landed trout, trying to avoid the flailing hooves. He was making an eerie crowing sound as he tried to force some air back into his empty lungs until, with a superhuman effort, he managed to breathe again.

'Who in Hell's name is that?' he grated to Allys. 'He could have killed me.'

Allys, having freed his foot, turned round to face the newcomer. It was true that she herself had been berating her husband moments before, but now that someone else was putting him at risk, she was like a wildcat defending her young. The man now visible round the corner of the lane was well known to her and she walked up to him and swung a mighty slap around his head which made his ears ring. Taken off guard, he fell to his knees.

'Are you some kind of idiot, Robert Scoggins, to go round the countryside shouting like that. Look at my husband!' Allys pointed a dramatic finger to where the Constable still lay in the dirt. 'He could have broken his back.'

The man looked from horse to man and back again. 'Why is he riding the Wasp?' he said. 'Nobody ever hires her, everyone knows that.'

Allys looked at him with narrowed eyes. 'That has nothing to do with it,' she said. 'It was your shouting and hallooing from miles away that made her skittish; Joe was doing well enough until you came up the lane behaving like a fool.'

'No.' Robert Scoggins shook his head. 'The Wasp is a mad 'un. Old Hobson only keeps her for loaning to any idiot that's fool . . . enough . . .' His voice trailed away. Joe Fludd's wife had been boxing his ears since they were children together but then he suddenly remembered why he was there. 'Gammer Harris's been murdered!' he said, raising his voice again as the news seemed to warrant. 'Lying stiff and cold and all blood bespattered and beaten in her own kitchen. And no sign of old Harris, her husband. You know, the hedger. We reckon he be dead, lying in his own blood somewhere we haven't found him yet. It'll be the Egyptians, now that's for sure.'

Fludd raised himself up on one elbow. 'Robert Scoggins,' he said severely. 'This won't be the first time you've come shouting up the lane with some tale that wasn't true.'

Scoggins looked down and scuffed the dirt with his toe and muttered something indistinguishable.

'Well may you mutter,' Fludd said, getting up with a wince. 'I called my constables out to prevent a murder last Plough Monday and all it was was Butcher Nevitt killing a pig.'

'It sounded like screaming,' Scoggins said, hotly. 'And I could smell the blood.'

'Yes, pigs do scream,' Fludd said, brushing himself down, 'as no doubt you've noticed before and since. And they do bleed when the butcher is at his work. Now, if I send a Constable to the Harrises, will they find old Mistress Harris sitting in her chair by the fire knitting with some nice red wool for some winter stockings?'

'No!' shouted Scoggins. 'She is dead. Dead as a nit. I swear to you, Constable Fludd. Dead of them Egyptians, as I stand here, she is!'

Fludd prepared to get back on the Wasp, just to show he could, but stopped as the sound of shouting came up the lane. Once bitten, twice shy, although so far about the only thing the animal had not done to him was bite and he was sure that was only a matter of time.

'Constable Fludd, Constable Fludd,' called a voice. 'Come quick, we've found . . .'

'. . . old Gammer Harris, dead as a nit and covered in blood,' the Constable completed the phrase.

'I think dead as a nit is a little tasteless,' said his new informant. 'But the poor woman is weltered in gore, I would be the first to concede.'

'Sorry, Reverend Mildmay,' Fludd said. 'I'm having a rather trying day.'

The Reverend Mildmay was a nice old boy, not given to the Gospel craze that marked a cleric as a Puritan and his frumpy old wife proved that he was not of the Catholic persuasion either. He helped the great and good of Trumpington in and out of the world; nobody could ask more of him.

'You're very muddy,' the vicar said. 'Have I interrupted anything?'

'Not at all,' Fludd said. 'I am about to leave Cambridge on an urgent errand and from what I hear it may not be unconnected with your own. As I pass the castle I will alert my men and they will come and see what is to be done. I'm sorry I can't stay, but I have wasted enough time already.'

He leapt on to the back of the Wasp with a flourish that surprised everybody. The animal galloped madly away down the lane, with Fludd clinging to her mane and desperately trying to get his other foot into the stirrup.

'But surely,' the vicar remarked to Allys and Scoggins, 'the Constable will not be passing the castle going in that direction. Should we perhaps . . .'

But he needn't have worried. After a series of furious oaths from down the lane, the sound of galloping hoofs gained in volume again and Fludd and the Wasp hurtled past them, heading for the town. Fludd had many thoughts sleeting through his head as he dashed headlong down Silver Street and across Magdalene Bridge, but foremost among them were the choice phrases he would be using at Hobson's Stables when he went there to exchange this nightmare for a horse a man could actually ride.

The golden Lion of Nassau flapped in the wind above the cupolas of the Prinsenhof that Tuesday as it had done since William the Statholder had taken the town when Kit Marlowe was still a pot boy at The Star in Canterbury and gentlemen threw him a farthing to hold their horses.

The wind, like everything else in Holland, blew in over the flat land, bringing rain as the darkness descended. All day William had sat in his robing room, the vaulted chamber where the nuns had worked on their altar cloths before the ideas of John Calvin had changed their lives for ever. Most of them had left the town years ago, although a few still worked and prayed in the Papist Corner. One of them even prayed for the soul of the Statholder, although he didn't know it.

William was tired. He'd spent the morning with his generals, looking at the troop dispositions he'd have to use against Parma. Why, he had asked himself for the umpteenth time, had God placed him across the barricades from the greatest soldier in the world? He took his meals with his men as they clucked around the models and the maps. They reminded him time and again that he wasn't facing the Duke of Alba now and that hit and run tactics would not suffice. What use were the sea beggars against a man like Parma? And what use were they anyway – the murderous bastards killed friend and foe alike. They were not patriots, not Dutchmen worthy of the name. They were murderers pure and simple. Ditch them and move on.

It was well and truly dark when their business concluded. They saluted him as their Statholder and commended his soul to almighty God before taking their leave. They bowed to the Statholder's wife as she swept into the chamber, muttering their goodbyes.

She smiled at her husband as she crossed the floor, still strewn with the planning of a campaign.

'Charlotte of Bourbon-Menpensier,' he croaked, his voice, like his body and brain, tired and old. 'Did I ever ask you, Lottie, what you saw in an old husk like me?'

She laughed and poured him a brandy from the ewer on the sideboard. 'I saw a rebel,' she said. 'A man who stood in the dykes and said "No". When Philip of Spain clicked his fingers and said "Jump" most men asked "How high, Your Majesty?" You –' and she kissed the top of his head as she reached his chair – 'just said "No".'

'"No".' He smiled ruefully, sipping his drink. 'And how many Dutchmen have died because I said "No"?'

'They died free men,' she said, smoothing his temples with her fingers.

'Ah, not yet.' He frowned. 'And there's the pity of it. Hence –' he gestured to the scrolled papers – 'all this. I say "No" and they send the Iron Duke against me. No sooner has he gone, they send Don John of Austria. And now Parma, the anti-Christ himself.'

'Parma is a fine soldier,' Charlotte said. 'I've heard you say so yourself.'

'Oh, he is.' William nodded. 'He's an Italian prince of charm and diplomacy; but the man is as rabid a Papist as you'll meet in many a long day.' He looked at her sideways, a glint in his eye. 'As were you, once upon a time.'

She pursed her lips and then laughed. 'Was I?' she asked.

'A nun, no less,' he whispered, looking round to make sure there weren't any still lingering in the darker corners of their old convent. 'A bride of Christ.'

'It may be blasphemy to say so, William,' she said, pouring wine for herself, 'but it's rather more fun being married to you.' And they laughed together, touching heads.

'I beg your pardon, my Lord.' An official in state robes stood in the archway that led to the chamber. 'I can come back if this is not a good moment.'

'No, no, Hans. What is it?'

'The petitioners, my Lord. They have been here all day.'

'Oh, my God, yes of course. I'd forgotten. Lottie . . .'

'I know,' she said. 'Kiss the children for me.' She whispered in his ear, 'But you promised Emilia the Pied Piper story tonight.'

'I did,' he remembered. 'I can tell her or anyone else that story in my sleep.'

His wife laughed and kissed the top of his head, running her hand down his neck lovingly. 'It's her favourite,' she said.

'I know.' Her husband smiled. 'Just go and tuck her in and I'll be along presently.'

Charlotte of Bourbon-Menpensier had heard that one many times before. If only the Duke of Alba and John of Austria and the Duke of Parma and even that mad old bastard Philip of Spain could see her William telling Emilia her favourite bedtime story, perhaps they would all just go away. Perhaps they would see the Low Countries as a land full of people, good people just like themselves and stop just thinking of it as so many miles of soil to be won. Perhaps they would just go away and leave the Dutch alone, to their endless battle with the sea. At least the sea played fair and used no mercenaries but the wind and the tides.

'I know you will,' she said, and kissed him again before leaving to be with her children.

Hans, like the good steward he was, waited until the Princess of Nassau had left the room before ramming his staff of office down on the polished floor. A servant was rolling up the maps and lacing them together. Another was lighting all the candles and a third drawing thick velvet curtains against the lashing rain and the threatening night. Not a night to be out. A night to be in, in the warmth of the fire crackling in the huge grate. A night to be safe.

The first petitioner crossed the floor and knelt before the Statholder.

'Who are you?' William asked.

'Jean Jaureguy, my Lord,' the man answered.

'You're a Frenchman?' the Statholder wanted to know.

'A Fleming, sir.'

William nodded. 'And what can I do for you, Monsieur Jaureguy?'

The Fleming suddenly stood up and flung back his cloak. 'You can die!' he shouted and levelled a wheel lock at the Statholder. The gun barked and flashed in the man's hand and a gash of scarlet sprayed out from the Statholder's head as the ball crashed through his skull.

Helene Dee was sitting by the fire, frowning a little as she turned the heel of a stocking. Her husband was not so busy, but he was concentrating just as hard, gazing at her beauty from the other side of the fireplace. His eyes, which had burned into many a soul in their time, were burning now into her temple but she didn't seem to notice. He upped the psychic pressure and eventually she responded.

'John,' she said calmly, not looking up. 'Are you just practising or are you . . . one, two, three, slip one knit one, carry slip stitch over . . . trying to attract my attention?'

Dee immediately looked away. 'Hmm, sorry, my dear,' he said. 'I was miles away. What did you say?'

'I said, you old fraud,' she said, with no malice, 'are you staring at the side of my head because you are practising a bit of magic, or are you trying to attract my attention?'

Dee sighed. Helene was beautiful and that was why he had married her. A lovely young wife gave an old magician a credibility that no phantasms of the living and dead could bring. The men of the court, seeing her beauty, believed that he had used the strongest magic to bind her to him; they couldn't see any other reason why such a lovely thing would shackle herself to such a dried out man when they, in all their youth and vigour, were available. The women knew why she was married to Dee; clearly he had magic powers which could bring pleasure to a woman beyond her wildest dreams. He could conjure incubi by the score and so when he was unavailable or unable, she could while away the midnight hour in ways no man could match.

They were all wrong. Helene Dee was married to the magus because he had rescued her from a life as a hedge witch, with only stars for her roof and ground for her bed. She had been unkempt and filthy when he found her, her beauty hidden to all. But he saw her inner beauty and it was a happy extra for him that when his cook and valet had washed and polished her, she shone like the stars she had once slept under. She was grateful. He was undemanding and so they rubbed along. But he should have known that a witch, even a hedge witch who made a living with potions and charms, would be more or less immune to all but his most complex conjuring and the outcome of a simple staring match would never be a foregone conclusion between the two.

'I was trying to attract your attention,' he said. 'I was also wondering . . .'

Helene did not help him by finishing his thought for him, although she easily could have done so. She held up a finger. 'I'm counting stitches,' she said. 'Wait.' She muttered the numbers under her breath and when she had finished the row, she laid her four needles in her lap, the filmy stocking knitted in the finest linen thread bunched beneath them. 'Now –' she smiled at him dazzlingly and her blue eyes danced – 'what were you wondering, my lord?'

He smiled back at her. All men smiled back when Helene Dee was smiling. Then, his face became serious. 'Let's see if you still have the knack,' he said. 'Come here and kneel, Nell. Look into my mind.'

'Oh, John,' she said, laying aside her knitting. 'Do I have to?'

'Humour an old man,' he said. He clapped his hands lightly and extended them, open, towards her. He shifted in his chair and opened his knees, patting down his gown between them, so she could come in close. When she still hesitated, he clapped his hands again and patted the insides of his thighs.

With a sigh, she got up and with languid grace knelt between his knees. She put two fingers of her right hand on his brow between his eyes and two fingers of her left hand on her own forehead. She muttered a low incantation.

'What's that you're muttering?' Dee asked, pulling back. He was as credulous as the next man, despite knowing every trick in the book and some others too frightening ever to write down.

'Oh, sorry,' she said. 'Did I speak aloud? It was just a list of the laundry that needs to be sent to the washerwoman. I'll be quiet. Come forward. We'll start again.'

She repositioned her fingers and pressed lightly on her husband's brow, the pressure making his skin go numb and a slight pain run along the sinuses of his face. She stayed like that for two minutes, counted by the second and then she let her fingers drop to her lap.

'You were wondering,' she said, 'whether I have been bedded by Edward Kelly.'

Dee pushed her away, not roughly, but purposefully. 'I do believe you really are a witch,' he said. 'That *was* what I was thinking.'

She sat back in her chair, made herself comfortable and reached for her knitting. She started counting stitches again and the minutes ticked by. Dee looked round the room of this rented house. It had none of the glorious eccentricity of his home in Mortlake, destroyed by fire not six months since. It had been a place of wonders, of cockatrices, of flagons of potions, of alchemists' retorts blown of glass so thin it was scarcely there at all. It had grown around him as a caddis grows its coat, in the still pools of night when he could commune with spirits best left in the vasty deep. He missed his house and was looking for another home, perhaps not so near to neighbours who took exception to his nocturnal noises and his not inconsiderable reputation. Ely, in the county of Cambridge, had attracted him for many reasons. The cathedral was unlike any other in the country, floating like a caravel in the mists of the fens, built by the Normans with their iron coats and strange tongue. The countryside was eerie, flat as a plate with skies much bigger than they ever seemed in London. It was a country that gave a man space to breathe, to think. It also gave Dee more time to be with Helene, without the distractions of his constant calls to court. Every time the Queen needed to make a decision, she called Dee to cast a rune or plot a chart. Helene joked that Elizabeth asked Dee before she took a piss. The call had not been for so trivial a reason yet, but that day was probably not far off. Pleading a vital piece of research which would strengthen his ties with the world beyond, Dee had taken his little household off to the Fens and so here he sat, on the horns of his dilemma. Was Helene faithful to him, or not?

Eventually, he could bear it no longer. 'And so, madam,' he said, 'have you?'

She looked up from her stocking, the heel now successfully turned. 'I told you what you were thinking,' she said. 'I didn't say I would tell you the answer to your question.'

'But you must tell me,' he said. 'I have never asked such a question before, although you must know I trust no man with you. You are the most beautiful woman any man has ever seen. To see you must be to want you.'

'Think of it from my point of view, then,' she said. 'I am the woman looking out from the tower of my beauty. There are few men who match my charms, if what you say is true. Why should the most beautiful woman in the world have anything to do with Edward Kelly, with his clipped ears? What could he offer such a one? You are a magus. He is a trickster with a silver tongue, one who mocks people's credulity, who turns their wishes to his own advantage. I have the magus. Why would I want a fraud?'

Dee settled back in his chair. He could see into men's hearts and see their innermost desires. He could bring men back from the dead to tell who sent them there. He could turn lead into gold . . . well, not that, but surely that secret was not far from his grasp now, if his calculations were correct. He looked at his wife, sitting there demure with her knitting. He decided to believe her.

She decided not to disabuse him.

'Kit?' Michael Johns popped his head around the scholar's door that morning. 'Leaving so soon?'

He took in the heavy leather haversacks, the extra rolled cloak, the provisions for the road laid out on the bed. Particularly he took in the sword with its swept hilt gleaming like mercury at the man's hip. The grey fustian of Corpus Christi had gone and Marlowe wore a black doublet with scarlet slashes, buskins of leather and a colleyweston cloak embroidered with spiders' webs in silver. Professor Johns would need to work for ten years to earn enough to buy all that.

Marlowe looked up at him, stuffing books into his satchel as he was. 'For the journey,' he said, waving a copy of Homer at his tutor.

Johns mentally listed the books the man was packing – Cicero, Aristotle, Ramus, the anarchic *Prince* of Machiavelli, the banned love poems of Ovid. 'By day,' he murmured, 'Christopher Marlowe, scholar and graduate of Corpus Christi, Quartus Convictus . . .' He saw Marlowe smile, 'Sometime playwright, sometime poet. And by night . . .' Johns' smile had suddenly faded and he was deadly serious. 'What are you by night, Kit Marlowe?'

The scholar, graduate, the playwright and poet looked up at him, then he slammed shut the last book and shipped it away in his pack. 'Better you don't ask, Michael,' he said. 'I couldn't lie to you and I would rather not have to try.'

'Couldn't you?' Johns asked. He had known this man for over three years, ever since he had come as a gauche pot boy from the King's School in Canterbury, a chorister and the son of a cobbler. And very quickly, Johns had realized that there was a fine brain there and a deadly, indefinable something that drew men to Kit Marlowe. In his own way, his quiet, scholastic way, Michael Johns loved Kit Marlowe. But who knew who or what Kit Marlowe loved? His eyes were shadows that afternoon, dark voids that gave nothing away. He didn't answer Johns' question directly.

'Let's just say I have business overseas.'

'Overseas?' Johns frowned. He didn't like the sound of that. 'Can you be more specific?'

Marlowe shook his head.

'How long will you be gone?'

'I shan't be gone,' Marlowe said and watched confusion cloud the older man's face. 'In fact –' he hauled his saddle bags on to his shoulder – 'I was just on my way to see you. Parker and Colwell have a purse to spend in the Buttery in my name. As far as the records show, it will look as if I have never left Cambridge. That just leaves you.'

'Me?'

'You and Dr Lyler,' Marlowe said. 'I have lectures with no one else until the end of the Lenten Term. Lyler, saving your colleague's professionalism, won't notice if I'm there or not. Colwell and Parker will string him along with more excuses than you've had college suppers. Which just leaves you . . .'

Johns held up his hand. 'Kit, I will not be party to subterfuge. If you are not there to say "adsum" at my lectures, I am bound to say so. You will not get your Master's degree.'

Marlowe looked levelly at the man, one of the very few he would trust with his life. 'So be it.' He shrugged.

'Can you at least tell me . . .' John's voice rose.

Marlowe spun back to him, already halfway through the door. 'Are you a patriot, Professor Johns?' he asked. 'Do you love your Queen?'

Johns was nonplussed. In all their discussions in the Schools, in Rhetoric and Dialectic, Marlowe had never asked him that or anything like it. Johns was only thirty-five, yet the world he knew was spinning away from him already. He knew suddenly how Doctor Norgate felt every day, with something that yesterday seemed as fixed as the firmament flying off the surface of his world. He opened his mouth but nothing came out.

'Let's just say –' Marlowe's voice was softer now – 'I am away on the Queen's business. Let that be enough. And, Michael, let it also be enough that you are the only person in this world who knows that, apart from the one who sends me.'

He clapped a fond hand to his teacher's shoulder and brushed past him to the stairway and the outside world. Johns watched from the window as Marlowe strode away into the closing light of the cold November afternoon. He saw him greet his old King's scholar friends, Parker and Colwell, drab beside him in their college grey as sparrows are to a flashing magpie. He hugged each one in turn and was gone, under the archway, out of the Court, his footsteps echoing into silence.

FOUR

Nathaniel Hawkins wasn't happy with any of this. 'Sort it out,' Trumpy Joe had said to him as if it were leading a bullock to pasture. But this was murder and Nathaniel Hawkins was out of his depth.

He looked at Jabez Hazel, his fellow Constable of the Watch, trudging through the Trumpington mud alongside him, their breath smouldering on the air like the smoke at stubble-burning time. The mud had a crisp top to it, ice which wouldn't carry a duck, and it gave a crackle to their steps that reminded them that winter was well and truly here.

'Didn't he say where he was going, Jabe?' he asked.

Hazel shook his head. 'Not a word, Nat,' the younger man grunted. 'But he was making for the north.'

Hawkins shook his head. 'It's not like Joe,' he muttered, listening to his staff clatter on the frozen ruts at the edge of the road, where the ice was harder and unyielding. 'Going off like that. Maybe we should ask Allys.'

'We will,' Hazel told him. 'But we've got a job to do first. Is that it? Left of the road?'

The smoke drifted up from the chimney of a cottage, old thatch dark and damp in the grey of the afternoon. A cart with an ox in the harness stood sentinel outside and a knot of villagers stood whispering in a huddle. The priest of Trumpington saw the constables and crossed to them.

'Master Hawkins, Master Hazel.' The man nodded to each. 'Has Constable Fludd sent you?'

'He has, Vicar,' Hawkins told him, 'in a manner of speaking.'

Both men had pulled off their caps in the priest's presence and stood a little sheepishly. They'd seen death before, even violent death with its blood and its suddenness. A knife flashing in anger outside in the street after men had been drinking all night, a cudgel against a skull too thin to withstand the blow; the usual free-for-all at the Stourbridge Fair; these they understood. But clandestine murder left them uneasy and without Fludd they were rudderless.

'I rather hoped that the Constable would after all come in person.' Henry Mildmay was scanning the road that led from the town but it was deserted at that time of day.

'He was called away, sir,' Hazel volunteered, 'sudden, like. Left it to us.'

Mildmay's raised eyebrow said it all. He'd baptized Jabez Hazel and laid his father and mother in the little churchyard where Gammer Harris would soon lie. But now she lay in the dark little hovel she'd called home, unwashed and unblessed. The priest pushed past the villagers who nodded at the constables, and leaned on the low door. He felt his feet dip into the greasy mud at the entrance and steadied himself against the beam. There had been no fresh straw on this floor for weeks and the room was acrid with smoke. There were just the two rooms, the one in which the three men now stood, with its single table and two chairs, and another off to the left, where a solitary candle now guttered and a low crooning seemed to drift with the fire smoke.

'Who's there?' the priest called, frowning. That was no Christian hymn he heard and it frightened him. The low wail stopped and Mildmay pushed the door back.

Nathaniel Hawkins caught his breath and Jabez Hazel, for all he swore to himself that he wouldn't, turned aside to heave his dinner all over the floor. There was that sickly smell of death, of blood, of the end of all things, and Hawkins and Mildmay found themselves staring down at a body on the bed. It was that body that held Hawkins' gaze. It was naked, glistening with warm water and there were blood-soaked cloths around it, like a baby in swaddling bands. Hawkins couldn't look directly at the head, because the head had been hacked down the centre. A mass of black blood and grey brains and white bone disfigured the features of the woman who had once been Gammer Harris.

But it wasn't the dead woman that Henry Mildmay watched. He was scowling at the shadowy figure in the corner, 'Mother Moleseed?' he said. 'Is that you?'

A crone of indefinable years hobbled into the half light,

tugging on her cap. 'Your worship, Reverend Mildmay,' she lisped.

'What are you doing here?' the vicar wanted to know.

'Preparing the dead, sir. You know that. I lays 'em out, sir, as I have for many a long year. And my mammy before me.'

'What were you singing?' Mildmay asked her.

'Just an old tune, sir,' she said, mopping the blood where it had seeped on to the headboard.

'There are tunes for the dead,' Mildmay reminded her, 'God's tunes. My tunes. I shall do the singing for Ann Harris when the time comes.'

Jabez Hazel had come into the room again, but how long he'd be able to stay was anybody's guess.

'Take her out, Jabe,' Hawkins whispered. 'Mistress Moleseed, is it? Take her outside. The vicar and I will cope in here.'

'But I have my work.' Mother Moleseed's reedy voice rose higher as she attempted to stand her ground. 'It's not right to leave a woman like that . . . not in front of men.'

'We all came naked into the world, mother,' Mildmay reminded her, 'and it is how, one day, we'll stand before the Lord.'

Hazel took the woman by the arm. He knew Mother Moleseed. He'd known her since he was a boy, bouncing on the hay cart at harvest time and scrumping apples from the squire's orchard. She'd caught him once and put the evil eye on him, or so he'd thought. He hadn't slept for a week and was careful to say his paternoster with more than usual fervour for a while.

'I know you, sonny . . .' she peered up at him with a tooth-less grimace and his heart sank.

Nathaniel Hawkins had watched Joseph Fludd do this, the two of them alone with the dead. He hadn't known what Fludd was doing, so he knew even less what to do now. 'Everything you see, Nat,' Fludd had told him. 'Say it out loud. It will help you remember at the coroner's court.'

'Her head's been cleaved,' he heard himself say as Mildmay wandered the room, muttering his prayers for the dead, closing his eyes and making the sign of the cross. 'But with what? Axe? Billhook? Sword?'

Nathaniel Hawkins knew what an axe could do. He'd watched Joe Fludd many a long day, hacking his way through oak and elm to fashion his carpentry for the great and good of Cambridge. He'd watched the bark bite and the chips fly and listened to the thud as the iron blade hit home. He knew what a billhook could do too. Old Jem Harris was a hedger, he used one of those all his life – and he had two fingers less on his left hand to prove it. But a sword? Hawkins had never owned a sword. If he saved all his life to buy one, he'd be in his box before he could; the box Joe Fludd would make for him one day. Could a sword do this? A broadsword might. Or one of those hand-and-a-halfs he'd heard the Germans carried. But who would old Gammer Harris know who owned a sword?

Hawkins looked up at the priest. He was still busy sending the old woman to her Maker, praying for her soul, interceding. Hawkins would have to do the hard work himself. 'Was she found like this?' he asked aloud. Mildmay didn't answer and Gammer Harris didn't either. He rummaged at the foot of the bed to find the dead woman's clothes. Her shift was covered with dark blood. Her shawl was folded on top of her pinafore; both were stiff and dark with drying and clotted blood. Hawkins unpacked the neat parcel that Mother Moleseed had made of the thin, worn fabric. Inside, the blood was brighter red, still sticky and wet; Gammer Harris had lost almost all of her lifeblood to whatever weapon had cloven her head in two. He barely recognized her cap because what was once white was a ripped shred of crimson, the ties stiff with blood.

So the woman was fully clothed when she died. Mother Moleseed must have stripped the corpse as she laid the woman out with all that keening and nonsense. Hawkins wanted nothing to do with that. That was the vicar's job. He looked at the pillow and the headboard, all of it dark and bloody. Whoever had killed Gammer Harris had hit her as she stood by the bed, or perhaps as she sat on it.

He could do no more for the woman in that room and he left the priest muttering over her and made for the fresh air. 'Where's Jem Harris?' he asked the knot of neighbours. 'Does he know of this?'

'In the Lammas Field,' someone told him. 'He's been sent for.'

'And what about the Egyptians?' Hawkins asked, 'Has anybody seen them?'

The tent had gone up in lightning time, even for the accomplished Egyptian camp-builders. No one had to give an order, everything just seemed to happen by itself. The teeming children – eight in all but sometimes seeming like eighty as they swarmed around the onlookers, dipping in the odd pocket here and there to keep their hands in – had disappeared to a quiet wagon. The tale of the child crushed to death by a falling tent pole was true enough. It hadn't happened to a child in this troupe, or to any child known to anyone there. It had probably not even happened to a child in this cold and frosty land, but that it had happened to a child somewhere, somewhen there was no doubt at all and so they instinctively kept out of the way. As the tent rose, to the rhythmic cries of the men, the women started the cooking fire and the bread making. The next thing that would happen, they all knew, was that the locals from Reach and Burwell would come skulking round, not making eye contact, not even being civil. The person you hate the most is the one who knows where the bodies are buried and ten minutes in a smoky tent with Balthasar Gerard was enough for him to know the innermost turnings in your very soul.

The camp was a tiny huddle of civilization in the vast unforgiving sweep of the lonely fens but within easy reach for superstitious country folk who needed their ten minutes with Balthasar. Since the caravan had passed through the town, people had been quietly falling into step behind and so by the time their camp was complete, with the single domed living tent in the middle, the smaller ones for cooking and for Balthasar's secret work around it, the crowd was considerable, although thinly spread around the perimeter, no one wanting to catch the eye of anyone else. Hern got his tumblers together; townsfolk who were after a potion or a reading could justify their presence there if they were watching a show. The men called the children out of the wagon. They could all tumble almost as soon as they could walk and with their ribbon-covered clothes looked like tattered butterflies spinning through the air as the two strongest men threw the children from side to side of the area they used in lieu of a stage. Boys and girls, curled into tight balls, flew so fast the colours merged and the crowd soon grew, pollarders, hedgers and shepherds, lured away to the tune of the pipes and the thump of the drum. And if some of them melted off from the edges at a gentle touch on the arm from one of the women, it was a secret no one had to share.

The group of Egyptians that had got the Mayor in such a fury was small as such troupes went, with just eight children, five men and three women. No one as they watched them pass could tell which man and which woman each child belonged to and this gave extra weight to the rumour that they stole children as they passed through each town. Nothing could be further from the truth. Although the children were loved and cared for each one could only be another mouth to feed until they could earn their keep and even Egyptian children were not adept at picking pockets until they were at least five. Why steal a child when their own came along so easily? The women belonged to everyone and to no one except themselves. The children obeyed the men and ruled the women; some had forgotten who their mother was and their father was anyone's guess.

Balthasar waited patiently in his tent, for the first of the people to slip in between the coloured canvasses which hung in the doorway. There was no light in the tent except a single candle, burning in the centre of the table. The candle was made of black wax, not for any other reason than that it made the petitioning townsfolk feel they were getting their money's worth. Balthasar was an adept at reading people, their present certainly, if not their future, and he knew that it was all about giving value for money. The candle was part of the table top after many years of use. When the wick of the current one finally gave out, the next was placed on top of the shapeless corpses of its predecessors until a slick pile of black wax had formed, looking as if it had powers all on its own.

Balthasar half closed his eyes and waited for the soft flap

of the canvas. Through his slitted lids, he saw that a woman had crept in, a shawl pulled low over her forehead and tight around her shoulders. This was to be expected – the evening was very cold – but she was wearing clothes to hide in, not just for decoration, vanity or warmth. He reached out to show her into her seat and managed to get a fragment of her shawl between his fingers for a second or two. Thick wool, not worn thin by years, so there was at least enough money in this woman's household, and more likely money to spare. Her hands grasping the edges of the cloth were smooth and white, so she had at least one servant in her house. Balthasar sniffed. There was a soft warm smell of roses, powdered in frankincense which filled his little tent every time she moved. She was going up the social scale with every second which passed. This one would be easy; she either wanted to be with child or wanted not to be with child. A few simple questions and he would have a gold piece in his palm, or he was not Balthasar Gerard.

He did not break the silence; that was not his way. He preferred to let his petitioners start the conversation. This gave him another opportunity to find things out. How they spoke to him, how they addressed him would give him more clues as to their social standing. A tremor in the voice, a clearing of the throat would also tell him much.

'Sir, what must I do?' she said. 'I expected you would ask questions of me, or make a pronouncement, perhaps.'

Her voice was low and clear, well spoken, but she had called him 'Sir' which he had not expected. She knew someone who had been to him already, perhaps here, perhaps in Cambridge, as it was often his custom to ask questions or make a sudden remark if the petitioner did not speak.

'What is the purpose of your visit, Madam?' he asked. 'I can make no pronouncement until you speak to me.'

'I have heard that you . . .' She paused, finding the next bit difficult. '. . . I have heard that you can foretell the future.'

'The future shifts, Madam,' he said carefully. 'I do my poor best to see beyond the veil.' He had learned not to promise too much. Men – and women – who had parted with a coin were often remorseful later. This was not like buying a loaf

of bread. They had little to show for their expenditure after a
visit to Balthasar and waiting to see if his auguries would
come true was not much to get for a groat.

'My life is a burden to me,' she said, leaning forward towards
the candle. 'If you can see no change, then . . .'

He looked up at her and saw in the faint light that she had
a bruise down one cheek and an eye swollen and black in its
socket. He gasped and reached for her hand. It was as cold
as ice and the pulse at her wrist was racing and thready. 'Who
did this to you?' he asked. 'I feel that it is your husband,' he
rapidly added. If he couldn't tell that, he was not much of a
soothsayer.

'I have no husband,' she said.

'I feel that this comes from a man who loves you, who you
love,' Balthasar floundered on. This must be a father, or a
lover perhaps, but why would such a lovely woman not be
married?

She sat back and put the shawl back over her head. 'I can
see that I was mistaken,' she said, acidly. 'I was desperate
and my maid told me you could see the future. You told her
that she would meet a tall, dark man and that she would live
happily ever after with many fine sons to make her old age
comfortable.'

'And so she will,' Balthasar said. 'She will look for tall men
from now on when she dispenses her favours and tall strong
men are better surely than small, skinny ones. I always say
dark, because I find that women in general prefer dark men
to ones with carrots for hair.' He waited for her smile.

'But you cannot tell the future?' she said, with a sigh.

'I can tell the future, but you wouldn't want to take part
in that ritual,' he told her. 'I can call spirits to me and at a
price they will tell me what you want to know. But they
always tell the truth. Most people don't want their future,
they want a happy story. No one's future is all roses and if
they knew the thorns in advance, who would even bother to
get up in the morning? I could tell you your future now and
you could make it yours or not as you chose.'

'What is my future, then?' the woman said. 'My present,
and I give this information to you as a gift is that I am kept

by a man of Cambridge, a rich and powerful man, who likes to hit women. His wife he will not touch, and so he hits me in her place. When we met, he told me he loved me, so in that you may well be right. For a while, he kept his needs at bay and we had a child. When she died without a breath being taken, I turned to him and he punched me in the face. And this has been his habit from then on. Tell me my future, that he is not in it, or I shall go to the banks of the Cam tonight and make my future as short as I can.'

Balthasar Gerard was a man who lived on the edge. He had his future written in stone and he would not change a moment of it, thorns and all. But sometimes even an Egyptian needs a rose or two. He leaned forward and reached for her hand. When she gave it to him, he clasped it in both his own. 'Here is your future, then,' he said to her.

And so he added his Rose to the company, and the three Egyptian women became four.

Kit Marlowe had had dealings with the curmudgeonly groom at Hobson's Stables before and so he walked in prepared for the usual cut and thrust of non sequitur which seemed to be the unavoidable precursor to hiring a horse. Ignoring the poor spavined thing by the door, he walked into the fetid warmth of the building, calling for attention.

The groom lurched out of an empty stall, the sound of giggling in his wake. He was fumbling fruitlessly with the front of his hose, pulling down his groom's smock to hide his embarrassment.

'Please don't trouble on my account,' Marlowe told him. 'I just want to hire a horse.' He caught the man's glance towards the door and stopped him with a raised hand. 'Not that one,' he said. 'I don't know how far I will need to ride, but certainly further than that poor thing could carry me. I need a mount that can carry me far and fast.'

An outburst of more giggling from the stall made the groom blush under his stable grime.

'I'm sure she doesn't mean it unkindly,' Marlowe told the man. 'You are clearly needed elsewhere, so let's be quick. What do you have for me tonight?'

The groom knew Marlowe as a more than competent horseman and also, in recent times, a heavy tipper. So he was torn. 'There's the Wasp,' he said, uncertainly. He didn't usually hire out the Wasp for long loans; she was always back in the stable within the hour, led by her bruised and muddied hirer, demanding all sorts of compensation and threatening Messrs Hobson with the wrath of God.

'The Wasp! Ideal for my purposes. But, Harry, there is a possibility I won't be able to ride her back. I may have to send word to you as to where I have left her. Would that suit Master Hobson?'

'Nothing much suits Master Hobson,' the groom said. 'You'll have to leave a large deposit.'

Both men waited for the giggling, but the woman appeared to have fallen asleep as there was nothing from the vacant stall.

'I have gold here,' Marlowe said. 'I'll leave the full value of the mare and if she comes back to you, you are to give the money to Tom Colwell of Corpus Christi. Is that fair?'

'Fair enough, Master Marlowe,' Harry said, stuffing the scholar's sovereigns into his purse. 'Where are you off to, may I ask?'

'East of the Sun, west of the Moon, Harry, for all I know. But I will try to return the Wasp; I know how fond you are of her. Don't trouble yourself. I'll saddle her myself.'

'That's very decent of you, Master Marlowe,' Harry said. 'She fetched me a nasty one the last time she was out. Constable Fludd had her for an hour or so.'

Marlowe laughed. 'Now, that wasn't kind, Harry, was it? Constable Fludd is no horseman, as all of Cambridge knows. What did he need a horse for?' As they spoke, he was pulling wisps of hay from the manger at his shoulder and packing it into a net. He was pretty sure that his quarry would be equipped with horse fodder enough, but the Wasp was a picky eater and all the more bad tempered if she got hungry. Better to be safe than sorry.

'He didn't say, but everyone knows he's off after the Egyptians. He's to make sure they leave England, or his job is forfeit.'

Marlowe nodded. Another complication for his journey would be avoiding Fludd, then. The Constable was a fine fellow in many ways, but falling in with any kind of subterfuge was probably not his strongest talent. Disguise was an option, but Marlowe was too vain to change his appearance much. He didn't mind wearing a scholar's fustian, but he was happier in the clothes he was wearing for the journey. And he certainly wasn't going to shave his beard or cut his hair again, not for Francis Walsingham or the Queen herself. So he would have to avoid Fludd or face him down if he named him in the wrong company.

'Back to your lady, Harry,' he said, 'before she goes off the boil.'

'Ar, getting her to the simmer is hard enough, Master Marlowe, and more than enough for me,' Harry said, but he turned back to the stall nonetheless. 'You'll find the Wasp's bridle on the left-hand hook. Her saddle's still on her; she was in too much of a skitterish mood when she came back for me to do much with her but wipe down her hocks with a wisp of straw. Good luck with your venture, Master Marlowe.' He disappeared behind the partition wall. The last Kit Marlowe heard of him was his grumpy voice saying, 'Wake up, you drab. What am I paying you for?'

With a smile at the weakness of grooms and of men in general, Marlowe went into the Wasp's stall. She put her ears back and showed her teeth, stamping her feet impatiently in the deep litter of the stall. Marlowe ran his hand along her flank and checked her girth. As he suspected, just a touch too loose, so that the poor Constable would have yawed about like a yacht in a gale, making the horse even more skitterish, as Harry would have it, than usual. He tightened the surcingle one more notch and ran his hand under the saddle tree, checking for burrs. Harry's sense of humour ran to the slapstick and his hatred of the constables of Cambridge ran deep. But there were no little surprises there and the mare soon calmed down at the touch of someone who knew what they were about. Her afternoon with an idiot on her back had made her testy, but she was not averse to a good gallop with a proper horseman astride her and so she consented to having the bridle fitted and she let him back her out of the stall.

As they walked down the stable, past the stalls, Marlowe heard just one remark from behind the partition where Harry was taking his ease, if that was the word.

'Was that it?'

A groom's life was a hard one, especially if he worked for Hobson, and on this particular day, it wasn't particularly merry, either.

'Good night, Harry,' Marlowe called as he stepped out with the Wasp into the cold night air.

'Er . . . yes, good night, Master Marlowe,' the groom called back. 'Good luck to your venture.'

'Thank you, Harry,' Marlowe said to himself. 'I may need it.' And with a reassuring cluck to the mare, he sprang on to her back and they clattered away through the emptying streets of Cambridge.

The Gothic turrets of King's College were black against the purple haze of evening as he made his way north, heading for Magdalene Bridge and the road to the Fens, where he was hoping to catch up with the Egyptians. They had gone north, that was the rumour and if they were bound for the fairs of Flanders, they would probably sail from Lynn.

Two men who saw him go stood in the angle of Trinity Lane, one wrapped in a roisterer's doublet, the other in his academic robes.

'Marlowe,' murmured Robert Green. 'Going on a longish journey by the baggage and hay he's carrying.'

'Not if he wants to remain a member of Corpus Christi College, he isn't.' Gabriel Harvey was furious, his jaw rigid in the cold of the late afternoon.

'You can do something about that?' Greene wondered.

Harvey sighed. 'I am Assistant Master of Corpus Christi College, Dominus Greene. Were it not for the fact that you and I have a mutual bond in loathing Marlowe, I wouldn't be seen dead talking to you. The sad fact is, however, that even I cannot just click my fingers and have the abomination sent down. What I can do is hammer nails into the man's coffin one by one until even someone as obtusely obstinate as

Dr Norgate will see sense and expel the man. Follow him. See where he goes.'

'But I'm on foot,' Greene complained. Already the echo of the Wasp's hoof beats had died away and Marlowe could have gone on any of a dozen paths after he had ridden past. Greene could run round Cambridge and its environs for weeks and never get a sniff of him again.

Harvey rounded on the man. 'You fancy yourself a poet, Greene. A university wit. Conjure up some spirit, why don't you and fly through Cambridge town.' He scowled. 'Or, failing that, run like Hell and then report to me which way Marlowe's going. I'll add a little imagination to what you find and report to old Norgate. Another nail. Tap, tap.'

And he swirled away, gown flying, striding through the gathering gloom.

FIVE

Kit Marlowe didn't know exactly where the Egyptian camp was but it wasn't hard to trace their passage. They were not only conjurors and tumblers, they bought old rags and bones which they traded along their route with paper makers and glue renderers. Picking over the rags for anything wearable was a job for the children while the carts were on the road and many a fluttering ribbon on their clothes had come from an outworn or outgrown lady's kirtle. Their payment for the rubbish they removed was a bright doll of paper, or a folded windmill for the children which rattled and hummed when it was blown round on its stick. It was almost like a game for Marlowe to track these tawdry leavings; out past Stow cum Quy and Lode's Mill, through Swaffham and across the Devil's ditch, dark and foreboding as darkness fell; and to find, at the end of the fluttering trail, the camp.

As he rode, he planned his strategy. He knew he would scarcely be able to simply blend in. Even if he had changed his clothes, he knew so little of their way of life that he could never hope to pass as one of them. He knew this much, that although their travelling nation was spread throughout the world, they were like one large family and to fail to recognize a name, an allusion to a fact known to them all would be to invite immediate exposure. So he decided that his best chance to win his way into the clan would be as a man on the run. If he threw himself on their mercy, they may take him in, if not for the love of their fellow man, for the love of the gold in his purse, for the love of angels.

Lost in thought as he was he nearly rode over the outskirts of the camp before he knew it. The dogs were the first to sense his presence, followed swiftly by the children, who swung on his stirrup leathers and led him into the centre of the camp, whether he and the Wasp wanted to go there or not. He warned them of his horse's temperament as best he could; he didn't know if the children could understand him as they seemed to communicate in a complex patois of their own. By the time he was at the campfire and in the presence of Hern, Gerard and the others, he had one child in front of him on his crupper; a girl, he assumed, from her long hair. All of the young of the Egyptians wore the same clothes, a pair of wide pantaloons of patchwork material and a thick coat, in this weather at least, of woollen material, fluttering ribbons at every seam. The shortest hair was to the shoulders, but it seemed that the boys had it cut to keep it at that length and they wore it quite plain. The girls' hair, as far as he could tell, was left to grow long until it formed itself into fat plaits with ribbons threaded deeply within each ringlet. To have tried to remove the fabric would have been to unravel the hair as well. His question as to whether they ever washed was answered by the proximity of the child in front of him. The smell of wood smoke and exotic oils was almost overwhelming and he hoped that it was only the flickering torchlight that gave the impression of small creatures scurrying through the ringlets.

Five men and four women stood around the fire, the women further back in the shadows, with their faces seemingly deliberately hidden. Three of them had hair in the same style as the children; the fourth was, like himself, dressed quite richly and she shone out with cleanliness. Could it be true that they kidnapped people on their travels? But the woman didn't seem to be shackled in any way, so he could only assume that she was there of her own free will.

One of the men stepped forward and spoke with a commanding voice in which the playwright could discern more than a touch of the theatrical.

'My name is Hern. What business do you have here?'

Marlowe decided to go for the charming approach. After all, there were enough women present to possibly swing things in his favour if he needed more help, and he had not met a woman yet he couldn't charm.

'Forgive my intrusion, I had not intended to ride into your camp like this, but your lovely children –' he clasped his passenger under the armpits and handed her down to Hern, resisting with difficulty the impulse to wipe his hands on his doublet afterwards – 'brought me here. They are impossible to resist, the little dears.' He looked down at Hern and saw the man's eyebrow lift in disbelief. Looking beyond the flames, he noticed that the women were not taken in either. That they loved their children was beyond question, but that anyone else would think them anything other than gutter rats was just as certain to them all. He tried another tack.

'I have had a little . . . altercation with the Constable back in Cambridge,' he said. 'It would be quite a good idea for me to leave the city for a while and I heard from a friend that travelling with you might be a good way of covering my tracks.'

Hern stepped forward and grasped the Wasp's snaffle rein. 'We know the Constable and he is on our trail too. Hiding with us will get you nowhere but the nearest lock-up, Master . . .'

On the ride, Marlowe had already decided to keep his own name. Only once had he tried to use another and it had brought nothing but grief; he had constantly failed to answer to it and his signature was different every time he tried to use the damned thing. Also, he feared he might bump in to people he knew and it was best to keep the complications of that eventuality to a minimum.

'Marlowe,' he said. 'Christopher Marlowe. But you can call me Kit.'

'I don't think we will be getting to the stage of calling you anything, Master Marlowe,' Hern said, evenly. 'We don't take in waifs and strays.' And here he stared at one of the other men for a heartbeat or two, but he got the stare back, measure for measure. 'We are called in our language a *caravanserai*, but that does not mean that anyone can join us as they will. If you are indeed running from the Constable, your best course would be to go wherever we are not.'

Marlowe had not expected this to be so difficult. 'I write poetry,' he said. 'Plays and stories. With a little preparation, perhaps you can learn some and add it to the shows you give.'

'Shows? We give no shows,' Hern said. 'Surely you know that that kind of thing is forbidden.'

Marlowe heaved a sigh and played his last card. Reaching

into one of his saddlebags he extracted a purse, not his heaviest, but quite tempting, nevertheless. 'I have gold,' he said, jingling the sovereigns, 'and it will be yours if I can travel with you to the coast and maybe beyond.'

A glance flicked between the men and a tacit agreement was reached. Hern stepped forward and reached for the bag of money. 'Welcome to our band, Master Marlowe,' he said. 'Is the horse yours?'

'To all intents and purposes.'

'An answer I understand and applaud,' Hern said. 'Come with me and I will introduce you.' The children lined up in a ragged queue, laughing and nudging. 'Not you scarecrows,' Hern said, giving the nearest of them a flick round the back of the head. 'Even your mothers can hardly remember your given names and I'm sure I can't. Keep your hands out of Master Marlowe's bags, now, or you'll answer to me. Now, Master Marlowe, this is Balthasar Gerard, our soothsayer. A precious man in our band; if you want to know your future, speak to him. He will tell you what you want to know.' A gale of laughter from the soothsayer greeted the remark and Marlowe's hand was clasped in both of his. He felt the man's fingers stray to his wrist, where the blood pulsed near the surface. Other fingers felt his fingertips and his palm, all as quick and as light as a butterfly's kiss.

'Hello, Dominus Marlowe,' Gerard said, and passed him ceremoniously to the man on his right. 'This is Simon. As I remember, he is Greek, is that right, Simon?'

'Portuguese,' the man replied, in a heavy accent. 'As you know only too well, Balthasar. But, for giving me an opportunity to lie, *obrigado*. May I introduce you, Master Marlowe, to my friend Frederico, from Italy.'

'Austria,' the man protested, laughing, and so Marlowe was passed round the band, where no one was quite who they seemed. The women soon melted away and the smell of spices swept over the camp as the evening meal got under way. Marlowe could see how a man could disappear in the company of these people; he had only been there half an hour and he was already none too sure who he was himself. The only question was; were any of them Egyptians at all?

They might all be spies like him and no one would be any the wiser.

He decided to put aside the cares of espionage for the evening and eat their food and drink their wine and try not to lose too much at cards. He was usually on the winning side when he played with Colwell and Parker, but these men cheated for a living; he would have to keep the bets small and his wits about him, he could see. Although they were so dirty that the original colour of their hair and clothes were anybody's guess, although they were so far on the other side of the law that it was out of sight over the horizon, although they could not tell the truth if their lives depended on it, Kit Marlowe felt oddly at home with this motley crew and ate his supper with relish – but being careful not to ask what the meat might be, for fear of the answer. If it was chicken, he didn't want to know whose; if it wasn't chicken . . .

Balthasar Gerard nudged him in the ribs and gestured with a greasy hand. 'Don't worry, Master Marlowe,' he said. 'It is chicken.'

Marlowe looked at him in surprise. He had been eating heartily enough; surely the question in his head had not been written quite so clearly on his face?

'Or, shall we say, *mostly* chicken.' The man laughed. 'Don't mind me, Master Marlowe. I like to keep my hand in; like this stew, most of what I do is what you would expect. But you must learn when living with us to expect the unexpected.'

'Where are we off to next?' Marlowe asked. 'I need to be out of the country sooner, rather than later.'

'You can't be in a hurry if you travel with Egyptians,' Balthasar told him. 'I have been with this crew of Hern's for some years and have learned that they are strangers to the straight line. Watling Street is straight for many a mile but Hern won't tread an inch of it; superstition, long bred in him, I fancy. The rolling English road is more his line; a strange choice for an Egyptian.'

'Does any in this band come from Egypt?' Marlowe asked. He had a fancy for writing a play on Cleopatra and Mark Antony and a little local colour never hurt in these undertakings. He always thought of himself as a playwright who did a bit of spying on the side, never the reverse.

Balthasar Gerard laughed and clapped the scholar on the shoulder. 'Bless the man,' he said and turned his head to the others. 'Which of you comes from Egypt, Master Marlowe wants to know.'

There were shaken heads and offers of various countries, some far flung, but none it seemed hailed from anywhere near the Nile.

'Once upon a time,' Gerard told him, 'I'm sure that a band came out of Egypt, bringing magic and colour to the more desolate areas of the world. Here and there there would be a dreamer, a poet, a singer of songs, a man such as you and he would tag on to the end of the caravanserai as it left town and so the bands grew, broke up, reformed, but were always called Egyptians, the children of the moon.'

'And are they all soothsayers?' Marlowe couldn't help but be reminded of his old friend John Dee, who could raise the dead, at least to his own satisfaction.

'No, by no means. Many use the cards or bones to pretend to tell the future. Not all have an adept such as myself.' In the firelight, Balthasar's eye teeth gleamed. 'I am famous even with other bands. They leave messages on the road to meet with us, so I can tell them what to expect in the time ahead.'

Secretly, Marlowe thought this would be quite an easy task; hunger, cold, dirt and, if they met the wrong kind of Constable, death.

'I see that you have worked out our futures for yourself, Master Marlowe,' Balthasar said, with his usual uncanny prescience. 'But, as you can see –' he waved his arm over the camp – 'we are not hungry, not cold and, though we may be dirty, we have evaded the Constable who, I imagine, has gone ahead of us to the coast.'

'How can you possibly know that?' Marlowe said. 'He could be on our tail as you speak.'

'You are riding the horse he hired from the stables,' Balthasar said. 'That he couldn't manage it is the talk of Cambridge. He left again on a quieter mount, but that was a while ago. Unless he is carrying his horse, which is unlikely, even for him, he is ahead of us. Unless he doubles back – and why should he? – he will ride until he reaches the coast. There he will wait a while, or he will ride back towards Cambridge. But since we will not be on that road, he will miss us again. And unless we are very unlucky, we will be long gone before he knows what has happened.'

'Why won't we be on that road?' Marlowe asked. 'Surely, we are heading straight to King's Lynn. Don't you want to be in Holland for the holiday fairs and such? Isn't there money to be made there?'

Balthasar gave Marlowe a long look. 'Either you have been planning to join us for a long while, Master Marlowe, or someone has told you much about us Egyptians. I won't ask why you want to leave the country, but I think it is more that you want to reach Holland than that you need to leave England.' He laughed again and slapped Marlowe on the shoulder. It was beginning to get rather painful and the scholar wished he would stop doing it.

'Not at all,' he said, and even to his own ears it sounded unconvincing. 'Had you been heading for France, or Spain, I would have still come with you.'

Balthasar Gerard looked for a long while at Kit Marlowe without speaking. There was something about the man which he couldn't read, couldn't penetrate. Most people had two layers in his experience, the one they showed to the world and the one that lay beneath. The one Kit Marlowe showed to the world, the flash horse, the gaudy clothes and the money was not the real one, or even close to it. That he was a scholar was obvious from the callus on his finger from the quill and the softness of his hand. But then there was the rest. His speech had cadences in it that suggested a singer, yet when Balthasar had mentioned singers there had not even been a flicker of an eyelid. Whatever the man was hiding, he had built his walls thick and high. But Balthasar was good at what he did, and persistent. He would find out before they embarked at King's Lynn what this man was all about.

'As you say,' he said, turning back to the group around the fire. 'Is it time for tales, Hern?' he asked. 'If so, I fancy Master Marlowe has more than one to tell.'

The troupe took up the cry and Marlowe shifted round until he was facing them squarely. 'What kind of tale do you want?' he asked.

'Love,' cried one of the women.

'But sad,' another said, 'like life is.'

'No,' Frederico said. 'Let's have war and plenty of it.'

'Can there be a cat in it?' the little girl from his pommel said, snuggling in to his side. 'A kitten, a ginger one with white paws?'

Marlowe looked around the faces in the firelight and the spy dropped away, leaving the poet and playwright in full command. 'I'll tell you a tale,' he said, 'with all of those things. A tale of Dido, Queen of Carthage –' he looked down at the grubby, earnest little face under his encircling arm – 'and her cat.'

Christopher Marlowe had been in some sticky situations, from the College proctors to the silent men in Walsingham's employ, but he had always endured those situations in the comfort, if only relative, of rooms in Corpus Christi or a palatial home with the Shelleys. The Tower was an option that he knew was always on the table; Walsingham reminded him of it whenever he thought fit and he had heard enough of life in that cold, dank place to want to avoid it, although death in the Tower was probably worse than the life. But nothing had prepared him for a night spent with the Egyptians.

As a paying guest, in a manner of speaking, he was given the back of a wagon to sleep in for privacy, rather than share a space in the tent, as some of the others did. He was given a couple of dogs to share his bed, for the warmth. He was offered a woman as well, for the same purpose or any other he cared to name, but he politely refused the latter and the former were soon looking for other lodgings when the scratching and the passing of wind got too much. He hadn't the heart to eject the monkey, the parrot and the snake, as he had obviously usurped their usual bed.

The parrot he could come to terms with, as it was as sleepy as he was and he could also foresee some amusement to be gained from teaching it some words that the Egyptians might not expect. The snake kept itself to itself, by and large, and once he had got used to the occasional dry rustle as it moved around in its basket, he didn't mind it. At least it didn't smell as much as the monkey. While the dogs were still in residence he had hardly noticed it, but once they were gone to seek new lodgings, he became aware of the smell of a piss-soaked carpet, warming in front of the fire. Every time the animal moved, a new waft reached Marlowe's nostrils and he was soon wishing for the old aromas of his shared room with the Parker scholars, which had been known to make strong men weep, to improve the general atmosphere. But soon he stopped noticing even that, and slept deeply.

In the morning, he felt as though he had slept on a sack of stones and when he looked he found that in fact it had been brightly coloured balls, obviously for the use of the troupe when juggling. But although they were much more colourful than stones would be, the general effect was the same and he ached at every joint. It was still dark when the rough curtain at the back of the wagon was pulled back and his little passenger poked her head round it and poked him in the ribs.

'Master Marlowe,' she said, 'it's time to get up. We must be on the road, Hern says.'

'What time is it?' Marlowe asked.

The girl looked at him in confusion. 'Time to get up,' she said. 'Time to be on the road, Hern says.'

Marlowe realized that she had no idea of time as clocks dictated it; the sound of the ever-present bells from tower and steeple which drove everyone else's world had no place here. He rolled off his sack and nodded to show that he was ready when they were. The women had stoked up the fire and were using a twig to stir something in a pot slung over it on a makeshift-looking tripod.

'What's in the pot?' he asked the girl, hoping it wasn't breakfast.

'Breakfast,' she told him. 'We all have to have some, because we never know when we will get another chance.' She spoke the sentence in the sing-song way that children will who have learned something by rote. 'It's oatmeal.'

Marlowe knew oatmeal. They served it in the Buttery for

the sizars and he even had eaten it sometimes. It wasn't his
favourite way to start the day, but the child was right, it did
keep you going until something better came along, preferably
something sweet and tasty in the Copper Kettle around ten of
the clock. It was the twig that worried him a little. But if he
was going to be part of this band, he would have to learn their
ways.

'Mind out of my way, then, young Starshine. Let me get at
that oatmeal. I have some honey in my saddlebags somewhere.
Perhaps it will make it slip down a bit easier.'

'I hope you've brought enough for everyone.' Hern's voice
came from round the side of the wagon. 'We don't have treats
for one and not the other here.'

Despite the setting, Marlowe was transported back immediately to his days at the King's School in Canterbury. Old
Master Greshop had eyes like a hawk and woe betide the boy
who tried to smuggle in a tasty treat for mid-morning. Greshop
would winkle it out and its owner would have to stand at the
front while the schoolmaster sliced whatever it might be into
minute portions so that everyone could have a taste. Although
oddly, it never divided up into quite enough portions to give
one to its original owner. Greshop's Law, the school called it.

Marlowe smiled at Hern as he appeared around the sacking.
'I have almost a whole pot,' he said. 'I would be happy to
share with you all. I'll just get it for you.' And he delved into
the saddlebags which had shared his bed, and more pleasantly
than the dogs. He found the honey, next to the letters of introduction to the court of William the Silent. He pushed them
further down as he extracted the pot. He handed it to Starshine.
'Give this to . . .' he was stuck then, as he had no idea whose
child she was.

'Your mother,' Hern finished the sentence for him. 'All the
women are called mother here and none of the men are called
father.' He laughed. 'It's simpler that way.'

Marlowe looked over to the fire, where one woman stood
to one side, wrapped in a thin cloak and scarf which were
much cleaner and of better quality than those worn by the other
wives. 'Who's she?' he asked. 'She looks a bit lost.'

Hern snorted. 'She's Balthasar's latest fancy,' he said. 'He picked her up last night when she came to have her future foretold. She'll not last. She can't cook, for a start and as far as I could tell she didn't keep Balthasar very warm last night either. So unless she changes her ways, she won't be coming far with us.'

'That's a good black eye she has,' Marlowe said, peering into the dawn gloom. 'I noticed it last night, so it's not from Balthasar, I assume.'

'She came with that.' Hern laughed. 'And that's about all. But Balthasar is a good draw at fairs and he does his share of the work. None of the children are his, so I suppose we owe him a little leeway, but I will be watching Rose to see how she manages. Any trouble and she's out.' He gave Marlowe a long look. 'That goes for anyone, Master Marlowe, you know that I'm sure. No matter how much money they bring, they work for their living, or they're out.'

'I understand,' Marlowe said, jumping down off the wagon. 'Why are we off so early?'

'Early? This isn't early, man. There's light in the sky already. We have an appointment to keep today. That isn't like us, we like to stay free if we can but this day has been arranged since we were in London last and I don't like to upset a friend. Well, perhaps not a friend, but someone who will put us in the way of good food, some warm lodgings and perhaps a bath for the children, at least. I am beginning to have trouble telling some of them apart.'

'Who are we going to see?' Marlowe was intrigued as to who might have the power to keep Hern to a time.

'Balthasar is the reason, Balthasar and his soothsaying. Although I can say modestly –' Hern looked down momentarily and a less modest man it would have been hard to find in a day's march – 'that I have skills of my own which interest this man.'

'Won't you tell me his name?' Marlowe asked.

'You may know of him,' Hern said. 'He is in the Queen's household, although that means nothing to us. She is not the Queen of the Egyptians. But he is a great magus . . .'

'John Dee?' Marlowe said. 'Are we going to Mortlake then?'

'Yes, it is Dr Dee,' Hern said. 'Do you have powers of

divination too? But we are going to Ely, not Mortlake. He has taken a house there and we are to meet him this afternoon.'

Marlowe was glad he had decided to keep his own name. The thought of Dee crying out 'Kit!' and rushing out to greet him, grey cloak flying with his strange household at his heels would have made any subterfuge very short-lived indeed. 'I know Dr Dee well,' he said. 'We have . . . worked together in the past. It will be good to see him again.'

The noise around the oatmeal cauldron had been rising as they spoke and Marlowe saw his honey pot going round the fire not once but several times. If he wanted to make his breakfast edible at all, he knew he should get over there as soon as possible. He pushed the problem of Dee to the back of his mind; the man was after all a magus of the most elevated kind. Surely he would foresee that he must be circumspect when they met. He could only hope so. He concentrated on the image of the man from when they had met last and tried to send him messages in the spirit. It was hard to keep his concentration in the hubbub of the camp and hoped that anything that got through was clear enough; he was sure he had sent a jumble of honey, children and smoke rather than a subtle message of intrigue and plots. But it would have to do for now. Air and fire. Fire and air.

John Dee was getting quite excited now that the day of the Egyptians was here. Helene was more circumspect; in her life before she had met Dee she had worked with groups of travellers, on and off, and was not under any illusions about their timekeeping qualities. Nevertheless, she followed her husband around as he flitted about their rented home, adding touches here and there to persuade their visitors that here lived a magus of the first order. Although he had proved his skills time and again, he still had a touchingly naïve belief in appearances. When he raised the dead, for example, he used so many elements that he would never know which was the one that actually summoned the demon or spirit. Would it, for example, work just as well without the sprinkled blood, or was that a vital ingredient? He never dared to try it; an annoyed demon was the last thing you wanted in your house. Getting rid of the damned thing could take years. So, he hung stuffed lizards from the portraits of someone else's ancestors, he opened doors in the cellars to create just the right amount of dank draughtiness and he gave instructions to the cook that at least one dish should be a rather disquieting colour; blue food always looked a little magical, no matter how well it tasted. Then he settled down to wait.

From a distant door, a thumping shook the building and Dee started up from his chair. 'They're here,' he cried, all excitement.

'That's the front door,' Helene said, all disapproval. These travellers had better know their place or she would know the reason why. Her marriage was unconventional enough, God knew, but she was still the mistress here. 'Call Bowes and have him send them round the back, John. We can't have their sort at the front door.'

Dee looked at her reprovingly. 'They are my guests, Nell,' he said gently. 'Guests come to the front door.' He scurried through from their snug boudoir and into the Great Hall, soaring up three flights, heading for the door.

Helene Dee sat back in her chair, eyes closed. Although many decades separated their ages, she sometimes wondered in which direction. Still, it was good to see him excited about something. The fire at their house in Mortlake had taken a heavy toll and she had thought that he would never be like this again, ready to delve into the unknown and see what he might find. She got up and went to the door, pulling it open just a crack. When she had been working in the travellers' way, she had found a little prior knowledge could go a long way, and listening at doors was only the start.

What she heard was unexpected. Her husband was speaking to one person only, and he was keeping him strictly on the other side of the door.

'No,' she heard him say. 'You can *not* come in here. You left me and I was glad to see you go. It has taken me a good while to undo the damage that you did and you will not come in and start it all again. I will not have it!'

From the other side of the door, kept open just a crack to keep the frosty morning out, she heard a voice in protest, but she couldn't hear what it was saying. It was angry, and that was all she could discern. Then, the door started to shake, pushed inwards by whoever – or, in this household, perfectly likely *whatever* – was outside. Dee was not as frail as he looked, but even so he was having trouble with the power on the other side of the thick oak planks. Calling for Bowes to come from his kitchen fastness, she hurried forward to help her husband. As she got nearer, she recognized the voice, which was now hurling imprecations and ill-remembered incantations at Dee. In her surprise, she spoke aloud.

'Ned?' she said, and Dee stepped back at the sound of her voice.

Edward Kelly, clipped ears blue with cold, stepped suddenly into the Hall, with the pressure from within removed and stumbled on the uneven flagged floor. He looked older than she remembered him, meaner and tight of lip.

'Nell!' he said, and moved to hug her, but she stepped back, behind her husband. 'Oh, so that's the way of it, is it?' he said, with a sneer. 'She did marry you after all.' Contempt oozed from every pore.

'In church, before God and the priest,' she said. 'Not some jump over the stick or any of your nonsense. I am Mistress Dee all right and as such I don't want you in my house.'

Dee was proud of her in that moment. He had never been quite sure how much of a wife she thought herself. Theirs was not a conventional coupling in any sense of the word and even after all these years she could have the marriage annulled for reasons of non-consummation, but he loved her all the same and realized in that moment that she loved him too. It was as if a fire had been lit in his heart and he reached behind him and fumbled for her hand. She grabbed his and squeezed it tight. They were in this together, the Dees, for better or worse.

Edward Kelly looked at them and nodded. 'Well, I can't argue with that, then, Nell. But it is cold outside and I am newly come from Holland. I have ridden for days to find you and if I could just come in for a warm by your fire and a sup at your table, I'll be on my way.'

'If you have come lately from Holland,' Dee said, 'how did you know to find us here? We have been moving around since the fire.'

Kelly narrowed his eyes and said, 'The spirits told me, John.'

Dee laughed. 'Edward, don't forget who you are speaking to, now. I taught you the tricks of that particular trade and I know you can no more raise a spirit than you can fly. Or is the flying coming on better these days?'

Kelly gave a bark of laughter, but there was no humour in it. 'I don't bother with the flying lately, John, thank you. And you are right. On this occasion, it was not the spirits, but a contact of mine in Holland. He had heard from a contact of his at court that you were wintering in Ely. I admit I have been to two other houses this morning; this was my last possibility, so I claim no special powers. In this case only, of course.' Even though he was speaking to people who knew his limitations only too well, he still couldn't help but keep his options open.

'Wheels within wheels, Ned, as ever,' Dee said. He had still not moved back any further and Kelly was still more or less on the doorstep. 'Have you ever been honest?'

Kelly looked upwards, thinking hard. 'No, not as I remember,' he said. 'But let me change all that and be honest with you now, John. I am destitute as I have never been before. The Dutch are a pragmatic people, damn their eyes, and a poor seeker after the truth has slim pickings in the court of William the Silent. The Spanish are worse – I was threatened with the Inquisition whenever I strayed south into their lands. At least the Dutch just mocked me; they didn't seem to want to set me on fire.'

'Another of your best tricks, as I recall,' Helene said, still standing behind Dee and holding his hand. This man had nearly ruined her husband before and she mistrusted him, with his big innocent eyes and his honeyed voice. She raised her voice again and called over her shoulder, 'Bowes! Come here, now!'

Down in the kitchen, the cook kicked Samuel Bowes on the ankle as he dozed before the fire. 'Nell is calling you,' she said, as he opened one lazy eye. 'There's somebody at the door.'

'Can't she open it, then?' he asked, closing the eye again. 'Got legs, hasn't she?'

The cook gave him another kick and turned over her piece of toast. 'Go and see what she wants. It might be them Egyptians, here to give trouble.'

'They'd come round the back, surely,' he said, but grumbled himself to his feet and climbed the stone steps out of the kitchen and opened the door, which he slammed to again immediately.

'What's the matter?' the cook said, turning round in alarm and dropping her toast in the ashes. 'Who is it?' The woman could turn milk on the best of occasions, but when she was frightened, her blubbery lips hung loose and her chins wobbled. Not a pretty sight, except that Sam Bowes was used to it.

'It's only that Kelly,' Bowes whispered. 'Standing in the doorway and trying to talk round the Master.'

'Is Nell there?' the cook said, in alarm, wobbling more than ever.

'She is. Standing behind the Master and holding his hand fast. I'm not going out there, not for a ransom.'

The cook stood up, her ruined toast forgotten. 'Go out there, you craven bastard. We nearly lost our positions last time that Kelly was in the household. If we all stand together against him, we can get rid of him. I'd rather have a dozen Egyptians than him.'

Together, they climbed the stairs, the cook wiping her hands anxiously down her apron and tucking her elf locks up under her cap. She had memories of Edward Kelly that she wasn't prepared to share with anyone and although she didn't want him back in her Master's house, a woman wanted to look her best. Just to show him she hadn't let herself go.

In the Hall, little had changed, at first glance. But Balthasar Gerard would have immediately seen the difference. Kelly was now further into the room and the Dees, though still hand in hand, had less of the tiger-at-bay look about them; their bodies were more relaxed, they now seemed to think that the danger had passed. But Kelly had been waiting for just this change and he took his chance. Before Bowes and the cook were in earshot, he leaned forward and whispered something in Dee's ear.

The magus drew back and dropped his wife's hand. He turned to Bowes. 'Make up a bed for Master Kelly, would you, Sam?' he said, in his best host's tone. 'He is staying the night. Just one night,' he repeated, almost a statement, almost a question, almost a plea.

'One night is ample,' Kelly said, with a smile. 'Just for old time's sake.' He stepped in, closing the door behind him with a finality that sounded like a coffin lid being closed. 'Just to warm my old bones at the fire.' He looked round and caught the cook's eye. 'Or something warmer, if you have it.' She hoped no one saw her blush.

'Hell fire,' Dee said, crisply. 'You can warm yourself in Hell fire whenever you want to Ned, but just until tomorrow at first light, you may use my hearth instead.'

SIX

Marlowe was anxious to help pack up the camp that morning, if only to work off the effects of the oatmeal, which had formed a lining to his stomach of which any alchemist would have been proud. He felt that he might never be hungry again. But wherever he turned, someone was already doing the work; the yurt was down in a matter of minutes, and folded into the wagon he had slept in the night before, the pole broken down into three sections and stowed along the side in special brackets. The fire had been kicked out and covered with the sods which had been cut and carefully set aside the night before. The horses were in the traces and the dogs tethered behind, the children stowed in neat and relatively silent lines behind Hern, who drove the first wagon. The Wasp had been rubbed down and fed, and she seemed remarkably docile. Hern had obviously had a word in her ear.

Almost before he knew it, they were on the Ely road through the desolation that was Wicken Fen and, looking back, Marlowe could see hardly a sign that seventeen humans and many animals had spent the night there. The flattened grass where the tent had been would soon spring back and the Egyptians would once more have disappeared into the mists. Only the secret visitors of the night before would remember their passage; how kindly they would remember them would depend on how well the potions had worked, how well their futures matched their dreams, whether the charms to foretell the name of their husband to be showed that it was to be handsome Hal, from the inn, with prospects and a winning smile, or gawky Harry, the tanner, who smelt of dog shit all the time and had a stammer and five teeth missing from the front.

They passed one village girl on the road, who was trying, on this icy morning, to collect dew to make her love potion work. Hern turned to Marlowe, riding at his side. 'If there's one thing I have learned on the road, Master Marlowe, it is that there is one born every minute.'

Marlowe looked behind him, at the bemused girl standing there with her bottle. 'She will catch her death of cold if she isn't careful,' he said. 'Isn't it rather cruel?'

'Not at all,' Hern said. 'In the winter we don't tell them to go barefoot and sky clad, although the summer charm does tend to bring them a man sooner rather than later. In the winter charm, she may well catch a cold, and the man who brings her hot soup and brandy is probably a better prospect than the one who finds her out at dawn naked on a summer morning.'

'So . . .' Marlowe spoke as he thought things through. 'Your charms are just a way of helping nature along a little.'

'Smartly said, Master Marlowe.' Balthasar Gerard had drawn up on his other side, riding a beautiful piebald horse, hung with bells and ribbons on its bridle. 'We will have you thinking like an Egyptian yet. Although, I must warn you, some of our charms are more than words. And when you can tell them apart, you will truly be one of us.'

A tousled head poked out from behind Hern. 'Is that Master Marlowe?' Starshine asked. 'When can we have another story, Master Marlowe?'

Hern pushed her back, not unkindly. 'Leave the man alone, Star,' he said. 'We'll have more stories tonight, when we have met Master Dee. He may have wonders for us that will give Master Marlowe even more stories for us. Isn't that right, Master Marlowe?'

'Doctor Dee has many wonders to share, it's true,' Marlowe conceded. 'But if they are suitable for children, I doubt.'

'No children here,' Hern said. 'Just very small people. If we don't let them see wonders, how will we find out which of them has the skill? Think of the many children in great houses who never find that they are musicians, conjurors, magicians or something even more wonderful because they spend their young lives learning Latin and Greek. Everyone should try everything at least once.'

Marlowe thought of the Shelley girls, Jane and little Bessie, children in a great house, he hoped, but not their own. Children whose father was probably dead by now. But Marlowe the scholar put his head over the parapet. 'I can speak Latin and Greek,' he said. 'As well as French, a touch of Italian, some Flemish . . .'

'You speak Flemish?' Balthasar asked, reining in his horse.

'A bit. Mostly childish stuff which I learned at home from the weavers. But I can certainly get by. And where my Flemish won't serve, there's always French, or Latin at a pinch.'

Hern looked at him from the corner of his eye. 'What a very surprising man you are, Master Marlowe,' he said. 'Do you have yet more surprises in store for us? Can you, for example, juggle?'

Marlowe laughed. 'I can juggle with a total of one orange,' he said.

'Tumble?'

'Over, if necessary, after a hard night drinking.'

Hern and Gerard exchanged glances. 'You might be hard to hide, then,' Hern said. 'But Simon isn't very good at the physical stuff either. Perhaps we can work out some kind of strong man act between you. He is a head taller than you and muscular. It's been a waste using Ernesto as his partner; he is a fine tumbler and we can do with him in the show.'

'Not muscular. Fat,' said Gerard, waspishly.

'A little fat, perhaps, but still quite strong. Hmm . . . I think we can work something out.' Hern fell silent and something in his demeanour told Marlowe he was dismissed. He fell back and rode for a while alongside the women's wagon, but the only conversation there was giggling. He fell back further still and when he ended up riding behind the dogs, he spent his time wondering how he would find his old friend, Doctor Dee.

As the caravanserai made its slow way to Ely, Marlowe was increasingly glad of his oatmeal breakfast. As a scholar on short commons, he had often gone without the odd meal, but his midday luncheon was the one he tried never to go without. His head was hungry, even though his stomach had only nibbled at the sides of the solid mass inside. He clicked his tongue to the Wasp and went back to the head of the column.

'Hern?' he said, 'are we to stop for luncheon today?'

Hern looked at him askance. 'Luncheon, Master Marlowe?'

he said, in a mocking, cultured tone. 'What would Egyptians on the road have to do with luncheon? If your oatmeal is not still satisfying you, go back to the women. They may have an apple or two to share, or a slice of cold oatmeal if you still have an appetite for it. But you'll have to get used to eating when there is food, not just because of the position of the sun in the sky.'

Marlowe looked up at the unending low grey sky, with not even a faint white glow to tell where the sun might be. 'It's my guts which tell me it's time for luncheon,' he said plaintively. 'How do you know where the sun is on such a day?'

'We all know where the sun is,' Balthasar said, coming alongside him with his usually unerring timing. How could a horse walk so quietly, Marlowe wondered. He himself was known to be flannel-footed, but his horses made the same noise as anyone else's. 'Even the children could tell you the position of the sun, and at night, they can tell the time by the moon, even when there is no moon to see.'

'How is that possible?' Marlowe said.

'No trick,' Balthasar said. 'I will tell you one of our secrets if you like.'

Hern looked at him with flinty eyes, as grey as his hair and beard. 'Be careful, Balthasar,' he said. 'We have not known Master Marlowe long.'

'I know Master Marlowe as well as he knows himself,' the soothsayer said, 'but this secret is one that any man could know if he thought for a moment about it.' He turned to Marlowe. 'Imagine the moon at the full,' he said. 'Come on, now, Master Marlowe. Let me see you imagining. Close your inner eyes and see the sky at night. Choose a good frosty one, so that you can see the stars clearly.' He watched as Marlowe's eyes moved from side to side, seeing the picture in his mind's eye, high above the rickety roofs of Canterbury or the turreted splendour of Cambridge. 'Can you see the moon?'

Marlowe found his arm lifting involuntarily an inch or two, to point to the imaginary world above his head.

'You are a good subject, Master Marlowe,' Hern observed. 'If I can give you some advice, don't let Balthasar speak quietly to you in the dark. Before you know it you will be telling him all your secrets and you won't even know you have done it. Beware!'

Balthasar laughed softly and patted Marlowe's arm. 'You have nothing to fear from me, Kit,' he said. 'We all have secrets here and which of us would want them shared around? So . . . can you see the moon?'

Marlowe nodded his head. He was 'Kit' now or was this all part of the soothsayer's guile?

'Now, still looking at the moon, but keeping the stars in view, wipe out the moon's face. Start from the middle or the edge, it doesn't matter, but imagine a cloth wiping out the moon.' He waited a few heartbeats. 'Is it gone?'

Marlowe nodded again.

'So,' Balthasar said, leaning back in his saddle, 'what is there to see where the moon once was?'

'Nothing.'

'Good. Now, let your eyes wander across the sky. Can you see any other patches of nothing of that size? Use your eyes. Don't just see the twinkling stars, but look and see the stardust too. Can you see another dark patch that size?'

Marlowe's eyes wandered about again, raking the celestial landscape in his head and eventually he shook his head.

Balthasar shook his bridle, setting the bells jingling and the ribbons flying. 'So, on a moonless night, look for the moon, Kit, and you will never be lost, not for place or time.'

Marlowe smiled slowly. 'That is so obvious, I don't know why I didn't know that already,' he said.

'You did, once,' Hern said, as Balthasar rode back down the column again, checking, always checking. 'We children of the moon remember things we knew at our birth. The rest of the world begins to forget as they draw their first breath. We begin to remember.' He looked slyly at Marlowe. 'Has Balthasar's lesson made you less hungry, Master Marlowe?'

Marlowe listened to his stomach, which said he was full and then to his head, which said it was definitely time for luncheon. 'Not less hungry, Hern,' he said, 'but it may be that I am learning not to be.'

'Then you must remember today as your first step to being a child of the moon.' Hern laughed. He reached behind him and foraged in the dark wagon. When he pulled his arm free, there was a child on the end of it. 'Here,' he said to Marlowe, 'take –' he twisted the child round and looked into its face – 'Lukas here and tell him some stories. He might tell you some in return; we have hopes of him as a storyteller when he is older.' He stood the child, who was somewhere around six years old, on the edge of the seat and gave him a push in the small of his back. The child leapt across Marlowe's saddle and snuggled back against his chest.

'Tell me a story, Master Marlowe,' he said, lisping badly.

'What about?' Marlowe asked, glad that the boy was facing forward and so only the Wasp was catching the spray. 'Do you have a favourite animal?'

'I like to listen to stories of squirrels,' Lukas said.

As long as he didn't tell too many on the subject, Marlowe thought, or whole audiences may well drown before he got to the end. 'Once upon a time,' he began, 'there was a squirrel, the bravest squirrel in all Christendom . . .'

Hern smiled as the two fell back in the column. He liked to know where Master Marlowe was at all times. It took a trickster to spot a trickster, and behind the face of that handsome boy was an adversary worthy of the Egyptians. This journey might turn out to be their greatest show yet. He clicked to the horses. They ignored him. Egyptian horses on the move had but one speed and he would have been amazed if there had been any change of pace. But he did it every now and again for the look of the thing.

Slowly, into the gathering dark, the ragged crew made its way along the road from Ely as it led through the Fens, across the watery waste of Soham Mere. Although the dusk and mist prevented anyone seeing far on either side, the feeling of enormous, silent space was unnerving, especially to a man who was used to the closes and alleys of Cambridge and Canterbury. Marlowe could feel the ghosts of the past gathering at his back and he was grateful for the sleeping warmth of Lukas, still astride the pommel of his saddle, finally sated on stories of squirrels in every guise; soldier, lover, swordsman, sailor, explorer and fop. The child, with his musky, unwashed smell and small jumps and twitches of his sleep was a reassuring taste of humanity. When Marlowe had encountered John Dee the last time, his feet were firmly on the ground and still he found the old magus deeply unsettling. Now that a few of his ropes had been untethered and the everyday world had retired behind a veil of the Egyptians' weaving, he was not sure how Dee and his peculiar ménage might appear.

At the back of the row of wagons and horses, lost in his own thoughts, Marlowe didn't notice that Hern had taken a right turn with his lead wagon and had disappeared into the tree-hung gloom of a small orchard inside an elegant but slightly tumbledown archway in the wall along which they had been riding for some while. Marlowe did a hasty adjustment to his course and was grateful that whatever Hern had said to her, the Wasp had taken to heart. On another day a rapid about turn such as that would have made her bolt for her life. Ahead, on a small man-made rise, was a manor house, its ancient stones grey and unyielding across the Level winds. It had the ornate roof gables of the Flemish influence that had reached this far west in the days of the Staple when the Lord Chancellor of England first placed his feet on the wool sack.

As they rode in between the two encircling wings, the big door in the centre was flung open and John Dee came flying out, with his cloak swirling and his dark cap seeming to glow with esoteric figures on his head. Behind him came Helene, if anything more beautiful than before, Sam Bowes and the cook, carrying the inevitable smell of toast which lingered about her always. This was a magnet for the children and soon they were clustering around her, trying to understand why a woman so relentlessly homely could smell so nice.

'Don't be a bother, children!' Hern called. 'My apologies for the behaviour of my brood, madam. They are tired and hungry from hours on the road.'

The cook got all flustered. Egyptians they may be, but children were children wherever they came from and the man who led them was certainly rather attractive, in a half-magical sort of way; and the cook was used to half-magical. Whatever she had been expecting, it wasn't this. She sketched a curtsey, taking everyone, including herself by surprise. 'May I take them into the kitchen, sir?' she asked. 'I could give them something to eat.'

'By all means,' Dee said, flapping his hand at her. Kitchens and children were far from his mind just now. He was the only one in the courtyard who did not seem to realize that the cook had been addressing Hern.

The cook went back into the house, looking like a galleon in full sail surrounded by tiny pinnaces. The total noise in the echoing space was immediately reduced and everyone could hear themselves speak. Marlowe kept himself to the back of the line and watched as the others were introduced to Dee. Looking beyond Helene's beautiful head, he thought he could see someone else lurking in the candlelight from the porch. It was difficult to focus on, now here, now gone and it was even difficult to identify its size, age or gender. No sooner did he have it in his sights but with one blink it was gone. Balthasar's voice sounded in his ear.

'I see that you have spotted Master Kelly,' he said.

'To be honest with you, Balthasar,' he said, 'I'm not sure who or what I have spotted.'

'No,' Balthasar said. 'It is not an illusion. It is Edward Kelly as I live and breathe. Our paths have crossed now and then, but I would be happy if I never saw that particular gentleman again, and certainly not here. He used to be Dee's partner, in business if not in crime, and when the good doctor dispensed with his services, it was a happy day for him, I'm sure. But let's not let him skulk back in the shadows.' Raising his voice, he called across the courtyard, 'Master Kelly. Come out and meet my friends, new since we met last. Come forward, come forward.'

Out of the dark corners of the porch stepped an ill-favoured man with cropped dark hair and the clipped ears of a rogue. Marlowe had heard of Kelly, but only in passing in Dee's house, as one might speak of an invasion of mice or fleas, now departed. He seemed to sidle rather than walk and the general impression was of someone walking down a corridor lit fitfully by tallow candles; neither definitely there, nor definitely not. Marlowe found that his features were not easy to remember when he was not actually looking at his face and knew that here was a man who, like himself, made a living on the edge. But, unlike him, this man had taken the road of disappearance and disguise, rather than Marlowe's trick of hiding in plain sight.

'Balthasar,' he called, as though greeting a long-lost brother.

'Edward,' Balthasar said, reaching forward and pulling him towards Marlowe, 'please don't fear that I am going by another name these days. Balthasar Gerard is and always has been good enough for me. May I introduce you to a new friend of mine, Kit. Kit, Edward Kelly, who is . . .' he paused and turned his penetrating smile on Kelly. 'Edward, I fear I don't know what you are these days.'

Kelly waved an insouciant hand in the air. 'I do some of this, Balthasar, some of that. As ever.'

'So there you are, Kit,' Balthasar said, thwacking Kelly heartily on the back, 'Master Kelly is a some of this and some of that, so now we know. But, Edward, please enlighten me. Is the beautiful woman yonder the reason for your return to Dr Dee's fireside?'

Kelly spoke sulkily, but Marlowe could tell that when he wanted to, the crust could be covered with honey. 'She is Dee's wife,' he said to Balthasar, 'and for some reason loyal to him. But I see you have a beauty of your own, albeit a little . . .' he swept his finger in a circle round one eye.

Balthasar dropped his voice to a growl. 'Rose is also not for you, Kelly,' he said. 'The eye will heal and when it, and her heart and her head have healed as well, possibly then . . .' he turned his head to watch as Rose stood with the women, trying to blend in and yet standing out like a diamond in oatmeal, like a petal in a box of coal.

'Another of your rescues, eh, Balthasar?' Kelly said, but his eyes were hungry as they looked in Rose's direction. Then, with a blink, he turned his attention on Marlowe. The poet felt as if he was being examined with a lens. 'And what do you do, young Kit?' Kelly asked. 'And do you have another name, to go with Kit?'

'No.' Helene Dee was suddenly at Marlowe's side, squeezing his elbow. 'No one has names here, Ned, not for you. You have just one night here, don't forget. And now that dear Kit

is here, there will be no bed for you. You can sleep in the
kitchen, with the dogs. You'll be nice and warm there, and in
good company.'

Still holding his elbow in a vice-like grip, she led him away
from the two men, towards the house. 'Kit,' she said in his
ear, 'excuse me for my familiarity, but you should not let Kelly
know what your other name is; he finds things out, uses them
against people. What are you doing with these ragamuffins,
anyway? I understood you had returned to your studies.'

'My studies and I are occasionally in correspondence,'
Marlowe told her, 'but just now I have a fancy to a roving life
with the Egyptians.'

'Well,' she said, looking him up and down and fingering
the leather of his jacket appreciatively, 'whatever you are doing
seems to suit you well. Here we are, our home for now. What
do you think?'

'Nothing will ever be like Mortlake,' Marlowe said, looking
round at the towering Hall with its Gothic beams and Flemish
tapestries. They depicted the Trojan War, if he knew his Homer.
And Kit Marlowe did know his Homer. 'I dream of it still.'

'So do I, Kit.' She sighed. 'So do I. You will see that John
has put in a few touches which I doubt the Leslies would like.
They are of the Puritan persuasion, John says, and not at one
with nature. I fear they will think we are ruining their home.'
She gestured to the lizards hanging from various curtain tops
and the owl who turned its head to watch them go. Of Bibles
and plain clothing there was no sign.

'I see the doctor has tamed another owl,' he said, pointing
to it.

She glanced in its direction. 'No,' she said. 'That takes
years. That one is stuffed. How he makes its head do that is
a mystery.' Then she squeezed his arm again. 'Come on, Kit,
there is no sign of Sam, as ever. I will take you up to your
bedchamber myself.' She led him across the Hall. 'Mind that
flagstone just at the foot of the stairs. It is still wet.'

'Wet?' Marlowe said, skipping sideways to avoid it. 'What
with?'

'Blood,' she said, then, seeing his expression, 'from the
meat for dinner. But John is going to say it is the wet blood

spilled hundreds of years ago by the ghost which walks this house; the ghost of Lennox Leslie. Oh, Kit,' she said, 'he has a host of wonders planned for this evening. I hope your Egyptians are as good as I hear, or he will leave them gasping.'

'I think there will be gasps in both camps.' Marlowe laughed. He looked into her eyes as they prepared to go up the stairs. 'But what are you frightened of, Helene?' he said. Her blood was fluttering in her fingers like a trapped butterfly.

'Why, Master Marlowe,' she whispered in his ear, 'nothing at all. What would I be frightened of?' But the eyes which looked over his shoulder were big and her lip wobbled just a little. He looked behind him and saw the Egyptians outlined by the edge of the great door, with Edward Kelly lurking behind Rose, like a thief in the night.

The cook had made a special effort with the food that night and toast scarcely featured at all, unless it was sitting under a freshly roasted bird to soak up the juices. The great table had been laid along its length with plates for all of the Egyptians; no one was forgotten. Rose made an extra mouth, as did Marlowe, but they were easily accommodated by shunting everyone a few inches and with Helene at its foot and Dee at its head and village women from nearby Prickwillow serving, the feast was perfection. On Dee's insistence Sam Bowes and the cook had joined them for the meal and the woman's eagle eye watched the serving women above her increasingly greasy mouth; she was not a cook who only cooked to please others, as the width of her hips bore witness.

The children were along one side, flanked by Rose and Lily on one side and Maria and the shy Eloise on the other. Opposite sat Hern and Balthasar, whose glares kept the behaviour in check and the cutlery on the table and not in pockets. The littlest two, scarcely more than babies, sat on their mother's knees and watched with round eyes the food being passed up and down. They listened with ears almost overwhelmed to the chatter and occasional bursts of song that filled the room. Their mouths seemed constantly full of some special titbit, rammed in without favour from all along the table. The cook had taken a shine to Lukas and was passing him all the best bits of the roast capon in front of Bowes, who was never quite quick enough to stab her in the back of her hand when she was thieving.

Balthasar sat opposite Rose and drank in her beauty while she ate. Marlowe, two along from him on his right, so favoured with a good view of them both, was struck again as he had often been before that a man in love was truly blind, because although Rose was as lovely as the day, she ate like a swineherd or even one of his swine. She didn't look to right or left, just into Balthasar's face, but filled her mouth and cheeks constantly, barely stopping to chew. She was either brought up in a barn, Marlowe thought, or had known long periods of hunger. Or, alternatively, she just had the manners of a pig. To get away from the view of half-chewed food flying all over the place, he looked down the table to where Helene Dee sat, pale and cool as ice. She had not taken much on her plate, just a few slices of the breast meat of the capon and a little sallet. She toyed with her knife, balancing it on the point and twirling it round in her fingers as the blade bit into the wood. He hoped that the Leslies were charging John Dee a sensible rent; it would take a while to remove the traces of the Dee company, what with the stuffed lizards leaking everywhere and the holes in the furniture. Lennox Leslie must already be spinning in his grave.

He felt rather than saw Edward Kelly's eyes on his back, but did not give the charlatan the pleasure of seeing him turn round. Instead, he bent back to his dinner and, catching the eye of the cook, raised his goblet to her. She simpered and looked away but when she met the eye of Kelly, sitting opposite, she looked the other way in confusion and stuffed almost a whole roast apple into Lukas' mouth, so that she had something to do.

Just when everyone thought they couldn't eat another thing, Dee clapped his hands and a huge bowl of frumenty was carried in, all ablaze with the brandy poured over it in the kitchen. The two Prickwillow maids carrying it held it out to their sides, so that they didn't lose their eyebrows or even their hair. The flames were showing no signs of dying down as it was placed in front of Dr Dee, the Queen's magus.

'Good, thank you,' he said to the wenches. 'Who has the cloth?'

One of them, the one on his left and standing nearest the wall, unfolded it from across her arm. As she had practised all afternoon she flipped it with a flourish and offered the top corner to her friend standing on Dee's right. They pulled the cloth taut across the table, masking Dee and the pudding from view, although the tall blue flames were still visible above the top of the cloth. All eyes were on the white screen, through which trembling images were visible. Those further down the table could also just make out the top of Dee's head. Those close to him could see his elbow or feel the pressure of a foot under the table. Suddenly, there was a bright flash which printed itself on every eye down the table and when they could see clearly again the cloth, the two girls, Dee and the pudding had all disappeared.

But not for long. Balthasar and Hern each had a girl on their knee and, from the kitchen, two new maids carried a flaming dish of frumenty and leading the way was a triumphant John Dee. The girls put the dish in front of his place again, the flames still rising feet into the air.

The applause was deafening, as was the laughter, as Balthasar and Hern both got up from their seats with the maids in their arms and danced them up the table in a wild jig until they were level with the flames.

'Blow, my pretties,' Hern said to them.

The one who had been on his lap, a pretty little blonde with an angelic face, turned to him. 'That's brandy, sir,' she said. 'There'll be no putting it out until it's ready.'

'Blow,' Hern said, 'and see who is more powerful, you or the brandy.'

Laughing, both girls bent down to blow and the flames immediately went out. Their faces were a picture of confusion, and more so when Dee waved his hand over the dish and they sprang up again.

'Blow,' Hern said again and the girls and Dee were off in a whirl of flames and no flames until eventually the cook intervened.

'Now then,' she said. 'I didn't slave all afternoon to make

this frumenty for you to play with it all night. Bring the ladle and let's eat.'

'Well said, cook,' said Dee. 'Enough playing with our food – let's eat it.' And everyone's plate was in the air for a spoonful of the rich treat. Only Helene declined a portion and Balthasar and Hern; they knew what went into anything which would not be extinguished and eating it was not sensible. Dee caught Hern's eye.

'I think I have fooled you, Master Hern,' he said. 'This is not the everlasting frumenty. It is the perfectly edible one from under the table. As long as no one has trodden in it, I think you will find it quite palatable. Will you pass your plate?'

'That was clever, Doctor Dee,' Hern said. 'You have given us something to live up to tonight.'

SEVEN

After the meal was finished, down to the last nut and fig, the Egyptians went outside to construct their stage and get ready to perform. Dee likewise had preparations to make, less elaborate perhaps but just as vital for the final effect. As the Egyptians filed out, he stopped Marlowe.

'Master Marlowe,' he said, all formality. 'What will be your performance tonight?'

'I am to be part of a strong man act,' Marlowe told him with a smile. 'But to save my blushes in front of friends, I am to be only a storyteller tonight. I think that Simon will need practice before he can do much with me. I'm heavier than I look.'

'Christopher, you are as thin as a lath,' Dee said. 'But if you are not busy performing with your new friends, could you perhaps help me with a trick?'

'If I can,' Marlowe said. 'Does it involve . . . necromancy, at all?' Dee's skill at the art of raising the dead had never been proved to Marlowe's total satisfaction, but that he had links with worlds outside the one they all inhabited in the day to day was not really in any doubt. Anyway, this was the Queen's necromancer, her magus and if the Queen believed in him, who was a mere subject to disagree?

'No, no. Well, perhaps I should say, not really. All is trickery, Christopher, all is illusion. I won't need to practise with you; just do as I say when the time comes and we will do splendidly, I feel sure.' The magician clapped the poet on the back. 'How have you been, though? We looked for you in London, but although there were signs and portents, you never came.'

'I have visited London,' Marlowe said, remembering his few hurried secret meetings with Walsingham or one of his crew, always in darkness, always in an anonymous alleyway; the Clink Wharf, the Cranes in the Vintry. 'I have been working, though, as a tutor.'

'Not a scholar still? What a loss.' Dee looked at him from under his brows and it was impossible to tell if he was laughing at him or not.

'A scholar again, I hope,' Marlowe said. 'I am just . . .' he tried to think of a good reason why he should be with the Egyptians, but nothing sprang to mind. He had told Hern a vague tissue of hints and suggestions, but nothing concrete. He had hoped he would never have to give details.

'Just doing a little spying,' Dee finished for him, in a whisper. 'Don't worry, Kit, I move in higher places than you. I know not only where the bodies are buried but who wielded the spade. I won't let you down. Any secret you may have is more than safe with me.'

Marlowe looked at the man before him, in robes which had once been rich and beautiful but which had now seen better days. His eyebrows had grown back since his last alchemical experiment had gone skywards, but the acid stains on the front of his gown and the fact that his hair was noticeably longer on one side than the other bore witness to the fact that for him the search for knowledge never stopped; the elixir of life was a lifetime's work and a man could grow old looking for the fountain of youth.

'Will you let me know when you need me?' Marlowe asked him. 'I feel I should help outside. I am trying to become a part of the troupe in all ways. Standing in here in the warm while they work outside won't help me with that.' And he turned to go.

'Be careful,' Dee spoke quietly behind him. 'This troupe is tricksy and not quite what they seem. Or so I'm told.'

Marlowe continued through the door. How could the Egyptians not be what they seemed? They seemed to be a group of beggars and thieves with a spot of dubious magic thrown in. He had seen them practising. The card tricks, done slowly, were no more than tricks; the bent-up corner or the clever shuffling was all it took to fool a country crowd. He had seen one of the women, he wasn't sure of her name, possibly Lily or Rose, a flower at any rate, seem to cure a woman who was dying of childbed fever as they passed through a village on the way to Ely. But did she cure her? Was she dying? What was real and what was illusion? He couldn't tell, yet. In a while he would know, when he had lived with these people a little longer, learned their ways. But for now, just for tonight, he was determined to put aside Kit Marlowe, intelligencer, and become Kit Marlowe, poet and storyteller; just a man prepared to be amazed.

'Come on, Master Marlowe,' Ernesto said as he stepped outside. 'Don't just stand there. Put your finger on this knot here.' Marlowe wandered over and was about to comply when a sixth sense alerted him.

'Why?'

'Why not?' the man retorted. 'Why not, get it? Not. Knot. Oh, I really must try and sneak that into the act.' Then he looked at Marlowe seriously. 'Because I need to tie it up, of course. Sometimes things are just as they seem.'

Apologizing, he put his finger on the knot and within seconds was tied down tight to the top of the stage, by the end of one finger. The more he struggled, the tighter the knot became and the perpetrator of the joke had melted into the darkness of the court. Marlowe tried to attract someone's attention, but no one seemed to see him there.

'Come on, Master Marlowe,' a voice said. 'Don't just stand there. There's work to be done.'

Marlowe pointed to his finger. 'I seem to be a little tied up, Balthasar,' he said.

Laughing, the soothsayer leaned over and pulled one end of the knot, which immediately unravelled and fell away. 'Be careful with us, Kit,' he said. 'Sometimes things are not just as they seem.'

'I am learning that, Balthasar, thank you,' Marlowe said, rubbing the end of his finger carefully. 'What can I do to help?'

'I think we are almost ready,' the man replied. Torches had been lit at the entrance to the courtyard which had become the rear of the performing area. Seats had been brought out for the household and the wenches and men who had been brought in to serve the meal. The servants from the house did not come with the rent but even so some of them had crept back to the house as soon as they discovered there was a show to be seen. They had heard rumours about John Dee and the village was full of tales about plumes of coloured smoke rising from the chimneys and they were anxious to see what was to be seen. And if it annoyed their employer, the old skinflint Gregory Leslie, then the perfection of the evening would be complete. They were spread out along the front of the house, on boxes and blankets to keep the chill of the ground from their bowels. They all knew from their grannies that sitting on the cold ground would make your bowels fall out and that didn't sound at all a pleasant thing. Finally, everything was ready and the small audience was hushed.

When the silence was about to degenerate into a hiss of mutterings and shiftings, Hern stepped forward. A torch in front of him sprang spontaneously to life and illuminated his face from below, giving it sinister hollows and highlights that it did not usually possess. Having gained their attention, he waited again, and again judged the perfect psychological moment, when their nerves were twanging at their utmost, but before the nervous laughter could begin.

'Good evening, ladies and gentlemen,' he boomed, throwing his arms wide. 'And thank you, Dr Dee, for your hospitality tonight. My band of Egyptians has fed royally and won't need to pick a pocket or steal a fowl for a day or two. What do you say, boys?'

A gaggle of children broke cover from under the stage, juggling with purses and bags which all looked familiar to the crowd, because it was from them that the children had lifted them not half an hour before. An angry muttering started, stilled by Hern.

'Give them back, my lovelies, give them back and with no less in them than you found there.'

As the audience looked into their purses, which had contained little enough before, each one let loose a pure white butterfly, which flapped into the air and disappeared into the dark sky. They followed their flight with eyes and mouths wide with amazement.

'A very nice touch,' Dee muttered to Helene. 'How did they do that, do you think?'

'Wires,' Bowes said, definitely. 'Wires, has to be.'

'Thank you, Samuel,' Dee said. 'Why is it that you always come up with the most difficult answer? Would magic not be easier than a dozen wires, so fine that they cannot be seen or felt? But, hush, there is more.'

Hern had moved to one side and Balthasar had appeared at the other side of the stage, blindfolded and led by Maria. 'Now,' Hern said, 'I introduce to you Balthasar, who can see into the innermost mind of man. Do not try to keep a secret, ladies and gentlemen, because the more you think of keeping it, the stronger the message will come into your mind. And Balthasar will pluck it from there and will display it to the world. So be careful what you think of. Eloise will guide him along the line and he will tell you your innermost thoughts. Are you all ready?'

He looked at the crowd and saw that most people were nodding. Dee was sitting with an amused look on his face, Edward Kelly was leaning against the door jamb, back inside the porch, half hidden from view and Helene was staring intently at Marlowe where he was standing at the side of the stage with the others, trying to blend in. They were ready, he could tell.

'Eloise? Is Balthasar ready?' The woman whispered in his ear and turned to Hern and nodded. 'Then, lead the soothsayer among us. See what he can find in the depths of men's minds.'

Holding Balthasar by the hand, the woman led him to the end of the line and began to walk slowly along. Balthasar's eyes were bound with many layers of thick multicoloured cloth and he looked down at the ground. A disbeliever, a groom currently unemployed thanks to the rental of the big house, jumped to his feet and threw a punch at Balthasar's face, pulling it at the last minute and the Egyptian didn't even flinch. The man turned to the rest of the audience and made a gesture to Balthasar, waving his hand in front of his own eyes. Clearly, he could see nothing.

'There is a mind here full of a man,' Balthasar suddenly cried, with his arm in front of him. No one moved as he inched along the row, feeling with his fingers, but not quite touching anyone. When he got to the cook, his hand darted forward and pressed down on the top of her head. She made an indignant noise and then spoke up.

'I am a respectable woman, I'll have you know,' she said, shaking him off. 'Widowed these many years. Men indeed! What would I want with a man?'

Balthasar spoke to the crowd. 'What she wants to do with a man is not for the ears of our children. I will whisper in her ear and then you can see if I have divined her thoughts correctly.' He leant forward and spoke quietly to the cook. The crowd didn't make a sound, hoping to hear a salacious comment but his voice was too low.

Suddenly, the cook got to her feet like a mountain surging out of the sea and slapped Balthasar's face. Without a word, she turned for the house, overturning her chair and dashed, head down, for the door. Seeing Edward Kelly there, she stopped, then fetching him a ringing slap as well, ran into the house and slammed the door.

The audience went wild and the laughter rang and echoed through the courtyard. Dee leaned over to Bowes. 'Wires?' he asked, with a twinkle in his eye.

'Not hard to work out, Master,' Bowes said. 'We all know what she would like to do with Edward Kelly.'

'What she has done many times with Edward Kelly,' Helene added, from Dee's other side. 'He has . . . unusual tastes, or so I hear.'

Dee gave her a calculating look but decided that the show was the thing. Time enough to winkle the truth out later. Balthasar was still making his way along the line, and the laughter followed him, although sometimes it was more than a little forced. With his impeccable timing, Hern stopped the show before the idea got stale and called for applause for the Amazing Balthasar, who swept off his blindfold and bowed low. He and Eloise ran round behind the stage, to get ready for their next performances. The Egyptians didn't waste a single person – they all had more than one trick up their sleeve.

'Well done with the cook, Eloise,' Balthasar said.

'Not difficult to see, that one,' she said. 'She had a guilty conscience a mile wide and jumped out of her seat when you spoke. But how did you know what to whisper?'

'Also not too difficult,' he said. 'I know Edward Kelly and his little ways. Know that, and the rest is easy.'

On the stage, the children were lined up in order of size. The only ones missing were the two who couldn't yet walk without falling over every other step. As soon as they could be relied upon to walk round an audience with a collecting hat, they would be put to work. But for now they were asleep behind the stage, being watched by anyone who was not actually performing. Marlowe wondered how they could sleep with so much going on; in fact, they couldn't sleep when it was quiet.

First, the tallest child, still only about twelve years old, climbed up on to Frederico's shoulders. Then Simon stood alongside Frederico and invited the next in size on to his shoulders. At a couple of inches taller than Simon, Hern came next and linked arms with Simon and the next tallest child took a run up and jumped aboard, springing off Hern's knee. The next two children made the next level and finally Balthasar threw little Starshine into the air where, after a somersault, she landed on the shoulders of those two. The audience went wild and wilder still when Simon braced himself and took the weight of Hern and Frederico on their linked arms at both sides.

'Very interesting,' Dee said to Helene, 'but when will we see magic? As yet, I have seen nothing but common tumbling and common sense.'

'I'm sure they are building up to it,' Helene said. 'Look – what is happening now?'

One of the mid-sized children, who Marlowe had learned was called Bracket, had appeared in the middle of the stage, with a snake wrapped around one arm. A large jar was brought on stage and Hern picked up the boy and put him in it, sealing it with an enormous cork at the top. Then Simon jumped on to the stage from the other side with a huge mallet in his hands and, taking a mighty swing, smashed the jar to smithereens. There was a gasp from the crowd as the snake slithered out of the shards to be caught by Hern. But of Bracket, there was no sign. Some people sitting against the wall of the house crossed themselves surreptitiously. Others closed their eyes and muttered prayers. Dee nodded sagely, but muttered, 'Conjuring. No more, no less,' to his wife. But even he was surprised when Bracket popped out from under his chair, sketched a bow to Helene and ran up to Hern to reclaim his snake.

And so the show went on, with firecrackers, flaming hoops through which the men threw the children, curled into tight balls, juggling with knives and Frederico's sword-swallowing and fire-eating act. But finally, Hern walked solemnly on to the stage and waited for silence.

'Thank you, ladies and gentlemen,' he said. 'I hope you have enjoyed our show. We have certainly enjoyed entertaining you in this lovely setting and, thanks to the generosity of Dr Dee, we will not need to pass the hat.'

This was met with a storm of applause which Dee acknowledged with a small bow.

'Although,' Hern added, 'the hat will be on the edge of the stage, should anyone feel like adding a few groats to it as they go out.' In the silence which met that statement, it was possible to hear the plink of the stones of the courtyard cooling now that all the torches were out. Finally, the audience realized that they would not be getting any more and started gathering their things together to leave and in a very short while, the courtyard was empty, save for Dee, Hern, Balthasar and Marlowe.

'Well, gentlemen,' Dee said. 'Thank you for a wonderful evening's entertainment. It was certainly the best night that this old house has seen for a while, I should imagine. But where is the real magick?'

'You saw Bracket disappear,' Hern said.

'I saw a child appear to disappear,' Dee said. 'I saw some things from a distance and in dim light. I saw sleight of hand, I saw clever conjuring. Come in to my house now, now that all is quiet, and we will show each other magick.'

Hern glanced at Balthasar. 'Are you ready to show Dr Dee a secret?' he asked.

'I will show him a secret, willingly,' Balthasar said. 'But I will not explain to him how it is done. He will have to work it out for himself.'

'That sounds fair,' Dee said. 'Where do you prefer to work, Master Gerard?'

'Balthasar, please,' the Egyptian said. 'I don't mind where I work. This is magick, don't forget, Dr Dee. Not a trick to deceive a few country folk.'

'My retiring room, then,' Dee said. 'There is a good fire in there, and Helene is waiting to be amazed.'

'Your wife?' Hern asked. 'Does she have an interest in magick, then?'

'Indeed. She has a not inconsiderable talent of her own in that direction. If you would like to invite your . . . wife, Balthasar?' Dee said, politely.

'I have no wife,' the Egyptian replied.

'I'm sorry,' Dee said, watching from under his lashes, 'I thought that you and . . . Rose, is it? There seemed to be . . . something.'

Marlowe smiled to himself. Balthasar was up against a worthy opponent here, if all he intended to do was watch the play of a man's feelings on his face, as he did when telling the future. Dee could see into a man's soul and out the other side. And that was on a bad day; when his reputation was at stake, the man was terrifying.

'She is not my wife, Dr Dee, but she would welcome a warm by the fire, I am sure,' Balthasar said. 'I will fetch her and then we can begin.'

'Helene will wait in the Great Hall, to bring you to the right room,' Dee said. 'I will just have a word with my cook. I will still be needing meals when you have moved on and I fear she is a little unnerved by this evening's revelation.'

'She would have done well to stay away from Edward Kelly, then,' Balthasar said. 'And I would say the same to you, Dr Dee. I was surprised to see such a one here.'

'Charity,' said Dee. 'I have given him charity just for tonight. And Christopher here has ousted him from his bed, so not so much of that, even.'

'He will bite the hand that feeds him,' Hern said. 'He was ever thus.'

'I am pleased to hear you all think so well of me,' a voice said from the darkness.

'An eavesdropper never hears well of himself,' Dee said, without turning round. 'I think that it is time that you settled yourself down for bed, Ned. The straw in the stable is clean and I believe Helene has put out a flagon and some bread for you, should you still be hungry.'

'How kind,' said Kelly, in a sneering mimicry of Dee's voice. 'I'm off to bed, then.' He tapped Hern on the shoulder. 'Any of your women need warming, Hern? As Balthasar knows, I can teach them a thing or two.'

In a flash, Hern was behind him, twisting his arm up behind his back and pressing a blade to his throat.

'I am assuming that your answer is not,' Kelly said, carefully, trying not to move his throat too much. 'If you could perhaps let me go, I can be away to my bed.'

Hern dropped him and aimed a kick as he slunk around the front of the house, heading for the stables. 'Charity?' he asked Dee.

'Christian charity.' The magus nodded. 'He was my friend, once.' Dee turned and walked across the Great Hall towards a small door in the corner, which led to the kitchen. Balthasar went out to the wagons to fetch Rose; Marlowe and Hern waited for Helene. It seemed only polite to be escorted by the lady of the house.

'Master Marlowe,' Hern said. 'We must have a talk, you and I, before we go much further.'

'Why?' Marlowe said. 'I thought my purse was all the conversation we needed.'

'I have been thinking things through. You are a man with a mission; I see it in your eyes. I don't want that, whatever it is, to bring trouble to us.'

'The trouble, if it comes, will come but singly,' Marlowe said. 'You and your troupe will not be dragged into it. I have . . . friends.'

Hern looked dubious. 'What friends are they?'

'If I told you, then they would be of no use to me, would they?' Marlowe told him. 'They are the kind of friends who lose their power if everyone knows them. Don't worry, Hern. It will all be well.'

A soft footfall behind him made him turn.

'Helene,' he said, 'you made me jump.'

'I'm sorry, Master Marlowe,' she said. 'I am naturally very light on my feet. Come, let me take you to John's room. We can choose the most comfortable chairs. And I have this bottle of brandy here.' She raised it to show them, a cobweb clinging to the side. 'I am no expert, but Gregory Leslie had hidden it well, so I think it will be of some quality.' She took Marlowe's arm and led the way, but he could feel her trembling. 'Mind the wet patch at the foot of the stairs,' she said over her shoulder to Hern. 'Oh, too late. There is a cloth over in the corner there. Cook hung it over that statue. It gave her . . . ideas.'

Hern half hopped over to the dark space under the stairs and whipped the cloth from the statue. It had been hiding a very obvious attribute and he thought he could see a theme developing. The cook was clearly mad; Dee was rather soft in the head, whatever the Queen may think; the manservant was obviously simple. The brains in this house belonged to Helene, without a doubt. A beautiful and very accomplished woman. No wonder Edward Kelly had come back, like a pigeon to its nest.

While he blotted the blood from the sole of his shoe, a small door opened behind the stair. A blast of cold, musty air which came with it suggested cellars, long unused. Simon the strongman slid along the wall where the shadows were longest and slipped out of the front door without a word. Hern did not call out although a quiet word with the man later would be more than necessary. This was not a house in which to be caught out in clandestine behaviour. He waited in the shadows and after a few minutes, the door opened and shut again, but this time the shadow was a woman, one that Hern did not know. With her head down, she also made for the door and was soon gone. Hern sighed. Yes, a word would certainly be necessary in the morning.

'Gentlemen and ladies,' Dee said, looking around his fireside. 'I am so glad to have you all here, old friends –' he smiled at Marlowe – 'and new, I hope. I am anxious to learn from you but first I would like to demonstrate my small skill. Helene has told me that she is somewhat tired and I don't want to keep her up longer than I need.'

It was true that Helene Dee did not look at all well. She was pale and quiet but she smiled at her husband and then at her guests. 'Today has been quite tiring, yes,' she said. 'A lot to take in. So, if you don't mind . . .'

Rose leaned towards her from where she sat on a short bench, next to Balthasar and whispered in her ear. Helene flushed a little, but shook her head. The men looked away, as men will when women whisper.

Dee looked a little askance and then cleared his throat. 'May I ask Master Marlowe if he will help me?' he said.

Marlowe looked at him nervously. He knew this man and the kind of thing he liked to do. If demons were involved – and knowing Dee, there would be at least the hint of a demon somewhere – then he was not sure his doubts were strong enough to defend him. Dee read his mind.

'No demons, Kit. But I think you will find it interesting.' He held out his hand and pushed a bench back from the fire to clear a space. 'Will you help? Helene will be here. And as you know, I would have no harm come to her.'

Marlowe stepped forward reluctantly and stood side by side with the beauty and faced Dee.

'As you can see,' Dee said to Hern, Balthasar and Rose, 'Master Marlowe and my wife are much the same size, although I would estimate that Master Marlowe weighs an ounce or two more. But I can make my wife weigh nothing so that she will float to the ceiling. And I can make Master Marlowe weigh so much he will not be able to move a limb.'

Hern and Balthasar exchanged looks. 'I would like to see that,' Hern said, politely. Rose smiled at Helene and sat back to watch.

Dee turned Helene and Marlowe so that they faced each other and joined their hands. They were almost the same height and they stood toe to toe, looking into each other's eyes. Dee stood behind them, facing his guests. Raising one hand, he pressed down on Marlowe's shoulder, whilst holding the other hand about six inches above Helene's head. He spoke in a low whisper and Marlowe was amazed to hear that he was simply reciting the Collects for the Sundays of Lent, in Latin. But somehow, as he identified the words, they seemed to slur together and his view of the world became very limited until all he could see were Helene's eyes, boring into his.

And something very strange was happening. He was having to look up to look into Helene's eyes. He was having to tilt his head right back to keep her eyes in his view. She was at the end of a light-filled tunnel, she was far away, she was drifting off, further and further away. He tried to tell her to stay still, but there was something wrong with his mouth. His tongue was stuck to the bottom of it, lodged beneath his teeth and his lips were glued shut. But although he was rather puzzled, he wasn't frightened. He felt instead as though he was sinking into the floor, which was made for some reason of the softest feather, very warm and comfortable. His eyelids were really heavy, and he could only see Helene now through the slits that his eyes had become. So heavy. So very heavy.

To the watchers, it looked no less impressive. As Dee muttered behind the pair, Helene rose inches and then feet into the air. She floated up to the ceiling and hovered there, her clothes wafting on an unfelt breeze. Marlowe had sunk to the floor and was unable to rise. Even his hair, the locks usually in motion around his face, hung as though lined with lead. His eyelids drooped over his large brown eyes and his bottom lip hung and drooled.

Dee looked up at the Egyptians. 'Please step forward,' he said, 'and try to lift Master Marlowe from the floor. I can guarantee you will be unable to do so. As for my wife, you may walk beneath her if you wish, although gentlemen, I would urge you to respect the fact that she is a married woman and of a chaste disposition.' He looked closely at Rose. 'I'm sorry, my dear,' he said. 'Did you speak?'

'A cough,' she said, 'nothing more. I apologize, Dr Dee. Do go on.'

'Erm . . . yes. Please, do come and examine my wife and Master Marlowe.'

Hern walked over to Marlowe and pulled at his arm. Nothing happened; not only did it not wake the man, but Hern could not make the arm move even an inch. He tried the other, with the same result. He picked at a lock of hair, but it was as if the man had been turned to stone. Balthasar was walking around Helene, his head below the level of her feet, which were not dangling as if she were hanging, but flat, as though she stood on a glass floor above him.

'Can she move?' he asked Dee.

'Indeed,' the old magus replied. 'My wife is weightless, Balthasar. It is Master Marlowe who weighs as much as the world we stand on.' He raised his voice. 'Helene,' he said. 'Can you walk towards the window, to show Balthasar that you can move.'

Helene Dee walked across the room, seven feet up in the air, her feet bending and straightening on her invisible floor. Then she turned and came back to her starting place.

Hern and Balthasar felt the hairs stand up on the backs of their necks. They knew some tricks, God knew, but nothing like this. This was breaking all the laws that God had ordained and while they didn't bother with laws as a general rule there were some, one of which is that women don't walk on thin air, which they had always tried to obey. They glanced at each other; there was nothing in their repertoire which would impress this man. They had lost the race, without having moved from the starting place.

Dee was almost dancing with pleasure. 'Well, gentlemen,' he crowed. 'Can you tell me how it is done?'

Hern had to admit defeat and Balthasar just shrugged his shoulders. 'You are a true magus, Dr Dee,' he said. 'You have me foxed.'

Suddenly, Rose stood up and walked across to where the men stood. 'Helene was doing this trick before she met you, John Dee, Queen's magus,' she said. 'Has she told you all her tricks?' Then she turned to Balthasar. 'I sought you out because I thought you could truly tell my future, could help me change it to something I wanted it to be. But you are just a man, like all the others. Credulous, fooled by a pretty face. I won't be coming any further with you, Balthasar, you and your troupe. I saw that in my future, even when you couldn't. Something is wrong here. Someone has done evil. It can't be put right.' She looked up at Helene Dee, who now hung in the air like a rag doll. 'Something is wrong. Look at her.'

Dee wrung his hands. 'What is it?' he cried. 'Helene? Helene? Come back to me. Wake up!'

'It's no good, Dr Dee,' said Rose. 'Evil has been done. Helene is dead.'

And as she spoke, the woman, light and air and beauty, turned once as she hung there and fell like a stone into Hern's arms.

EIGHT

John Dee was taken away by Lily, fished out of her bed by Hern for the purpose, and put to bed. The magus was a magus no longer, just an old, grief-stricken man. He, who could bring the dead back to life, or at least thought he could, had said goodbye to Helene as she lay cooling in her bed. She looked even more beautiful, if possible, as she lay there, her face free of the slightest worry, her skin wiped smooth by the deep sleep of death. Only her bluing nails and lips and her stiffening fingers gave any clue that she was not just sleeping soundly.

Marlowe was curled up in a ball on the floor of the retiring room. He had come screaming out of his trance as soon as Helene fell and every fibre of his body hurt as though he had been trampled. Whatever the secret of the trick, whoever had been in control of it, Dee or Helene, or even Rose, it had never been intended to end so suddenly. The weight which had been transferred to him should have been lifted, ounce by ounce and given back to Helene, so that she gently came back to earth and he could get up and move around. When Dee and Helene were on song, it sometimes worked that the light became the heavy and so on until everyone tired of it. Dee had even used the Queen herself in the trick one night at Placentia and had almost been skewered by Sir Christopher Hatton for his pains.

Lily came to him after she had lulled Dee to sleep. Passing her hands over him, she had looked up at Balthasar, looming over the boy as he lay and whimpered in pain. 'I'm trying my best, Balthasar,' she said, as though he had spoken. 'Everything inside him feels wrong to me. As if his bones are not in the right place.'

'It was the damnedest thing, Lil,' Balthasar said, chewing his lip. 'She just dropped like a stone and he just came up on to his feet with such a scream that I felt my bowels turn to water. And then he dropped again and he has been like this ever since.'

Lily carried on stroking Marlowe's back, because it seemed to ease him. 'I gather Rose knew Mistress Dee,' she said, somewhere between a question and a statement.

'I gather she did,' Balthasar said.

'Is that why she sought you out, do you think?' Lily said, kneading the muscle in the small of Marlowe's back, and being rewarded by a small scream. 'I am so sorry, Master Marlowe,' she muttered to him, moving her hand. 'To bring her here,' she carried on, not looking at Balthasar.

'I don't know,' he said. 'I thought I could see into her soul, Lily, but her soul is not what I saw. I don't know who she is or why she sought me out.' He drew a huge trembling breath. 'I thought . . .'

Lily got up, dusting off the front of her skirt, for all the difference it made. 'Balthasar,' she said, 'any one of us would be proud . . .'

He shook her off, but not unkindly. He had often thought that if he ever took a woman, it might well be Lily. He gave her a smile, but not his usual one which was like the moon coming out from behind a cloud, tinting everything it shone on with silver. 'I will find another rose,' he said. 'She can't be the only one in the garden.' And he walked away, leaving Lily and Marlowe to stay together through the night, until in the dawn he finally relaxed and fell asleep. Lily got up from where she had been shielding him with her body from the terrors which shook it and went back to the camp, to stir oatmeal with the women.

It took Joseph Fludd quite a while to fix his eyes on the horizon. The cold pearl of the sky stretched out beyond the breakwater where the grey surf lifted and the gulls wheeled overhead. This was only his second time out of his county of Cambridge and he felt uneasy. The sky was too big out here, the wind even more chill than at home. He had no jurisdiction here, no edge. Even the limited powers he had as Constable were denied him and he had left his tipstaff at home.

For three days he'd haunted the dockside taverns of Lynn,

buying a draught of local Norfolk ale and making it last. His ultimatum from the Mayor had been clear enough and there would be no expenses. He'd toyed for a while with tethering the old nag Hobson had hired him on the waste ground beyond the church of St Margaret but he knew there would be laws against that and however his search went he would never be able to afford to replace a horse. So his money had to last and his lodgings in a lean-to behind the Grey Goose did not come cheap.

Fludd was used to the cold of his native Cambridge, the unforgiving wind that crept round Petty Cury and across the bridge at Magdalen. The draughty, crumbling castle barbican that was his constabulary home above the cherry orchards had sudden cold spots of its own, when the wind currents eddied up the shafts of the old garderobes, now disused. But nothing had prepared him for Lynn in the grip of winter. Men he had drunk with the night before, narrow-eyed men with leather faces and sour looks, men who worked on the barges on the Broads and fished the sea off Brancaster Bay, spoke of this being nothing. Back in . . . and the year changed with the telling . . . the sea itself froze, with ice mountains lining the sands that stretched on forever. Birds, the gulls with their tragic cries and the curlews on the heathland, dropped dead from the sky with cold. And they had lowered their voices and closed to him when they spoke solemnly of the *Jesus of Ely*. The ship came in, they had told him, on a winter's day just like this one, when the sky was lead and death moaned in the wind. No birds followed the *Jesus* home and no one waited on the shore to welcome her. The *Jesus* was not due back for a month or more from Flushing over the unforgiving North Sea; yet here she was, her sails furled and her anchor trailing. When they boarded her, still drifting in the narrows, there was not a soul on her. The charts lay on her captain's table, bread and cheese, nibbled by the ship's rats, scattered the crew's quarters. Her hold was empty, though it should have been full of woollens and grain. It was the cold, the fishermen told Fludd, the ice fingers of the sea that had done for them all. And it would all be explained one day when the sea gave up her dead.

He had endured the silence, noted the nodding heads and dipped his lips again into the Norfolk ale. Fludd had waited for a suitable moment, then he raised the subject, casually. Had anyone seen any Egyptians? Those weird folk who rode piebald horses and told the future, those horse thieves and tinkers? Most had shaken their heads. One or two had told him tall tales of elsewhere in the county, how Egyptians had been hanged in Norwich not long since and one had disappeared in the market square there in a cloud of purple smoke. There were no Egyptians in the county now; the constabulary had driven them out. One thing they did well, the constabulary, the *only* thing the constabulary did well, was to move on Egyptians; whip them at the cart's tail, then hang them. And what, the drinking fishermen wanted to know, was Fludd's interest in all this? He wasn't a Constable too, was he?

Marlowe and Balthasar Gerard sat in the kitchen of the great and silent house, trying to warm themselves on the embers of the fire. The cook was prostrate with grief and no one begrudged her that; she had known Nell since she had been brought in by Dee one wet night, soaked to the skin and filthy. It had been the cook who had wrapped her in a blanket and warmed her by the fire while Bowes and Dee had prepared a bath for her. Not usually what she would call men's work, but they had remembered a herb or two to perfume the water and Dee had even remembered some cloths to dry the girl with. They had been the finest towels, brought from Turkey at great expense and were usually kept in the linen press against the day that the Queen might come – although the likelihood of her visit coinciding with her annual bath was not strong.

Finally, they had got through the layers of caked mud and there she was, as beautiful as the day and with a nature to match, sunny and happy almost always and if she ever felt a little cribbed, confined in her marriage to the magus, no one ever knew. She treated the cook and Bowes as if they were her friends, she treated Kelly with gentle contempt and she was the most beautiful and also the most silent hostess in London. In all, the day Dee had found her and looked beyond the mud to the jewel beneath had been the household's happiest day. And now the saddest day had come, one which none of them had thought to see. They were all old enough to be her parents and had all thought that one day she would see them severally into their graves.

'Did you know her well, Kit?' Balthasar suddenly dropped into the silence.

'Not well, no,' he said. 'But to see the outward Helene was to know the inner, as I have understood it. I have never asked, but I felt that the marriage was . . .'

'I understand that kind of marriage,' Balthasar said. 'Many hands which are offered to me to read have been given into that kind of marriage.'

'But they were happy, though. This household will never be the same, now she is gone. The three will be but perfect shadows in a sunshine day.'

Balthasar looked at him. 'Is there nothing that is not a subject for your poetry, Kit? Do you keep a notebook somewhere, to write these things down as they pop into your head?' The smile softened the phrase.

Marlowe smiled at him. 'They just come to me, Balthasar. If they stay of their own free will then yes, you may see or hear them again. If they don't stay – then perhaps they should not have been in my head in the first place.'

'Like Dido Queen of Carthage and her cat?'

'Dido has been with me for a while,' he said. 'I even wrote a play about her once. She didn't have a cat, that time. But she will live on, if only in the memory of Starshine.'

'So Helene will live on?'

'In the memory of John Dee and all who knew her. She was a lovely woman, in every way.'

Balthasar looked from side to side and leaned forward. 'But cannot Dr Dee . . . bring back the dead?'

'He says so. He thinks so. I have seen . . . I'm not sure what I have seen, but I don't think that what comes back is something I would want to have as hostess at my table, for companionship at my fireside. Death may be just a door, but it is one no one should come back through.' He leaned back. 'That may be just my opinion, though. What about Lily? Can she . . . ?'

'No. She can only heal the sick, and then only sometimes. I have never personally seen her fail, but she says it has been known. Another one where the beauty is not just skin deep.'

'And Rose?'

Balthasar leaned back. 'What of her?'

'She knew Helene, that much was clear. She knew her in her hedge witch days and she knew the trick, so Hern told me.'

'What was the trick, do you think?'

'I think you are asking the wrong person, Balthasar. I remember feeling very heavy and then waking up. I didn't know that Helene was dead until this morning.'

'It was . . . very convincing. She flew in the air. You were as heavy as lead. It wasn't possible, and yet we all saw it.'

Marlowe looked at him. He had not known these people for long, but he knew that they had more tricks up their coloured sleeves than they would ever let him know. But the man seemed genuine enough. Rose was the fly in this ointment; she was the stranger among them but Balthasar would see only good in her until she told him with her own lips that she was a murderess. 'What do you know of Rose?'

'She came to me. She was distressed. I thought I could . . . no I *can* mend her heart and soul.'

'You don't think that she might have used you to get into this house?' Marlowe suggested, gently.

'Why would she want to? Dr Dee is the Queen's magus. Rose is a beautiful woman and she could get into the court and find him that way.'

'But if she wanted Helene, not the magus?'

'Why would she want Helene?' Balthasar was puzzled and also getting rather angry.

'To kill her,' a voice said from behind him.

Marlowe looked up and Balthasar turned round to see a man they didn't know standing in the kitchen doorway. He was square and solid like the Norfolk brogue that tumbled from his lips. 'I hope this is not an intrusion, gentlemen,' he said. 'My name is John Sedgrave and I am the Constable of Ely.' He flashed a painted tipstaff at them. 'Dr Dee's man, Bowes, came to fetch me at first light, something about his mistress being murdered. Poisoned, it appears. There was no one at the door so I have let myself in. There are . . .' The question lingered in his voice. 'Egyptians in the courtyard.' He looked Balthasar up and down. 'And in the kitchen, I see.'

Marlowe stood up. 'My name is Christopher Marlowe,' he said, 'of Corpus Christi College. Dr Dee invited this gentleman, Balthasar Gerard is his name, and his companions to the house and they remain his guests.'

'Strange guests for a house such as this,' Sedgrave said. 'The law demands we hang Egyptians in the country. Does Gregory Leslie know they are here?'

'Who is Gregory Leslie?' Balthasar asked. 'If I knew that, I could tell you if he knows.'

'He doesn't know,' the Constable said, firmly. 'Because if he did, you would all be hanging from trees in the orchard, and that would include your brats. Master Leslie hangs first and asks questions later.' He gave them a twisted smile. 'I have been here before on many an occasion, and know it to be true.' He looked at the two. 'My men have searched the house and we have the woman, Rose, in irons in the Great Hall.'

'What!' Balthasar was on his feet, fists balled at his sides.

'Would you like to join her?' Sedgrave asked. 'Because if so, it is the opinion of my men that she did not plan this alone.'

'Plan? Plan what?' Balthasar shouted. 'Kit. This man is an idiot. Speak to him for me before I knock his head off.'

'Master Gerard is distraught,' Marlowe said, leading Sedgrave further away from him. It was a difficult task, as he was at least a head taller and as broad as a barn. 'We have only just met Rose, but I can't imagine that she is a killer. How would she do such a thing?'

'She is skilled in potions. One of my men recognized her. The women around here . . . well, they visit her from time to time, shall we say? She told me that she knew Mistress Dee in the old days, when their lives were very different. And now, here we find her. Mistress Dee, the wife of a powerful and rich man. Rose, living a hand to mouth existence, dependent on one man and then another. That's a nice black eye she has,

don't you think?' He spoke over his shoulder at Balthasar but
got no reply. 'Hmm, yes. A nice black eye. Where was I?'

'Rose knew Helene in the old days,' Marlowe said, helping
him out. With his long experience as a student of Dr Lyler he
was adept at keeping a man's wandering mind on its path.
Hebrew and Rhetoric were sometimes strange bedfellows.

'Thank you, Master Marlowe. Yes. And so, I believe, she
was jealous and poisoned her. She no doubt had a plan to
usurp her position as the wife of the Queen's magus, Dr Dee.
She had powers that would interest him, just as the late Mistress
Dee had.'

'You are clutching at straws, Constable Sedgrave,' Marlowe
said. 'Do you have knowledge of poisons?'

'No more than the next Constable,' Sedgrave admitted, 'but
I know when a woman is dead.'

Marlowe changed tack. 'How could Rose know we were
coming here?'

'We?' The Constable was on the word like a cobra striking
home. 'We? Are you one of these Egyptians, then?' He looked
him up and down and saw only a rich young man in fancy
clothes. These scholars were above their station, these days.

'I am proud to be travelling with Master Hern and his band,
yes,' Marlowe said, standing straight and unconsciously pulling
at his clothes to tidy himself up.

The Constable looked him up and down. 'Well, that is of
course a decision for yourself to make, sir,' he said, strangling
the language in his attempt to keep things formal. 'But to
return to the matter to hand, you know nothing of this Rose,
not even her other name or where she comes from or any fact
about her. Is that not so?' He turned to face Balthasar.

The Egyptian faced him but did not speak.

'Is that not so, Master Gerard?' he repeated, still polite.

'It is so,' Balthasar muttered, his eyes on the ground. He
turned to the fire and poked around in the ashes, lost in his
own thoughts. Marlowe expected more from the man, a token
resistance if nothing else, but there was nothing else. Perhaps
knowing the future had made him fatalistic.

'Master Marlowe,' Sedgrave said, 'I must tell you that we
have found some things in this house which have disturbed

us, but I have been told that they belong to Dr Dee, so unless you have reason to suppose that he killed his wife . . .'

'Dr Dee adores his wife. He would die for her.'

'As I thought. The woman, Rose, had herbs in her possession which she refuses to identify. She knew Mistress Dee. She is a stranger to you all and to this household. As far as I can tell, she is the only suspect in this crime.'

'What about Edward Kelly?' Marlowe said. 'He is a criminal and he was here.'

'Edward Kelly? Is he with your band?'

'No. He is a . . . not a friend, an acquaintance, an old acquaintance of the doctor.' Marlowe, thinking on his feet, did not want to make too much of the link between Dee and Kelly, with his clipped ears.

'We have not spoken to a Kelly.'

'He was sleeping in the stable,' Marlowe said.

'Not so much of a friend, or even an acquaintance, then,' Sedgrave said. 'The stable is where charity cases are put in houses such as this.'

'It is a very long story,' Marlowe said, 'and I don't know the half of it. But Edward Kelly is your man. I would stake my life on it.' He raised his finger in the air, excitedly remembering something. 'I remember seeing Helene looking out through the doorway, staring at Kelly. She seemed nervous all evening.'

'Was he the only one in sight?'

'Well, no . . . the others were out there, too.' Marlowe was not naturally truthful, but this man seemed to create an aura in which the truth was the only language spoken.

'Including Rose?'

'Yes.' There was no other answer. The poet heard Balthasar's grunt behind him.

'And was Master Kelly in the room when Mistress Dee died?'

'No.'

'We believe the poison to have been very quick in its action, whatever it was, as she complained of no pain; there were no signs but sudden death. It must have been given to her within minutes of her dying and Rose, by her own admission, was standing nearest. So, I am sorry, but unless you can produce this Kelly, Master Marlowe, I will have to take Rose back to the town. I have no choice.' He turned to Balthasar. 'I am sorry, Master Gerard. It gives me no pleasure.'

Balthasar shrugged his shoulders, but did not turn round.

'Would you like to come and say goodbye?'

The man shook his head.

'In that case, we will be away. Good morning to you, gentlemen. And, Master Gerard?'

'Yes?' the man muttered.

'Please get your people on the road as soon as you can. Master Leslie is not the only man in these parts who thinks trees look better with an Egyptian or two decorating the branches.'

'Thank you for your advice,' Marlowe said, ushering him out. 'I don't think we will be lingering. Dr Dee needs to mourn in his own way, and I suspect that is quietly.'

'Master Marlowe,' said Sedgrave, 'if you will take my advice, you will leave these people. They can only bring you trouble.'

'I like trouble,' Marlowe said. 'But thank you for your concern, Master Sedgrave.'

'It's no trouble to me, sir,' he said and touched a finger to his cap. 'Mind how you go.'

Marlowe went in search of Dee, the cook and Bowes to tell them that the camp was packed up and that they were leaving. The house was as silent as the grave and with the big oak doors shut tight little sound filtered through from outside. He crept quietly up the curving stair and found the three of them surrounding Helene's bed. She lay as though carved from marble, a look of total peace on her face. Dee sat at one side, with a hand gently cupped over one of hers where it lay on the embroidered counterpane. On the other side, the cook and Bowes were a little more restrained and did not venture to touch her, but the cook's face was bloated with weeping and Bowes looked as though he was made of oak. He certainly didn't seem to notice the tear that crept down his cheek.

Marlowe walked softly up behind Dee and placed a gentle

hand on the man's shoulder. Whenever they met, there seemed to be loss and this time it was very great. Even for Marlowe, there were no words.

Dee reached up with his free hand and patted Marlowe's. 'Isn't she beautiful, Christopher?' he said, almost in a whisper, the tears making his voice thick. 'Did you ever see anything so lovely?'

All Marlowe could think was that the living Helene, with her mischievous face and ready smile was more beautiful by far, but to say that would be to finish the old man by the bed. 'She is beautiful,' he said. 'She is fairer than the evening air, clad in the beauty of a thousand stars.'

'Poetry, Kit?' Dee said, with a faint pressure on his hand.

'It's all I have to give you,' Marlowe said, 'and her.'

'Make her immortal,' Dee said. 'One day when you have time, sit in a sweet garden and bring her back to life for me, with your words. In the meantime, I will try to keep some warmth in her, just for a little while. She always hated to be cold.'

His hand dropped from Marlowe's and he joined it to the other, holding Helene's hand, keeping her warm. Because when she was completely cold, men would come to encase her in oak and bury her and he wasn't ready for that yet. He would never be ready, but he would allow it.

'Goodbye, Kit. Safe journey to you all.'

'I'll see you again,' Marlowe said, 'and I will show you Helene's immortality.'

'When you have time.'

'Yes. When I have time.'

The camp had been made late and lazy. There were no fires and the Egyptians were sleeping tumbled together in the wagons, wrapped up in their cloaks and each other to beat the chill. They had not bothered to erect the yurt; time was pressing, they were tired and the death of Helene and the arrest of Rose had plunged them all into a low mood. Marlowe found himself sharing the wagon not just with the various livestock from his first night, but also Simon, who took up more than his fair share of room and had a tendency to mutter in his sleep. At least the parrot was quiet once it had a cloth over its wicker cage. The monkey, at the furthest extent of its leash, was pressed up against Marlowe's back, where he exuded enough warmth to pay for the inconvenience of the fleas and the smell.

At the edge of the huddle of wagons, the horses stood quietly, too cold to toss their manes, just intent on huddling together for as much warmth as they could muster. The blankets over their backs were something, but the frost coloured their breath silver as they waited for dawn. The dogs had slunk into the wagons one by one and were twitching in their sleep amongst the children.

Only one pair of eyes was watching the road from Ely, watching for followers, flannel-footed and evil. There was no reason to believe that all the trouble had been left behind the doors of Dee's grieving house and it was not possible to be too careful. But the soft hoof-beats which finally broke the silence of the night came from the other way, from the Fens and the coast and the heaving North Sea. The rider was not making an effort to be quiet, he was almost asleep in the saddle and the horse had settled into an uneven walk, with one loose shoe giving a double clip to every clop.

The watcher in the hedge peered closer in the starlight and drew back as the rider came closer. It was Trumpy Joe Fludd, on his way back to Cambridge, empty-handed and despondent. His head lolled and every fourth nod woke him sufficiently to stop him falling from the saddle. His empty purse was at his belt and his empty future as Constable reached ahead of him on the curve of the frosty road. He didn't look to left or right and so he never saw his quarry sleeping on the other side of the hedge. So, like two galliasses passing in thick fog, oars muffled and sails hanging slack, the Egyptians and Joseph Fludd met and parted for one final time.

'Who are these people, Hern?' Bracket wanted to know as the Egyptian caravanserai rattled into the little seaside town.

'Fishing folk.' Hern turned to the boy on the wagon beside him. 'Ship-men who cross to Holland and France. I expect . . . what? Ten purses from you and Tomaso. Twelve would be better.'

'Why twelve, Hern?'

'You'll need that many to match one taken in London. They're poor. Take Starshine with you. Get her to limp a little, turn in her feet. And only go for couples. The men won't soften like their wives and the wives won't be carrying any money.'

The smoke drifted lazily up from the chimneys of Lynn, made the King's since Lord Harry's day.

'Drums!' called Hern. 'Music!'

And the sleepy, stunned caravanserai thumped into life, the women shrilling and the children cartwheeling in the road, streaming their bright ribbons into the sky.

NINE

Joseph Fludd stood over the little mound of earth that marked Ann Harris's grave. Beside him stood his under-constables, Nathaniel Hawkins and Jabez Hazel. The winter ground was like iron, the ice lying in rivulets in the ruts of the road. A single posy of dead flowers lay at the grave's head below a small wooden cross.

'Who put that there?' the Constable wanted to know. He still ached from his hours on the road and had barely had time to kiss his Allys and the children before he had returned the horse to Hobson's stables and made his way in the raw morning to Trumpington churchyard, in the care of St Mary and St Michael.

'The Reverend Mildmay,' Hazel told him. 'We were all here, along with half of the village.'

'Nobody from the town, though,' Hawkins mumbled. 'Bastards.'

Fludd nodded. 'They're urban, squat and packed with guile,' he said. 'What did you expect?'

Nat Hawkins knew Trumpy Joe Fludd of old. They'd grown up together, learned their letters from the same schoolmaster. Except that Nat hadn't learned that many. Still, some things needed to be said. 'I expected you to come back with an Egyptian or two,' he blurted out. 'To pay for this.'

Fludd turned to the man. For a second, he contemplated flattening him, then he relented. 'Why?' he asked. 'The Egyptians had nothing to do with this.'

Hawkins looked at Hazel. Had Trumpy Joe gone mad? It *had* to be the Egyptians.

'Know what I think?' Hazel crossed to the others. 'It went something like this. One of 'em, the moon children I mean, would have got her talking, old Gammer Harris, telling her fortune, filling her head with all sorts of nonsense. Then, another one, one of the kids I reckon, would have been ransacking the house. She heard 'em, did old Gammer, and would have set off a-shouting, like she did. You must remember, Joe, when we were children and scared to death of Gammer Harris and her tongue.'

The Constable nodded. She'd certainly had a pair of lungs on her, had Gammer Harris.

'So,' Hazel said, looking solemnly into Fludd's face, 'she had to be silenced.'

'Where was Jem while all this fortune-telling, shouting and stealing was going on?' the Constable asked. 'Where was her husband?'

'In the Lammas Field,' Hawkins told him. 'Hedging. Like what they pay him for.'

'Who told you that?' Fludd wanted to know.

'Everybody,' Hawkins said.

'Did everybody see him?' Fludd asked.

'Er . . . Well, he's always there.' Hawkins held his ground. 'There or not far away. The Lammas field has got a lot of hedges. No sooner's he got round it once, it's time to start again, more nor less.'

'Did anybody see him?' Fludd repeated, slowly and deliberately. There was no answer this time. Least of all from Gammer Harris.

A cold rain thudded into the thatch of Jem Harris's hovel that night. He and the Constable sat in front of a roaring fire, one of the few benefits of being a hedger. The trimmings had to be burned anyway, so why not on his fire?

'So –' Jem was sipping an ale he kept for special visitors – 'you saw him hanged, then?'

'With my own eyes,' Fludd lied. 'After he'd confessed, of course.'

Jem looked at him, eyes bright in the firelight. 'Why did he do it? Did he say? Did he tell you why he killed my Ann?'

'You know these Egyptians.' Fludd shrugged, though clearly Jem Harris didn't. 'Moon-driven. Mad as corn hares in harvest time. I expect you miss your Ann, Jem?'

'Oh, I do, I do,' the old man said, helping himself to another draught from the pitcher.

'Her nagging.'

'Yes.'

'Some women.' Fludd laughed. 'My Allys is the one. Got a mouth on her like Hell in those old mystery plays. Remember them?'

'I do,' the old hedger crowed. 'I miss all that, you know. The good old days.'

'Yes.' Fludd was in full flow now. 'Still, you won't really miss old Ann's whine, will you? There are some days I could take hold of Allys and beat her backside raw. It's "Joe, have you done this? Joe, where's that? Joe, when are you going to get round to the other?" Drives you mad, doesn't it?'

'It does,' Harris enthused. 'It does.'

'Is that why you did it, Jem?' Fludd was suddenly quiet, staring at the man sharing the fire with him. 'That morning? Had she nagged you once too often? Is that why you took your billhook to her head?'

Harris blinked, then swigged from the pitcher. 'What about the Egyptian?' he whispered.

'There was no Egyptian, Jem,' Fludd told him. 'There never was. Why should an Egyptian set foot here? Man, there's nothing to steal but a flagon of ale and some firewood. Those people live by their wits. They don't need to kill. Especially some harmless old woman like your Ann.'

'Harmless?' Jem exploded. 'Harmless? Are we talking about the same Ann Harris? Nag, nag. She never shut up. I'd flogged her, beaten her. Even had her put in the scold's bridle once – before your time, young Fludd. You're ma would remember, God rest her soul. I just . . . just lost my temper, that's all. The red mist just came up and then, when it was over, I pulled the billhook out of her head and went hedging. It's quiet in Lammas Field, you know, Joe. Peaceful. No nagging.'

There was a silence and the two men looked at each other.

'What happens now?' Harris hardly dared ask.

Fludd stood up. 'Now, you'll come with me, Jeremiah Harris,' he said, 'on a charge of murder.' He patted the man's bony shoulder. 'And we'll find you somewhere quiet.'

The servants were used to it, of course; the master ambling around the knot gardens on his grey old mule. His robes hauled up over the saddle and his feet almost touching the ground, he was usually to be found letting the animal wander while he had his nose in a book. Cicero from the saddle. He meandered in the scent of box, rosemary and thyme, depending on the taste of the mule that particular day. The animal's browsing defined the flavour of the air.

This morning was a little different. The hoar frost lay thick on the low, trained hedges and jewelled the spiders' webs with a sparkling faerie dust. The master was wrapped up against the cold, a huge woollen cloak trailing the ground as he rode, the capacious hood over his head, shading his face. Beside him strode Sir Francis Walsingham, who would rather cut off his own arm than ride a beast of burden such as this. He had rather hoped to have this conversation in the man's library, warming his arse before a roaring fire and borrowing a book, or in his study or even his private chapel – *anywhere* with walls and a roof. But this was William Cecil, Lord Burghley, the right hand of the Queen and no one, not even Francis Walsingham, called the tune in his presence. So the pair plodded their way past the sharp, red brick of the North Front, the frost sparkling on the broad steps in a band where the sun had not reached.

'So, it's treason then, you're sure?' Burghley asked, looking at the ice thick on the carp pond and his breath snaking out from under his hood into the morning air.

'We have Throckmorton's confession. I felt a little sorry for him in the end.'

Burghley halted the mule with a sharp tug on the rein. He leaned back in the saddle so that he could look into Walsingham's eyes without giving up the warmth of his hood. 'You won't lose sight of the point of all this, Francis, will you?'

'My Lord?' the spymaster frowned.

'The bigger picture,' Burghley told him. 'The continued safety of Her Majesty and the peace of her realm.'

'My every waking thought,' Walsingham said and he meant it, even if it did mean trudging through a frosty morning in air that froze the blood. 'Shelley and the other conspirators in Sussex are under lock and key, awaiting the Queen's pleasure.'

'Kill them.' said Burghley. 'We're not playing games here, Francis. We must cut out the canker in this country's heart. I don't care whether it is Catholic or Puritan. I'll draw up a Bond of Association.'

'A bloody process, my Lord,' Walsingham observed.

Burghley nudged the mule on again. 'What news from Delft?' he asked. 'Nothing gets to me here at Hatfield. I must get back to Whitehall.'

'By some miracle, my Lord, the attempt on the life of the Statholder failed.'

'Miracle, Francis?' Burghley didn't look at him. 'What do you and I know of that?'

'I know that a wheel-lock pistol fired at point blank range should have blown the head off William of Nassau, but it didn't. The man yet lives.'

'By a hair's breadth, I heard.'

'True, but his wife nurses him day and night.'

Burghley smiled. 'They're good like that, wives,' he said, smiling up at the leaded panes of the east wing where Lady Burghley, his Mildred, still lay wrapped in her eiderdown. 'So what should we do?'

Walsingham found himself chuckling. 'My Lord, it is not for me to dictate the policy of the state . . .'

'Policy of the state, my arse,' grunted Burghley. 'Walsingham, we *are* the state. One slip from us, one wrong judgement and we may as well kneel before the Bishop of Rome and pay court to any Catholic Johnny-Come-Lately who doffs his cap at the Queen.'

It was Walsingham's turn to stop and he turned to face the Chief Secretary. 'But surely, the Queen won't . . .'

'Succumb to marriage?' Burghley reined in the mule again and eased his backside from the leather, letting his frozen toes touch the ground. 'I gave up on that one long ago. I leave predictions to wizards like John Dee, men who read the weather and the stars and the way bones fall. I deal – as do you, dear Francis – in reality. And the reality is that the Queen is the most eligible ruler in Europe if you discount Philip of Spain.' He looked into Walsingham's eyes. 'And we all *do* discount Philip of Spain, don't we?'

Walsingham smiled and walked on. 'If William survives?' he asked.

'If the Statholder survives and lives to take on Philip and Parma and the whole Godless tribe of them, I for one will be amazed. If he doesn't and if the Low Countries should fall to Spain . . .'

'Then we're next,' Walsingham said, finishing the Chief Secretary's sentence for him, even without the prescience of the Queen's magus.

'There'll be other attempts,' Burghley said. 'Other Juan Jaureguys to break through the cordon of the Statholder. And William the Silent will be silent for ever.'

'I have a man for that,' Walsingham said, 'to watch his back.'

'Oh? Who?'

'A new face. Name of Marlowe. It was he who closed the Shelley business. You'll have read my dispatch.'

'Of course.' Realization dawned on the Chief Secretary. 'Is he sound? One of us? Can he stand on his own two feet?'

Walsingham smiled. 'I prefer men who can think on their feet while they are standing on somebody else's.'

'Good,' Burghley said. 'Good.'

'I sent Faunt to him, but of course that was before recent events in Delft. I still intend Marlowe to go, but his brief is ever more desperate now.'

'I don't need the details.' Burghley waved the man aside. 'That's what we pay you for. Come on, Walsingham, time for breakfast. We've braved this ghastly weather for long enough. The cold gets to my bones these days.' He looked up at the turreted splendour of his house and the grey clouds building from the east. 'What will it bring us, do you think, this new year of our Lord?'

Walsingham smiled. 'I never think of that before the Christmas fires die. The Lord of Misrule has a habit of making a mess of things.'

'He does.' Burghley sighed. 'He does indeed.'

It took Hern several hours to negotiate with the master of the *Antelope* to take his menagerie across the North Sea. There were the horses and the dogs, the two monkeys, the parrot and the snake. And then, there was the nature of the human cargo to be reckoned with. These people were Egyptians, weren't they? On the run from something or other. The Master of the *Antelope* wasn't a religious man. He followed the laws of God and Elizabeth when he could by attending church once a month, but everybody appreciated that running with the tides off Norfolk carried a schedule of its own and he couldn't always arrange time with his Maker. So it didn't matter to him whether his passengers were Egyptians, Calvinists, Lutherans, Papists or Anthropophagi with their faces in their chests; it was just a matter of cash, pure and simple. And everyone had his price.

Hern, on the other hand, had done this before too and he had a knack of getting discounts for this or that reason, even when the price of the crossing was fixed and there was no room for negotiation. There had even been one spectacular occasion when a particularly unwary Master had paid him for the privilege of transporting his people.

It was another grey day when the *Antelope* sailed, canvas tumbling in the raw wind and the ketch coming about to hug the Norfolk coast. All that first day they followed it, the Master tacking to take advantage of the wind as little fishing villages came and went.

'Is this your first time in the Low Countries, Kit?' Balthasar Gerard stood on the forecastle in the raw morning air, tugging his cloak around him against the weather.

'It is,' Marlowe told him. 'You know it well, I suppose?'

'I am a Frenchman,' Gerard said, although his accent seemed universal, 'but in my calling, I go anywhere. Everywhere.'

'I have been impressed by what I have seen,' Marlowe said, 'but I still can't see where the trickery ends and the real fortune-telling begins.'

'As Hern told you,' Gerard said, 'when you can do that, you will truly be an Egyptian.'

'Do you forget nothing you hear?' Marlowe asked him. Hern had said that as a throwaway line, weeks before, when they were first on the road and before everything else had happened; Helene, Rose, all the bad things.

'I remember everything,' Gerard said, 'in one part of me, my heart, my head, my guts. I am the only true teller of the future in this band, although other troupes have others. Not as good as me, I must say, in all modesty.'

'So . . .' Marlowe knew he must tread warily. 'You knew about Rose and what would happen?'

'Not in exact terms,' Gerard said. 'I try not to see my own future. What man could stand to do that? But I knew our time together would be short. Yes, I knew that.'

Marlowe pressed a little harder. The more he probed these people, the less he seemed to know. 'So, although you knew she would kill Nell, you still took her to Ely?'

'Did she kill Helene Dee?' Gerard asked. 'I am far from sure, but when I try to look, all is mist, turns and twists and I can see nothing.'

Marlowe was unimpressed. How often the fog came down when the soothsayer was forced to look into something he had not already arranged to happen and, the oddest thing of all, Balthasar had done nothing to save the girl. When he realized that Constable Sedgrave had her in his clutches, he just meekly let her go. 'Couldn't one of the others see into that part,' he asked, 'if you yourself can't? Surely, you all have the skill of prophecy, to a greater or lesser degree? That's what Hern says, at any rate.'

'Hern speaks for Hern,' Gerard said. 'It is true that the children of the moon are as varied as the colours of the rainbow. They all have their skills.'

'If you are the best, then,' Marlowe said, 'tell my fortune, soothsayer.' And he pressed a groat into the man's hand.

Balthasar Gerard looked into Marlowe's eyes. 'Are you sure?' he asked. 'I do not give readings to please the payer, except to the ignorant who couldn't face the truth. You might not like what you hear.'

'You have my money, Master Gerard,' Marlowe said. 'Time for your end of the bargain.'

The Egyptian held up his hand. 'Remember,' he said, 'I am only Balthasar. We have no surnames here. Our pasts are behind us. We have only the present and the future. Today and tomorrow.'

'So be it,' Marlowe said.

The soothsayer took a deep breath and held Marlowe's hand flat, palm uppermost. He looked up into his face for a moment. 'There is greatness here,' he said. 'You will be remembered for all eternity.'

Marlowe laughed. 'I'm flattered,' he said, when he realized that Balthasar wasn't smiling. 'Go on. How shall I be remembered?'

'A line,' the other continued, tracing the lines in Marlowe's palm. 'A mighty line. There is a thump, a rhythm. I cannot describe it. No one has heard it before, but others will claim it as their own.' He suddenly faltered. 'I see blood,' he said, 'much blood. Paris. Do you know Paris, Kit?'

The scholar gypsy shook his head.

A strange look flickered across the grey face of Balthasar Gerard. 'Near the bed,' he said, in a voice that didn't sound like his own.

'What?' Marlowe didn't understand.

'There is a place,' Balthasar said, speaking slowly, tasting each word for sense as it left his mouth and finding little, 'a place where great ships come, some in pieces. There is . . .' he shut his eyes tight, his grip firmer on Marlowe's hand, 'a stream, a raven.' He opened his eyes suddenly. 'Does any of this make sense to you?' he asked.

Marlowe shook his head again.

Balthasar let his hand drop. 'That is where you will die, Kit,' he said, solemnly, 'where the great ships lie, by the raven's stream.'

'Near the bed!' Marlowe reminded him, smiling.

The Egyptian smiled too, the dread moment gone. 'You don't believe me.'

Marlowe slapped the wooden rail that ran around the *Antelope*'s deck. 'I believe in this –' he reached out to the rough hemp of the rigging – 'and this. What I can see and smell, taste and feel.'

'Liar!' Balthasar Gerard laughed at him. 'You are a dreamer, Kit, a poet. When I heard your tale of the Queen of Carthage, I knew that. You and I are both children of the moon in our different ways.'

'Are we?' Marlowe asked. 'Well, then –' he turned his face into the wind of the North Sea – 'amen to that.'

Night found the *Antelope* butting through the breakers, her compass holding as she ploughed south-southeast. Kit Marlowe was asleep in his bunk at the stern when he heard it, a low chanting like a dream from his childhood. For a moment, he was back in Canterbury, jumping the puddles in the cobbles as he ran to school, past St George's Church and on into Mercery Lane, with his old friends Henry Bromerick, Tom Colwell, Matty Parker. He heard the bells of the cathedral clash and call, prisoners in their great stone towers and he heard the hiss of the cane as a scholar stumbled late under the Dark Entry that led from the cloisters; Master Greshop flexing his muscles.

Slowly, his dream faded and he was aware of his surroundings. Above him the timbers of the deck were black with pitch and the beams were thick and knotted to his left. The bunk was narrow, a makeshift bed wedged between the frames and the horse hair pillow flat and unyielding. He popped his head over the side to where Balthasar Gerard snored softly in the bunk below. Across the narrow aisle where the night lamp swung, its tallow candle spent, he could make out the shape of Hern on the top bunk opposite his and Frederico on the bed below.

'Near the bed.' Balthasar's incomprehensible words moaned in his head with the roll and roar of the sea and the creaking of the timbers. He propped himself up on one elbow. There was no mistaking it. He wasn't dreaming now. It was a paternoster, half sung, half whispered, and in Latin. It had been a long time since he had heard this, the prayer of hope but in the language of the damned.

As silently as a shadow, Marlowe hauled on his breeches and slipped his dagger into the belt at his back. Then he slid off the bunk, landing on bare feet and padded his way towards the bow. The swell caught him as he reached the galley and he steadied himself, hissing an oath as he nearly fell. He passed the bunks of the women, their hung dresses swaying in the ship's movement like ghosts. He recognized the cherub face of little Starshine who wanted nothing but stories about cats. She lay cradled in her mother's arms, this child of the moon, dreaming of who knew what.

Still the prayers called Marlowe on, drawing him deeper and darker into the bowels of the ship. The stench from the animal deck was grim, ammonia reeking from the straw in which the horses slept standing up. He gripped the rope rail and went down, where the bilge water rolled with each sway and lapped over the keel timbers with each thud of the breakers on the bows. There was a faint light ahead, blue and secret and he followed it, like the wise men and their star. Three people knelt in prayer in the circle of light, in that makeshift stable between the bales of wool and barrels of ale. Two women who Marlowe had only seen in passing amongst the other passengers, eyes closed, their mouths moving in silent adoration. Simon was the third, the Greek who was really a Portuguese, or some such complicated genealogy. He was speaking in Latin now, the words of the Mass long outlawed in England wherever good Christian men met.

Simon's eyes flew open and he dropped the Bible and the chalice, both thudding to the bilge-wet deck, the goblet rolling away to the rats' nests in the corner. The women opened their eyes too and crossed themselves, gasping as they saw Marlowe standing there, watching them. His finger flew to his lips, 'Calm yourselves,' he said softly, 'we are at sea. The Queen's writ cannot reach you here.'

Simon retrieved his Bible, made the sign of the cross over the frightened women and sent them on their way. They bobbed past Marlowe, anxious to be gone, back to their beds, back to the dark.

'So, you know,' Simon said, kissing his rosary and folding it away into his robes.

'I had my suspicions,' Marlowe said, 'Ever since Ely. An Egyptian who doesn't speak the language, a juggler who doesn't juggle, a card sharp who doesn't touch the devil's pictures.'

'Are you hunting me?' Simon asked.

Marlowe chuckled and helped the man to his feet. 'You

flatter yourself, Master Jesuit,' he said. 'As our brethren in the crew might say, I still have other fish to fry.'

'So I am safe?' Simon asked, more for the sake of the women than himself.

'Simon, we are rolling about on a widow-maker full fathom five in a boat made of pieces of wood tied together with rope and canvas. How safe we are is anybody's guess.'

'We are in God's hands,' Simon assured him.

'That's a comfort,' Marlowe said. The priest made to brush past him, but Marlowe placed a hand on his chest. 'Not so fast.' He smiled. 'I know some Puritans who would have slit your throat by now for what they've seen and heard tonight. The fact that I'm letting you live means a few words of explanation are owed to me, I think. *Quid pro quo*, Father.'

The priest smiled. 'Very well,' he said. 'But I must have your word that those women will not be harmed. They are of the true faith. I offered them succour. Why is that a burning offence?'

Marlowe laughed. 'It is not for us to debate the temper of the times, sir,' he said. 'We are survivors, you and I, each in his own way. Tell me how you survived.'

To his dying day, Simon never knew why he told Kit Marlowe the truth. There was something about the man, the deep, dark eyes, the soft mouth set in the hard jaw. Something about him which hinted that he already knew and was just seeking confirmation.

'My name is not Simon,' the priest said, sitting on a bale of wool, greasy and smelling of sheep and ancient hay. 'It's Father Belasius. I am from Oporto, from the Jesuit College there.'

'And are you part of Campion's mission in England?'

Both men knew the story of Edmund Campion, the Protestant who had joined the scorpion's nest at Douai and kissed the Pope's arse before bringing the Papist word back to England. It was the talk of every tavern in Cambridge when they broke the man on the rack and hanged and quartered him at Tyburn.

'That man went his own way,' Belasius said. 'I am not made of the stuff of martyrs.'

'Remarkable you've survived so long, though,' Marlowe said.

'Circumspection.' Belasius shrugged. 'I have had to be careful. My guard was down tonight. You caught me in a weak moment, Master Marlowe.'

'We all have those.' Kit nodded. 'Happily not when you were throwing me into the air.'

'That trick only worked the once.' The priest smiled. 'You always led off the wrong foot.'

'We'll do better in Delft,' his tumbling partner said, 'assuming you will still be with us.'

Belasius shrugged, then looked at him seriously. 'Tell me about the other fish you have to fry – what are they?'

Marlowe looked at the man, long and hard. Circumspection was his middle name too and bobbing about on the North Sea where only God commands and no man's laws held sway would not let him relax his guard for one moment. 'Ask the fortune teller,' he said, springing to his feet. 'Ask Balthasar Gerard.'

All that last day at sea, the Master of the *Antelope* kept a watchful eye and his iron fowler primed on the aft castle. The whole stretch of coast from the Zuyder Zee to the Scheldt was the domain of the sea beggars, Dutch patriots who cut a man's purse strings while cutting his throat and asking his race and religion afterwards. He breathed a sigh of relief as the Hook of Holland lay grey in the morning mist and that danger, at least, was past.

While Hern and his people hauled their animals and carts ashore, refitting wheels and axles and unfurling their flags and ribbons, Marlowe went in search of the sign of The Salamander, a dark inn on the edge of the town quay where fishermen jostled with dockmen and sipped the froth from their ale.

He tried out his rusty Flemish on the innkeeper who gave him a royal reception. Travellers came and went through the Hook all the time, but few men of this quality ever crossed the threshold of The Salamander. The man's doublet and cloak were of the finest Italian weave, his buskins Spanish leather. A gentleman in The Salamander, even one who spoke Flemish so uncertainly, was doubly welcome and the whores clustered round him. Marlowe made his wishes known and the innkeeper

shrugged before leading the way up the rickety back stairs to
a low, wood-panelled room under the eaves.

'Are you Marlowe?' a voice growled in Flemish from a
dark corner.

'I was when I last looked,' Marlowe said, in English.

A tall man emerged from the shadows. He wore the dull
smock of the artisans of Zeeland and a pair of uncomfortable-
looking clogs. His pantaloons were enormous, hiding, as they
did, a brace of pistols.

'You're taking a chance, speaking English,' the man said,
in English this time.

'You're taking a chance carrying your guns so close to your
manhood. Not loaded, I hope.'

The tall man looked at him grimly, then burst out laughing.
'Yes, you're Marlowe, all right. Faunt warned me about you.
Ralph Minshull.' He extended a hand. They sat down opposite
each other at the table in the corner and waited while the
landlord supervised a couple of maids serving beer, cheese
and salt fish. Minshull waited until they'd gone.

'You came over with the Egyptians?' he asked.

'Yes. They're preparing for the road as we speak.'

'Tell me, do they still hang those people at home? I've been
away for a while.'

'They hang them when they can catch them,' Marlowe said.
'But they're like quicksilver. You think you have them in the
palm of your hand . . .'

Minshull nodded, breaking his bread and hacking off a hunk
of cheese with his knife. 'The authorities over here are more
tolerant. At least, the Dutch are. Further south, though . . .
you're not going south, are you?' He noticed Marlowe looking
suspiciously at the cheese. 'It's called Gouda,' he said, 'from
a town nearby. Oh, it's not Stilton, but it will do.'

'Don't you know where I'm going?' Marlowe asked, wiping
the ale's froth from his upper lip.

Minshull looked at him. 'You're new at this, aren't you?'

'I'm a graduate of the University of Cambridge.' Marlowe
shrugged, all innocence and wide eyes.

'Yes, and I'm the Pope's left tit,' growled Minshull. 'How's
the cheese?'

'Good.' Marlowe nodded, chewing. 'As you say, not Stilton, but I'll get used to it, I'm sure.'

Minshull leaned in to him, waving his dagger point around, greasy and smeared from the cheese. 'In our business,' he said, 'we only know what we need to know. We are all just cogs in a great machine. I go from here –' he pointed at an imaginary point in mid air – 'to here. And no further. Whereas you . . .'

'Whereas I was delayed by murder.'

'Oh?' Minshull was mildly curious. It took a lot to shake him out of his calm ways. He had seen most of what the world had to show and murder was almost the least of it.

'The wife of the Queen's magus.'

'Oh!' Minshull was suddenly all ears. 'Dr Dee's wife a murderess? This tale will run and run.'

'Dr Dee's wife a victim,' Marlowe corrected him. 'I am travelling with her murderer.'

'Oh?'

'The authorities back in Ely took a woman called Rose into their safe-keeping. They got the wrong woman.'

'You seem very certain of that,' Minshull noted.

'There's nothing certain about the Egyptians,' Marlowe said. 'Let's just say I have a sense beyond the five about this.'

'Yes.' Minshull nodded wisely. 'You do get that in this business. Do you know for certain who it is? Why did you let them leave Ely?'

Marlowe smiled enigmatically. 'Let's just say I prefer to keep them close. There is no telling what they might choose to do if left behind. But, enough of this – Nicholas Faunt said you'd have news for me,' he said.

Minshull leaned back, sampling the ale, taking his time. 'Faunt,' he said. 'I haven't seen him for a while. Still licking Walsingham's arse, is he?'

'The man's private life is his private life.' Marlowe shrugged. 'I came here to do a job.'

Minshull looked at the man before him. He was – what – twenty years his junior? Armed. Professional. Ready. Or at least as ready as you ever could be in a job like theirs. 'All right,' he said, and began to rearrange the objects on the table

between them. 'This –' and he pointed to the unused napkin
in its wooden ring – 'is Parma. His forward lines are two days'
march from here with his headquarters at Antwerp. At least
they were last week, but he's a tricky bastard and likes to keep
one jump ahead – to keep his own people guessing as much
as ours. This –' he placed the pewter salt cellar to the left of
the napkin – 'is the Spanish Road. It keeps a line of supply
all the way from Spain and it's in Parma's interest to keep it
open. If he loses that, he's sunk.'

'Can't he supply his troops from the sea?' Marlowe asked,
with only the vaguest working knowledge of the Dutch coast.

'He could,' Minshull told him, 'but the sea beggars would
make life difficult. Two or three of their damned barges could
probably board a galleon of Spain. And they'd make short
work of a galliass.' He caught the confusion in Marlowe's
face. 'Lower in the water, you see,' he said. 'Easier to board.
Anyway . . .' He suddenly broke off. A creak of a floorboard
had alerted him that they may no longer be alone. He got up
as stealthy as a cat and crept to the door, opening it a crack.
He sat back down behind the table. 'No one there,' he said.
'This old place creaks like Hell in winter.' He paused to get
back his flow. 'Yes, anyway, they say the King of Spain has
other uses for his Navy.' He tapped the side of his nose.

'What of William the Silent?' Marlowe asked.

Minshull's face darkened and he shook his head. He thumped
his flagon down near Marlowe, away from the napkin. 'He's
here,' he said, pointing a finger at the froth on the table. 'Quite
a formidable town, Delft, especially on the South side –' he
narrowed his eyes at Marlowe – 'unless you happen to
be the Duke of Parma, of course, in which case nothing is
formidable. And the Statholder is not a well man.'

TEN

The fire crackled and spat in the bedroom in the Prinsenhof. Beyond the convent walls, the city of Delft settled down to sleep, the carts rolled to their starting places for the morning, the market stalls silent in the darkness. Candles were lit in the tall houses and the Night Watch prowled the streets, their boots clattering on the cobbles and their pikes heavy on their shoulders.

Charlotte of Bourbon-Montpensier sat by her husband's bedside, as she had this past month, talking to him, stroking his forehead, now hot, now cold, patting his still hand. The doctors had told her that he would live and yet he looked so still, his eyes shut, his lips just slightly parted as though he might yet speak, although no sound ever emerged except an occasional shuddering sigh which nearly stopped her heart each time; the sighs sounded like the last breath of a dying man, and yet there was always one more breath. Only a pulse, which beat steadily in his neck, seemed to prove the doctors right, that he would recover, that he would live. For his faithful Lottie, it was enough, but watching over him like this, hour by hour, day by day, was taking a heavy toll. A tear ran down her cheek. If only he would wake, open his clear, grey eyes, smile and whisper, 'Lottie, *lieveling*, Lottie,' as he used to every morning when they were together. If only Hans had checked the robes of Jean Jaureguy that cold evening when he'd come calling as a humble petitioner, a devil in disguise. If only there was no war beyond the convent walls, no Duke of Parma, no Philip of Spain.

She pulled herself together sharply, brushing the tear away and she got up, bending to kiss her husband gently on the forehead just below the bandages and she made for the door. Her waiting women closed in on the bed as she left. They operated in shifts, two for the day and two for the night. Only Charlotte stayed for both, nodding asleep for minutes at a time, upright in her chair, before sitting by her husband again and chatting to him. She hadn't brought the children to see him. Little Emilia would not understand why Papa was sleeping all the time and she would jump on the bed and cause who knew what damage. The others would understand and the sight of their darling Papa so hurt and lying so still would terrify them.

Charlotte reached the bottom of the stairs. She had people to see, documents to sign. No one beyond the walls of the Prinsenhof knew of Jaureguy's shot, about the fragment of lead that still lay in the brain of the Statholder. Nor must they ever know. The private papers that he signed by hand she read carefully, telling his private secretary to amend here and there. She signed them herself with a flourish approximating to his and trusted that no one would look too closely. The state papers, the edicts and orders that went out to his troops she checked too, but these were appended with the wax seal of Nassau and she had no need of forgery here.

Even so, she knew perfectly well that this subterfuge could not last. It had been four weeks since anyone outside Charlotte, her maids, Hans and the doctors had seen the Statholder and in the streets of Delft and the flat levels of the Netherlands, rumours would be spreading like a mutinous rumbling. The Statholder had gone mad. The Statholder had fled the country, leaving his people to the Spanish Fury they all knew would come. The Statholder was dead; had in fact died years ago and it was an impostor who sat on the throne at the Prinsenhof. William the Silent was silent for ever, while the rumours grew louder, enough to deafen a whole country.

At the turn of the stairs, Dr van der Buick bowed low to the princess of Nassau. 'Rudi –' she took him aside into the antechamber which had once been a Catholic chapel – 'you saw His Highness this afternoon. Is there any change, anything at all you can tell me?'

Van der Buick was a clever man. In the university of Leyden there was no one better known. He had become famous throughout the land in these years of war for his treatment of the wounds war caused. If anyone could save the life of William the Silent, it was Rudi van der Buick. But Rudi van der Buick was a politician too; you didn't become physician to the Statholder without that. He knew when to be circumspect and he knew when to change the subject.

'I am concerned for you, Highness,' he told her. 'You have not slept . . .'

She held up her hand. 'Answer my question, Rudi,' she insisted.

'I can detect no change, Highness,' he said. 'The humours are unbalanced because of the shock to the brain. Only time will tell if His Highness will come back to us.'

'And there is nothing you can do?' It was a question she had asked him every day for a month.

'We have bled him, as you know.' Van der Buick had already tried every trick in and out of the book. 'It has had no effect. I can only suggest what I have always suggested. Talk to him, madam, let him hear your voice. Perhaps the children . . .'

'No.' She shook her head vehemently. 'I will not allow that.'

The doctor nodded. 'Then, Highness, the best service you can do for your husband is to go to sleep. You will do him no service by becoming ill yourself.' He led her gently by the arm, 'I will prepare a draught for you.'

'You will not,' she said, still patient, still strong. 'I will sleep when William sleeps and not the sleep he is in now. What if . . . ?' and her voice tailed away, full of unspoken fears.

'Highness?' Van der Buick waited.

Charlotte cleared her throat to compose herself again. 'What if my husband is locked in his silence for ever? What if he can hear and see what is going on around him but he has no way of responding to it, to show us he is still here, in his body? Could there be a worse fate for a man?'

Or a worse fate for the Netherlands, van der Buick wondered to himself. It was not the kind of thing a doctor of medicine said out loud, so he went further than he should and took the liberty of patting Her Highness's hand.

They held an ice fair that year on the Crow's Nest, shortly before Christmas, while the great and the good of South Holland tried to carry on as usual and forget there was a war on. Marlowe had toyed with saddling the Wasp and riding north to Delft while he still could, bearing in mind the constantly shifting front lines of the Duke of Parma, but an Englishman riding alone in the Low Countries would attract too much attention. Minshull had told him that the area was swarming with spies, intelligencers and projectors who listened at keyholes and whispered in corners, men like him and Marlowe but who served a different sovereign and spoke a different creed. The man with the halting Flemish would turn too many heads, pose too many questions. Better to stay in the exotic anonymity of the Egyptians. Simon thought that too.

Marlowe was surprised that Simon the Jesuit stayed with them at all; after all, this was Calvinist country and he would find few needing his particular comforts here. That day at the fair with the frost sparkling at the lake's edge and the locals skating with ease over the ice, he saw the priest hawking ribbons around the area in front of the stage where Hern and his people went through their paces, swallowing swords and eating fire to the gasps of the crowd and the rattle of their gelders. Why hadn't Simon gone south to Parma's lines where he could have thrown off the bright ribbons of his disguise and become Father Belasius again, all black and velvet and incense? Something was holding Simon the Jesuit here, on the cold flat fens of the north, and it wasn't the quality of the cheese or the ale.

'A gelder for them, Master Marlowe.' Hern sat down on the blanket next to the scholar who was scratching with his quill on parchment, his fingers numb with cold. 'Another story?'

'A poem,' Marlowe told him. 'A sonnet.'

'What's that?'

'A poem.' Marlowe smiled.

Hern laughed that deep bass laugh of his. 'Why weren't you born an Egyptian?' he said, slapping his man on the shoulder. 'Is this one for tonight?'

'I thought I'd try it out,' Marlowe said. 'Looking at this lot, the locals of South Holland could use some culture.'

'Ah.' Hern smiled. 'Creatures of the clay, Master Marlowe, creatures of the clay. They've been holding fairs like this since

Jesus was a carpenter's apprentice. They don't look like rebels, do they?'

Marlowe had to agree that they didn't. Knots of portly men, blue-nosed and pot-bellied, stood around braziers at the water's edge nattering away in Flemish and northern Dutch. Vats of boiling oil balanced on the grids above the flames disgorged baskets of crisp *bitterbollen* on to their waiting plates while a child offered up pots of the mild mustard for dipping. Women in their wide white hats were admiring the silks and satins that fluttered from the stalls all round. Blonde, grey-eyed children pushed each other on to the ice or dragged little sledges up and down while dogs yelped and ran in all directions. There wasn't a gun or a sword or a soldier in sight. Only Kit Marlowe felt the dagger nestling in his back under the bright reds and yellows of his Egyptian costume. He wondered if Hern felt iron too but he couldn't see any bulge in his doublet.

Hern whistled an Egyptian lad to him and whispered in the boy's ear. Marlowe had seen him do this before at many of their stops since the Hook and he knew what was going to happen. Like a ghost, the boy slid into the crowd at the edge of the Egyptian stage. High in the air, the streamers flew and twirled, spiralling in myriad colours to the boards, then flashing skywards again. And all eyes were on them, hypnotized by the sway and curl of the ribbons, their senses marching to the thud and rattle of the drums and tambourines, though their feet seemed glued to the grass. The boy moved through the fair, silent, like a will-o'-the-wisp that haunted the Stour in Marlowe's Canterbury.

In minutes he was back, beaming, and he quietly dropped six fat purses in Hern's lap. The lord of the dance swept them up and they were gone. He winked at Marlowe and ruffled the boy's matted hair. 'Try the ice, Tomaso,' he said, 'but stay near the edge. The Devil's in those depths. Don't let him catch you.' And the boy was gone.

'I saw him take four for certain,' Marlowe said, 'and I think I know where he took the fifth. But I didn't see him take the sixth.'

'Nor the seventh,' Hern said and threw Marlowe's own purse back to him.

The would-be Egyptian laughed.

'Take my advice, Master Marlowe,' Hern said. 'Carry that near your codpiece. You'll feel it if it shifts from there.' He swiftly stood upright. 'Ah, if I'd had you in my camp fifteen years ago, what I could have made of you. Good luck with your scribbling.'

And Marlowe checked his purse once more as the man disappeared like smoke into the crowd.

They came from the south on the road that ran straight and true through the *vennen*, the heather criss-crossed with dykes. The sky was leaden over the church spires of Delft and smoke drifted lazily from the ragged pauper hovels that ringed the town walls.

The Town Watch circled those walls, armed to the teeth and watching the roads intently, especially the roads to the south. That was the way the Spaniards would come, with their flags and their cannon, the oxen clashing on the road and the giant crucifixes black against the sky. Marlowe, bouncing on the lead wagon beside Hern, chuckled to himself at the thought of Joe Fludd and his lads facing this situation and not knowing one end of an arquebus from another. Different times. Different crimes. Perhaps an army just over the far horizon made learning happen quickly; learn quickly, or die.

The Egyptians began to beat their drums and blasted their trumpets, Hern standing up and waving his banner in both hands, feet planted firmly on the board of the wagon. The children dropped silently from the rumbling carts and grabbed the ribboned manes and tails of the piebald horses, springing up on to their backs and hauling the littlest ones up behind them, their shrill voices breaking into song to the drum's rhythm. Marlowe added his voice to theirs, the cadences and harmonies of church music chiming oddly but sweetly with their innocent melodies.

They entered Delft by the southern gate and passed unchecked through the narrow streets to the square in the centre where the Nieu Kirke loomed over everything, grey and squat like the burghers who had built it. A crowd of people and dogs began to coalesce around the caravanserai as it spread out ever more thinly to accommodate the narrow twists and turns of the lanes. In places, the houses met overhead and from every window an apple-cheeked head seemed to pop out, maidservants interrupted in their bed-making by the sound of the drums and singing, housewives and nursing mothers hanging out of the upper storeys, babies on their arms, waving and singing back at the children. Marlowe, still more used to the welcome they got in England, with rotten apples thrown by day and creeping figures needing potions and portents by night, felt his heart lift at the welcome, and almost forgot that he was here for another purpose than to entertain the crowd. The spy sank down lower as the poet, singer and temporary tumbler rose to the occasion.

Soon, Tomaso was about his sneaky business in the crowd and Hern was swallowing swords and fire, regurgitating lines of flags in the Statholder's colours. Balthasar's tent had gone up in double quick time at the edge of the square and a shifty line had formed at its door, each person in it trying to pretend that they were just standing there, there was no particular reason why they should be *there* rather than *here*, they were just resting there out of the bitter northern wind off the *vennen*. One by one, they disappeared into Balthasar's particular kind of darkness and, mostly, they emerged with a complacent smile on their lips. Balthasar was feeling kind today; he would not be dispensing death and destruction to the good burghers of Delft. They had enough of that a horizon away.

Marlowe crept away, skirting the edge of the crowd and disappearing neatly down a narrow alley. The Prinsenhof, which had stood out so boldly at a distance from the town, was not easy to find in these towering tunnels of houses. Whenever he got to where two alleys crossed he got a better view of the sky and so, by turning left and right and sometimes even going back on himself, he reached the wall of the Prinsenhof itself.

There was no gate or door along the whole length of the wall as far as he could see. The place had all the hallmarks of a nunnery, sealed and secret from the world. He swaggered nonchalantly along, turning each corner as he came to it as if there could be no danger around it, though he knew this was probably far from the case. The crowd the Egyptians had drawn was a two-edged sword for Marlowe. It had enabled him to slip away, but on the other hand it had almost emptied the streets and this made him all the more noticeable. Finally, he turned a corner and could see a gate ahead of him.

He approached it at a purposeful walk, trying to look as though he was on an errand of mild importance. This had worked often enough for it to be worth a try. The halberd heads clashed across his face as he stepped over the threshold. A guard snarled something at him and Marlowe summoned up his Flemish. He passed his papers across, the ones given to him by Faunt who in turn had got them from Walsingham. The guard didn't recognize the seal and couldn't read the language. He muttered to a third man who was pointing his arquebus at Marlowe and the scholar gypsy was pleased to see that the Statholder's security had clearly improved.

There were shouts and heel-clicking and an officer arrived in a plumed helmet, clanking down the stairs in hobnailed boots. He looked at Marlowe in his Egyptian coat of many colours and looked at the papers. He snapped at one of the halberdiers who threw his weapon to his comrade and patted Marlowe's clothing, his body, his arms, his legs. Then he stood back.

'This way,' the officer growled, but Marlowe stopped him, sliding the dagger from the small of his back where the guard had missed it.

'To show my good faith.' He smiled.

The officer rapped out a string of oaths that Marlowe didn't understand to the guards who looked suitably chastened. By way of explanation, he muttered, as far as Marlowe's Flemish could tell, 'You can't get the staff,' and he snatched the dagger's hilt. 'Pick this up on your way out.'

He led Marlowe through a tangle of passageways, the walls lime-washed like the Puritan churches back home and up a broad staircase. He was shown, beyond the huge double doors, into a lofty antechamber, where glittering-eyed burghers sat waiting to press whatever suit burghers the length and breadth of Europe waited to press. It would be about market stalls and grazing rights and trading concessions. Didn't they know there was a war on?

The officer had unbuckled and removed his helmet and was in earnest conversation with a court official, a tall, refined-looking man with a neatly trimmed goatee above his impeccably starched ruff. The man looked Marlowe up and down and immediately disapproved. The visitor looked like a wandering lunatic and they had enough of those in Delft already. He nodded at whatever the officer said to him and crossed to Marlowe, beckoning him into a side room.

There was a stir among the burghers. 'I've been waiting for nearly three hours.' 'That man's a tramp, what's he doing here?' 'I demand to see the Statholder.' The rumble of outraged citizenry throughout time. Beyond another set of doors, which closed behind him with a thud, Marlowe found himself alone with the tall man.

'Who are you?' he asked in the clipped dialect of the court.

'Christopher Marlowe.'

'Where are you from?'

'Cambridge University.'

'You are a scholar?'

'I am.'

The tall man sat quietly in a covered chair, poring over Walsingham's papers and proceeded to ask Marlowe questions in Latin, then in Greek. He answered them fluently. Then there was a silence.

'But personally,' Marlowe went on, still in Greek, 'I've always found Aristotle a little laboured on that point. Ramus says . . .'

The tall man held up his hand, smiling, and lapsed into surprisingly good English. 'All right, Dominus Marlowe. I have no doubt that you are a scholar. But what else can you do?'

Marlowe smiled in turn. 'I am learning new things all the time,' he said, 'but speaking for this moment, I can write a play, cut a reasonable rhyme, sing tolerably well. More recently, I have learned to turn a somersault, as long as some-body gives me a hand with the first bit, but I am improving. But most importantly and also, I hope, with a little help from you, I will keep your Statholder out of the clutches of Spain.'

The tall man stood up. 'I am Hans Neudecker, Chamberlain to His Highness the Prince of Nassau. You will wait here.'

Marlowe did, a large clock on the far wall the only soul for company as it chimed the hour. When the doors opened again, a lady glided into the room, followed by two others. Her dress spoke of finery and wealth, but she wore no jewellery and her face was sallow and drawn. Instinctively, Marlowe bowed.

She held out her hand to him. 'I am Charlotte of Bourbon-Montpensier,' she said in French, 'Princess of Nassau. You are Monsieur Marlowe?'

'I am, Highness,' Marlowe replied in the same language.

'We will speak in English,' Charlotte said. 'Even here, walls have ears.'

He nodded, grateful at least for that. She took a seat and ushered him in to one next to her while the ladies-in-waiting waited. 'I fear,' she said softly, 'you may have come too late. The doctors advise that my husband cannot recover.'

'Forgive me, madam,' Marlowe said, 'but time is of the essence. I heard at the Hook that the Statholder was ill. Do you rule in his place?'

'Rule?' Charlotte laughed bitterly. 'One town and miles of marshland, hemmed in on one side by the sea beggars and on the other by the might of Spain? Oh, yes, Master Marlowe, my kingdom knows no bounds.'

'Forgive me, lady.' Marlowe was still trying to find a way to reach this woman. 'Your husband's doctors will of course be the finest in the land?'

'I have no reason to doubt them.' Charlotte sat upright, suddenly on her dignity. The letters that Hans had shown her a moment ago bore the seal of the Privy Council of England and the lion and dragon of Elizabeth, the Queen. Yet the man before her wore the rags of a pedlar and a mad one at that. And here he was, questioning the ability of the royal doctors.

'Nor I,' Marlowe said. 'But I have people with me who may yet be able to help.'

'People?' Charlotte frowned. 'What sort of people?'

'Egyptians,' he said. 'Is that what you call them in this country?'

Hern looked at Marlowe sternly and put his hands on his hips. 'That is not how we work, Master Marlowe, and you know it. We never offer our services to people. They have to come to us, it is part of the cure. You know that.'

'But, Hern, this could do us a lot of good. Think how much the Statholder would pay the person who cured him. Soft beds and soft living for the rest of the winter, if that's what you want. I know the women would welcome it, especially Maria. Her time must be nearly here.'

'How did you know that Maria was with child?' Hern snapped. 'It is not the way with our women to let the child show. Her clothes should hide it from all eyes except the father's.'

'I have not been travelling with you all these weeks without learning some tricks,' Marlowe said. 'So, you have just told me for certain that you are the father. Thank you, I didn't know that for sure. Maria stands with her hands in the small of her back when she straightens from her tasks. I remember seeing other women do that; our women are not so shy about letting the child show. Also, she is given treats to eat by the other women, fruit when there is any, the inside of the bread, rather than the hard crust.'

'Clever watching, Master Marlowe, but that doesn't tell anyone when a woman is with child, just that she has kind friends.'

'Also, I happened to come upon you and Maria behind the wagon the other day. You were kissing her and stroking her belly. That was what gave me my biggest clue.' Marlowe waited to see if he had gone too far, but Hern threw back his head and laughed.

'At last, Kit Marlowe, you are a true Egyptian,' he roared. 'Yes, you are right, the child could come at any time. Maria is not young any more and this child may give her trouble. She would be glad of a safe home for a while. But if we fail to recover the Statholder's health, what then? If he dies, we will be held responsible. We could all dance on the end of a rope, men, women, children. You.'

Marlowe took this without a flicker. This was true, except that it was doubtful that he would ever dance on a rope. 'I have seen Lily heal the sick,' he said. 'In the house of John Dee, just weeks ago. I'm sure she can do this.'

'It will be Lily's choice,' Hern said. 'I will put no pressure on her. But, and I must ask this, Master Marlowe, how were you in a position to offer our help to the Princess of Nassau? The royal family of any country are not usually to be found at our shows. Simon missed you in the tumbling. He had to content the crowd with some shows of strength.' Hern pictured the debacle in his mind silently and shook his head. 'It was not a success, I must tell you. The vegetables are frozen hard in these parts in December. He is nursing his bruises.' He smiled in spite of himself. 'So that's where you were, was it? At the Prinsenhof?'

'A sister of mine is married to the brother of one of the maids in waiting to the princess,' Marlowe extemporized. 'I went to see if I could say hello. On my brother-in-law's behalf.'

'How kind. What a close family you must have,' Hern said, straight faced. 'And did you?'

'Did I what?'

'Say hello on your brother-in-law's behalf?'

'No, sadly. She was off duty today. But I did happen to bump into the princess. She was on her way from her husband's bedside and we got . . . chatting.'

Hern looked hard at the ragged thing in front of him, a sartorial shadow of his former self. And yet there was something in the soulful dark eyes and the angel's mouth which said that it was possible, *just* possible, that he could end up chatting to a princess he met in a corridor. Hern decided to believe him, just this once. 'And so, she mentioned . . . ?'

'Yes, she mentioned her husband was gravely ill, had been in a deep unwakening sleep for weeks and none could help him. She looks close to death herself, in fact. Very sallow and ill-looking. She perhaps needs some attention too. But if her husband could be woken, that would be a comfort to her, at least.'

'But again I say, what if he dies?'

'Why should he? Was Lily's performance a trick?'

Hern smiled. Lily's powers of healing was one of the Egyptian skills which was not a trick. But it wasn't foolproof, either. Sometimes, it didn't work and in this case it would not be a simple matter of being chased out of town in a rain of rotten fruit and imprecations.

'It was no trick, Master Marlowe. Lily is with the children in the middle wagon. Go and ask her if she will help. But no coercion, mind. And that means no fluttering those eyelashes either. Just ask her straight, and take her first answer, whatever it may be. And don't forget, I'll find out if you lie.'

'I promise, Hern.' Marlowe said. 'I'll just put it to her that there is a man out there in the town who has been the victim of terrible plots to kill him and he is lying close to death, wearing out his wife, breaking the hearts of his children and putting his entire country at risk of being overrun by Spanish troops intent on pillage, rape and driven by religious mania. Then she can make up her own mind whether to help him or not. Is that fair?'

Hern cast up his eyes and flapped his hand at the man to go and do as he pleased. Whatever else he had learned about Kit Marlowe, he knew that he would at least always do that.

John Dee always did as he pleased too, but at that moment, back over the lumbering, bouncing sea to Ely, he was incapable of conscious choice. Sam Bowes and the cook were worried about him, a more or less permanent state of affairs for any members of his household. That the man was peculiar, fractious, as demanding as any child was an undoubted fact, but Bowes and the cook loved him like a father; which was odd, as Sam Bowes could have given him ten years and kept the change. But even when he was so distracted that he forgot to eat, or speak and went about in sulphur-stained robes with half his hair burned off, he was still the Master in the house and no one made a move without it being the move he had told them to make. So, Sam and the cook were like kites with broken strings and no wind to speak of. They just bounced aimlessly around, never going far, never doing much, just watching their Master and trying to get him to eat and perhaps be interested in something.

The cook, the gossip of the party, had the women of Ely in for ale and cakes every afternoon. The women enjoyed it, as a chance to wear their best caps and sit in front of someone else's fire for a change. The cook, of course, was in search of an interesting conundrum to make her Master sit up and take notice. But humdrum not conundrum was what the women delivered and Sam Bowes was glad that Dee took no notice of the household accounts. The amount of butter, sugar and eggs that the cook was getting through was something amazing and yet still there was not a hint of a puzzle for their Master to solve. This was mainly because the murder of Helene Dee had been the most stupendous thing that had happened in the area for centuries and that was all they wanted to talk about. The cook decided to give up the afternoon meetings as a bad job and was looking for Bowes to tell him so when she bumped into her Master as he came round a corner at more than his usual speed.

'Where's Sam?' he asked, with no preamble.

'I'm looking for him myself, sir,' the cook said.

'Well, find him quickly, quickly. We're going back to Cambridge. I have decided that I am going to live at my old college, St John's, for a while. Perhaps I can forget . . .' he waved a hand over the Hall and the staircase. He seemed to conjure up the rest of the house in a cloud of memories streaming from his finger ends, as well as all the other houses they had lived in, finding Helene that first time, telling fortunes on a village green, seeing her in the smoke of his fire the night before, his lonely life before she was in it and since.

'I thought perhaps if I could go somewhere where she had never been, I might be able to forget her for a while.'

The cook understood that. She had had a family once, husband, children. But when they died of the sweating sickness she had shaken the dirt from her feet, left her cottage door open for whoever needed it and joined the mad household of Doctor John Dee. Edward Kelly had been with him then, and he had eased her heart for a while, until he had broken it all over again. She heaved a sigh. She had loved Nell like a daughter and missed her very much, in the evenings, over her endless slices of toast.

'A change of scene will do us all good, Master,' she said. 'Shall I pack?'

Dee waved his hand again. 'No,' he said. 'We're going now, as soon as you can find Sam. I want to be in my rooms by Christmas.'

'Where will we be?' the cook asked, panic seizing her by the throat. She was too old now to start again and the toast had taken its toll on her once girlish figure. There would be no Edward Kelly to warm her bed this time, she was sure.

'You can have rooms too, I'm sure,' Dee said. 'I am after all one of St John's most revered alumni. There will be no problem in finding room for us all. Quickly, quickly, fetch Sam and put on your cloak.' He looked at her, as if for the first time. 'You have grown portly, cook. Can you ride a horse?'

'If someone helps me up on one,' cook said. She had ridden bareback over the South Downs when she was a girl. She heard that riding a horse was something you never forgot how to do; she hoped that that particular old wives' tale was more accurate than most of the others.

Dee looked her up and down again. Twenty stones if she was a grain, he was sure. But that was what Bowes was here for. And sure enough, here was Bowes, running down the corridor on his bandy legs. Cook would make three of him on a good day, but he was probably stronger than he looked. Those wiry types often were.

'There you are, Samuel,' Dee cried, with something of his old animation. 'We're off to Cambridge, so fetch a coat for yourself, there's a good chap. It's freezing out.'

'What do I need a coat for?' Bowes was confused. It had taken two months to pack for this move. Surely, the Master couldn't mean that they were going to Cambridge today? For a start, there was a goose fattening in the barn, for the Christmas dinner and all sorts of gentry invited for the season. The Leslies would have expected as much.

'Because,' Dee said, enunciating clearly, 'we are off to Cambridge and it is freezing out.' Ye Gods and Demons! First the cook balloons up to a hundred times her original size and now Bowes has gone simple. He felt as if he was waking from a dream, some of it sweeter than sugar, much of it bitterer than gall. 'So, get your coats, cloaks and whatever you need. I am just going to pack a satchel with my essentials and off we go.' He turned and went back into the room he had been using as his snug, rubbing his hands together. 'It will be just like old times.'

Bowes looked at the cook. 'This is your fault,' he said severely. 'You would do it!'

'All I did was ask that Egyptian for a charm,' she said, her voice wobbling with emotion. 'It seemed polite, after they did all those tricks. It only cost me a groat.'

'And did you use it?'

The cook looked down at where she was pretty sure her feet were. 'Yes,' she said, sullenly.

'And what did you wish for?'

The cook mumbled, but Bowes could not hear what she said.

'Humph,' he said. 'All I can say is that you should have listened to what Nell always said. Be careful what you wish for. It might come true.' He looked at her as she stood there, head down, wringing her hands in distress. 'Now, then. Go and get your cloak and I'll get the horses round. How are you at catching geese?'

She looked up, alarmed.

'No, I thought not. I'll catch it, then. At this rate, it will be so tame none of us will want to eat the damned thing. Tell the Master the horses will be round the front. And bring a chair out with you. There is no power on Earth, in Heaven or Hell that will help me get you up on a horse's back. You'll have to climb up yourself. Quick now, shift yourself, woman.' He gave her a slap on the rump as he went round behind her and she stood quivering with indecision in the middle of the Leslies' Great Hall.

Bowes went muttering round to the stables and saddled up two horses. The third horse, because he was not an unkind man, he put in the harness of an old dog cart that was collecting cobwebs in the corner. If she asked, or went all coy on him, he could always say it was for the comfort of the goose.

ELEVEN

Lily was with the women, as Hern had said. She was massaging Maria's back, but stopped as soon as Marlowe poked his head around the sacking at the back of the wagon, parked in the angle of the courtyard walls.

He flashed a smile at the two. 'Congratulations on your forthcoming confinement, Mistress Maria,' he said, pleasantly. 'I wonder if I might have a word with you, Mistress Lily? In private?'

The two women were not sure what to make of this young man, who seemed to be in the world, but not of it. That he was not attracted to Maria, forty years old almost and pregnant, was one thing. That he had seemed impervious to Lily's grubby charms however had so far confused them. He had seemed very drawn to Rose, but then, who wasn't? Balthasar, hitherto as chaste as Marlowe, had behaved like a lovesick puppy whenever she was around, and had been distant ever since Ely. But now he had obviously come to pay what passed for court in the Egyptian caravan. Maria nudged Lily in the ribs and rearranged her layers of clothing to hide her pregnancy.

'Off you go, Lil,' she said. 'My back will wait. Perhaps Master Marlowe's need is more urgent than mine.'

'I hope so,' Lily said in her ear, hopping down off the back of the wagon. She had had her first child when she was just thirteen, an infant herself, almost, and had not had one for nearly four years. That first child had been Frederico's and he had only been fifteen. Fatherhood, even the Egyptian kind, had not suited him and he had not slipped his body into her sleeping place for years. Her body ached for a baby and this handsome lad would make fine and beautiful children, let alone that they would be clever and could become something special one day. Almost before her feet had touched the ground, she was rubbing against him and muttering sweetness in his ear.

He pushed her away, but not unkindly. 'Thank you, Lily. Very nice. But for now I have an important job for you.'

'What can be more important than what I can do for you right now? Right here, if that is your fancy.'

Marlowe looked around and saw at least eight pairs of eyes watching him, nine if he counted the cloudy gaze of one of the older horses as a pair. 'There are rather a lot of people around, Lily,' he reproved her. 'But even if we were alone, this is not what I want to ask you.'

Lily pouted and pulled away. 'What, then?' she asked, sulkily.

'Come for a walk with me,' he said, 'and I will explain.'

From the fireside, Hern watched them go. Lily was again pressed as close to Marlowe as she could get, without tripping him up in her flowing rags. She was looking up into his face, adoringly. Then, about twenty paces from the camp, she turned and faced him, looking up still, but now with a calculating look in her eye. Hern saw Marlowe cast his arms out, over the camp, the town, the whole country – possibly even the earth and heavens. Marlowe was good with words, but his body was just as eloquent. Hern sighed. Why could that boy have not been born an Egyptian? Surely, on the night his soul was ready to return to earth, it went to the wrong family. A cobbler would not know what to do with such a boy.

Then, Hern stiffened. Lily had agreed, he was sure of that. Marlowe touched her hair, tidying it around her face. He turned her hands over and smoothed the back of one hand down her face. He picked up a layer of ribboned rags and let them fall. For a second, Lily's face fell. Then, he reached into his belt and took something out, which he passed to the girl. She looked down at it, bit it and ran for the town. Hern shook his head and smiled to himself. He remembered that he had not forbidden bribery and reminded himself not to forget it again.

'The rooms are taken, Dominus Greene,' the proctor insisted.

'Taken?' Robert Greene narrowed his eyes at the man. For four years he'd known this idiot, boy and man and their true minds had never married. 'By whom?'

The proctor consulted the ledger with its spidery scrawl.

'Dr John Dee and two servants. And –' he squinted a little at the writing and held the book up at a different angle, hoping that might help – 'a goose.'

'A goose?' Greene was almost speechless.

'That's what it appears to say here,' said the proctor, putting the ledger down again. He pointed. 'One goose.'

'Is this or is this not, Master Proctor, St John's College of the University of Cambridge?'

'It is, Dominus Greene.' The proctor sighed, knowing exactly where the man was going with this line of unreason.

'And you are letting out rooms in this hallowed hall to a goose? The damned thing will be elected Master next and we'll have to kiss its wing feathers.'

The proctor held up his hand. 'I am merely a link in the chain, sir,' he told him. 'I do as I'm commanded by a higher authority. As do we all.' The emphasis was not lost on Greene but he had no intention of backing down now. His own rooms were not uncomfortable but they faced north-east and the wind blew the river smells along the cobbles and they eddied up into his apartments in the summer. In the winter, the wind just blew. To the north-west however lay a particularly imposing set of rooms belonging to Richard Clare that were the envy of every graduate and sizar in the college. And Richard Clare had gone of the ague not three weeks since. There had been a full college funeral, everyone in their academic robes laced with black and a suitably mournful-looking Robert Greene had composed a requiem. But all that was just so much show and *so* three weeks ago. The rooms had been thoroughly cleaned and Greene had watched the bedder in question with a hawk's eye to see how she fared. When there was no sign of sickness after three weeks, Greene decided that the time was right to strike, before anyone else got the coveted rooms. So now, here was Greene, on his dignity. In fact, it was not often he was off it.

'You do know, sir –' the proctor came over all conspiratorial – 'who Dr Dee is, don't you?'

'Of course I do,' Greene snapped. 'The Queen's magus. That doesn't give the man the right—'

'He *was* a member of the college, sir, before my time, but my old dad remembers him well.'

'Yes, well,' Greene sniffed. 'I'm very happy for your old dad's reminiscences, but I am a member of this college now.' He paused as that particular bomb merely bounced off the granite that was Proctor Boddington. 'Tell me, Boddington –' Greene only ever used the man's name when he wanted something – 'why is Dr Dee coming to St John's?'

'I'm sure I don't know, sir,' Boddington said, stern-faced.

Greene sighed and reached below the man's counter, jingling silver in his purse. Boddington caught the coins expertly, had the temerity to test them with his teeth and pocketed all but one. That one he pushed back towards Greene. 'Dud, sir, sadly,' he said and waited. Greene, with a sigh, replaced the forged penny with another which passed the molar test and Boddington went on. 'His wife's died,' he told Greene. 'At their house in Ely not a week ago. They do say . . .' He bent lower to the graduate, pausing in the hope of more inducement. When it was clear that none was forthcoming, he carried on nonetheless. Since Mrs Boddington had had it away on her toes with the dairyman, he had few to exchange gossip with, and this had been burning a hole in his tongue. 'They do say she was murdered.'

Greene's eyes widened. 'Do they now?'

'The old man's prostrate with grief. Coming back to his roots for comfort, they do say.'

'And do they say how she died?' Greene asked.

The proctor tapped the side of his nose. 'I know what you're thinking, sir,' he said, as if he and Greene were twins born in time, 'the husband did it. Whenever there's a domestic ruction such as this, sir, look to the spouse.'

'But you said Dee was prostrate,' Greene reminded him.

'A front,' Boddington told him flatly. 'He's blaming the Egyptians.'

'The Egyptians?' Greene repeated. This began to sound more and more like the weakest excuse in the world for not letting him have those nice, warm, west-facing rooms.

'You know, the band of ruffians who passed through the town. Constable Fludd was on their tail, they do say, but he might as well have pissed into the wind. Dee invited them to his place at Ely, to talk magic or whatever Devil-driven nonsense they speak. They say the constables at Ely have taken one of their women for the crime.'

'Who are "they"?' Greene asked.

Sometimes, Boddington wondered just how these scholars ever got their degrees. He spoke more slowly. 'Egyptians, sir,' he said, sounding every syllable with exaggerated care.

'No, you said "they say". Who are they that say?'

Boddington frowned and his disbelief that Greene was an actual graduate of St John's at all deepened. He threw up his hands. '*They*, sir,' he repeated. It would have to suffice. 'They also say –' Boddington's nose was almost in Greene's ear-ringed ear – 'that that Christopher Marlowe was with them. You know, the one they call Machiavel.'

The driving sleet had driven most of the good Cambridge folk off the streets by nightfall. The husbandmen had shut the cocks away, the market stalls had dropped their shutters along Petty Cury and the scholar roisterers had downed the last of their ale and had made for their colleges, ready to run the nightly gauntlet past their proctors.

The clock of St Mary's clanged the midnight chimes as the three men ordered more wine in the upstairs room of The Eagle and Child along Bene't's Lane. Dr John Dee, in his funeral black, had been drowning his sorrows in his old drinking haunt when he had been hailed by an acquaintance, Dr Gabriel Harvey of Corpus Christi and an Italian-looking fellow with an earring who, Dee was horrified to discover, was of Dee's own college. They had spent the evening talking of this and that, of the likelihood of war with Spain or France; of the foolhardy nonsense of sending Francis Drake to sea on some wild goose chase; on the cost of claret and the new trend coming from London, drinking smoke.

'Tell me, Dr Dee –' Harvey was as oily as ever – 'have you news of Kit Marlowe? I haven't seen him around the college recently.'

Now, John Dee was usually a reader of men's souls. His grey eyes glittered in the firelight and the candle's flame flared back at them in Harvey's vision. Robert Greene was peeling an apple with his dagger, apparently unconcerned. Normally,

John Dee would have read those two like a book, divined their joint intent, understood their common loathing of Marlowe. But tonight was not normal for John Dee. He had wandered Magdalene Bridge in the pouring rain, ignored the street vendors along the High Ward and had relived his youth. Thirty years ago, in the days of the stone-hearted Mary, he wore his ignorance on his sleeve, dared God out of Heaven with the best of them and had taken his life in his hands. Now he was older, sadder. Was he wiser? Perhaps not. Tonight, all he knew was that his darling Helene was dead and he desperately needed to know why. He desperately needed to talk to her, but his powers, those devils that sat on his hunched shoulders, had been washed away by rain and tears and he was alone.

So it was not the normally astute, second-guessing John Dee who answered Gabriel Harvey in The Eagle and Child that night. 'The last I saw of Marlowe,' he said, 'he was riding on a cart, travelling with the Egyptians. They were bound, I think, for King's Lynn and the Flemish coast.'

'King's Lynn and the Flemish coast?' Dr Norgate's tired old eyes fluttered up from the Ramus he was devouring. 'Marlowe gone with the Egyptians? I can scarcely believe it.'

'Nor I, Master.' Gabriel Harvey was rectitude itself. 'I was shocked. Profoundly shocked. After you gave him a fresh start, so to speak, agreed to let bygones be bygones—'

'Gabriel,' Norgate interrupted him. 'I may be creeping nearer to my appointment with the Almighty, but I cannot see St Peter's gates yet. You have no love for Christopher Marlowe and, I have noticed, seize every opportunity to blacken his name.'

'I, Master?' Harvey was outraged. 'Has Dr Lyler not mentioned that Marlowe is missing from his Schools? Professor Johns?' The name hung in the air like a poison. If there was one man in all Cambridge that Gabriel Harvey hated nearly as much as Kit Marlowe, it was Michael Johns.

Norgate hesitated. He knew what this meant. 'No,' he said quietly. 'They have not.'

'There is one thing more, Master –' Harvey was getting into his stride – 'though I hate to mention it.'

'I'm sure you do.' Norgate closed the heavy, leather-bound Ramus, sure that his researches would be ruined for the day now.

'Marlowe may be involved in murder.'

Norgate turned his head as well as he could, frowning. 'What are you saying?'

'Dr John Dee, the magus. He it was who told me about Marlowe. The poor man's wife died while Marlowe was under his roof. The next thing he knew, he had fled.'

'From which you deduce . . . ?' Norgate asked.

'You and I, Master, were weaned in the Schools of Logic. Doyens of deduction, we. And you are right. I have no love for Dominus Marlowe. Yet I cannot believe him guilty of this . . . whatever the evidence may say.'

Gabriel Harvey rose and took his leave from the man whose job he coveted. And as he left, he heard another nail thud into the coffin of Christopher Marlowe.

Marlowe waited impatiently at the eastern gate of the Prinsenhof for Lily to arrive. He had sent a message on ahead, for the Statholder to be prepared for Lily's visit. He had seen her heal the sick back at Ely and had a vague memory at the back of his brain of a soft and healing touch on his own damaged muscles, but was not sure what she would need in a sickbed setting. In John Dee's house, the woman she had healed had walked to the house herself, albeit using two crutches and help from her sons. This was different. He didn't want to put Lily off her stroke, but on the other hand, he wanted the Statholder and his wife to feel comfortable with what was about to go on. There was only a thin, a very thin line that must be trodden, and on either side of that safe line, the swamps of failure and the quicksands of disaster sucked and swirled silently, waiting for someone to put a foot wrong.

A tap on his arm brought him back to the here and now. He looked down and there was Lily, but a Lily in a new mirror, a clean Lily. A scented Lily for sure. He smiled to see her and looked her up and down, nodding. She was still, in essence, the same. Although the coin he had given her was large enough, she had not been able to dress herself from the skin out, so she had wisely chosen to deal with the most obvious problems with her dress. Not that they were problems to her; her clothes had taken years to get to the state of near perfection they were in, but she realized that her hair and general level of grime was something that non-Egyptians might find it hard to understand. So she had had her hair washed with fine herbs and dried before the fire in a friendly inn. It glowed tawny in the light from the guards' brazier as it tumbled down her back, held off her face by two tortoiseshell combs. Her face was glowing, not with lead or rouge, but just with the youth that was under the grime all the time, helped by a frugal diet and the wind in her face as they moved from place to place. She had trimmed her rags in places and had clean white lace at her throat, and her cloak, though not new, was clean and warm.

'Lily!' he said, with genuine pleasure. 'I would hardly have known you. You are beautiful.'

She looked at him sadly. 'Master Marlowe,' she said. 'Like everyone, you believe beauty to be skin deep. I am just the same Lily that woke this morning, covered in dirt, and when the dirt has gathered again, and this cloak is covered with mud and mire, I will be that same Lily again.' She smiled at him and at that moment, they each knew they had a new friend, come what may. 'Shall we go in? I am nervous, and waiting out here is making me shake with cold. I don't want them to think I shiver from fear.'

'There is nothing to fear, Lily,' he said. 'Do you have all you need?'

She held up a bag she had concealed under her cloak. 'All I need is in here,' she said, tapping her temple, 'but all that others need is in here.' And she raised her bag.

'Let's go, then, and heal a prince,' Marlowe said and, arm in arm, they entered the Prinsenhof's eastern gate.

The Princess Charlotte was waiting for them at the foot of the stairs that led to the Statholder's suite of rooms. She looked Lily up and down, then turned and led them up to the next floor. She opened the door and there, on the bed, Marlowe got his first glimpse of the leader of the Dutch. He was almost the same colour as the linen sheets he was lying on, and there was a bandage around his head. His hands lay limply by his sides, palms down and the pillows behind his head and back were not tousled and crumpled as they would be behind someone who was merely asleep; they were as smooth as if they had been ironed in place and no one had touched them since. The man's face was as smooth as his pillows. Marlowe felt Lily flinch at his side.

The Statholder's wife walked quickly through the room and climbed the single step of the dais that surrounded his bed. She smoothed his forehead and kissed his unresponsive cheek. 'William,' she whispered in his ear. 'Some people are here to see if they can help you. To see if you can be brought back to us.' She straightened up, with her hand still on his forehead, still looking down into his face. '*Lieveling*, let's see if you can come back to us, shall we?' There was a tiny splash as a tear met the starched linen of his sheet, but that was the only sound from the bed. The princess came back to the two in the doorway.

Marlowe reached for her hand, and squeezed it. 'We will do our best, Highness,' he said. 'But, you do know that it might not work?'

'Nothing else has worked,' she said. 'Why should this?'

Again, there was the flinch from Lily.

'Someone must believe,' she said. 'I cannot work against the stars. Do you have children, madam?'

'Six,' the princess said. 'All girls. They miss their father.' She sighed and passed a hand, almost transparent with fatigue, across her brow. 'As do I.'

'Then go to them,' Lily said. 'Gather them around you, all your girls. Ask them to bring into their minds their favourite day with their father, whether it was hawking, or reading, or walking or riding. Tell them to take that picture and enclose it in a globe, blown from the thinnest glass.' As she spoke, she moved her hands in the air, sketching the globe. 'Tell them to wrap the globe in the brightest colour they can imagine. Not red; that is for death in our company. Blue, or gold, or springtime green. Wrap the globe in the cloth and then throw it in the air.' She likened her actions to the words. 'And when the cloth comes fluttering down, empty, then their father will be well.' She stood to one side to let the woman pass. 'You will do it, madam, won't you?' she called after her.

The princess didn't turn, but with one hand over her eyes and the other flapping as if to ward off demons, she ran down the landing and disappeared up a stair in the corner.

'Does that work?' Marlowe asked the girl.

'Does what work?' Lily asked, striding forward, already delving in her bag.

'That globe. The cloth.'

'Let me tell you just one thing,' Lily said, turning to face him, at the foot of the Statholder's bed. 'I have never known it work without the globe, so why would I dispense with it now, at this most delicate time? Usually, it is the sick one who imagines the globe, and he puts his sickness in it. But who knows – it may work this way.' She shrugged. 'Why should it not?'

Marlowe stepped forward another pace and she stopped him with a gesture. 'Not so near, Master Marlowe. Things are not always pretty at the bedside of the sick and I may need you with a strong stomach later. Stay back. Stay back.'

'May I sit down?' he asked.

'By all means. But no nearer the bed than you are.' She turned to him. 'Do you know the Statholder?'

For a split second, Marlowe felt his heart thump. 'Nearer the bed.' That was almost Balthasar's phrase for the place where Christopher Marlowe would die. Then he checked himself and answered the girl's question. 'No,' he said. 'He has been unconscious since we came to Delft.'

'Why are we helping him, then?' she said, still busy laying out her herbs and cloths.

'He is on our side,' Marlowe said, knowing as he spoke that the Egyptians had no side to be on.

'The English side?' she asked.

'The side which doesn't want Philip of Spain and his Inquisition to sweep across the land carrying all before it. If the Low Countries fall, who will be next? Soon the Egyptians will have nowhere to go.'

Lily looked into the blank face of William the Silent. 'Sickness and sleep have wiped almost everything from his face,' she said. 'I doubt that even Balthasar could read anything from this page. But his wife seems a good woman and in my experience a man is seldom bad if a good woman loves him.'

'Your experience?' Marlowe said. 'How old are you, Lily.'

'This time, I am seventeen,' she said. 'But if you number all my years on earth, many hundreds.' She stepped down from the bed and walked over to where Marlowe sat on a couch by the window, lit from behind by the frost light. 'You are young,' she said, 'in these years and all years. But, you have great wisdom, Hern says. He says you will come again, or all is waste.' She pressed a finger lightly between Marlowe's eyes and ran it down his nose, over his lips and down to the point of his chin. 'Now, be quiet, and let me heal this man, if I can.'

Marlowe tried to concentrate, but as he had found in Ely, Lily's hands were everywhere over the length of the Statholder's body. She took hardly any notice of his heavily bandaged head and it was hard not to cry out to her that the bullet had entered his brain and not his gut. She placed coloured stones, about the size of pigeons' eggs, at intervals down his body and on the covers between his legs. She dipped a bunch of herbs in water from a flask and sprayed it over him, concentrating on his face this time. The man didn't even flinch. Then, she walked down to his feet and held out her hands so her arms were straight from her body. She put the right hand over the left and leaned down, arms still straight, until her left palm was about an inch away from the coverlet of the bed. Muttering quietly to herself, she moved very slowly up the bed, with her hands always the same few inches above the Statholder. When she reached the head, she hovered her hands over the man's face. She appeared to be pressing down hard, but against an irresistible force, because although the sinews in her elbows and wrists stood out clearly, she could not touch the living flesh beneath her palm. Then, as though he had struck her from below, her hands flew up over her head and she toppled over on her back, falling off the dais and landing with a crash on the floor.

Marlowe leaped from his seat and ran to the bed head. He instinctively leaned over Lily first; she was the one he knew was living. Of the Statholder he was still not sure.

The crash of her fall had brought people running. Hans Neudecker was first through the door and stood appalled at the sight of a dishevelled girl lying on her back near the bedside of his Master. Marlowe he knew, but could not work out quite what was going on; Charlotte had kept this attempt at healing from him. Hans was one of the pragmatic Dutchmen who had made Edward Kelly's life so difficult and would not understand.

'What is going on here?' he bellowed, his stentorian voice echoing round the simple chamber. 'Who is that woman?'

The doors behind him crashed back as Charlotte, followed by her children, came into the room, also alerted by the noise. 'Do not shout so, Hans,' she said mildly. 'This was all my idea.'

Hans turned round in confusion. 'Madam . . .' he began, but broke off as the children rushed past him, climbing on to the bed at the foot.

'Papa!' little Emilia cried. 'Papa has woken up.' She turned to her mother, beaming all over her face. 'You said he would, and he has.'

'We threw the globe up, Papa,' said another.

'Mine went highest,' said her sister, giving her a push.

'Hush, children, hush.' Charlotte wasn't scolding them. She just needed the quiet to drink in her husband, sitting up with a puzzled smile on his face. 'Don't hug Papa so hard. He is still not well.'

Marlowe looked up from Lily, who was beginning to rouse herself. From his vantage point on the floor, details were difficult, but one thing was in no doubt. William of Nassau, known as the Silent, was pushing himself in to a seated position in the bed, with his children clustered round him. He looked over their heads to his wife.

'*Lieveling*,' she mouthed silently to him. 'Welcome back.'

Marlowe, with his playmaker's sense of timing, knew when a quiet exit was called for and, helping Lily to his feet, he crept round the walls of the bedroom and slipped with the girl, still woozy from the effort, down the stairs and back out through the eastern gate.

'And so, the little princess, trailing light, lived happily ever after.' Marlowe's voice tailed away as little Emilia's head flopped back on her pillow for the umpteenth time. He patted her starfish hand and tucked the covers around her ears before tiptoeing from the room. The candle still glowed because this little princess was afraid of the dark, the dark that had nearly claimed her papa. Marlowe nodded to the nursery maid sitting by the embers of the fire and made for the door.

Here, the bandage still on his head, stood the lion of Nassau himself, a curious half-smile on his face. 'It seems my Emilia has a new favourite to tell her bedtime stories.'

'I do my best, Highness,' Marlowe said. 'But I think she finds my Flemish rather funny.'

William patted the man's shoulder. 'It's not many royal body-guards who tell bedtime stories to the children of their charges.' He walked with Marlowe to his oak-panelled study and poured them both a goblet of Geneva spirit. If truth were told, it was not one of Marlowe's favourite drinks, but the Statholder and most of Zeeland seemed to live on it, so it must suffice.

'Quite.' William the Statholder seemed to read his mind, but more prosaically read his face as the gin hit home. 'I'd rather some good Spanish wine, too, Christopher, but it's treason to say so in these unnatural times.'

'Does Emilia know her mother is unwell?' Marlowe asked. He had no children of his own, but he had been brought up surrounded by girls and knew how their minds worked.

'She is sleeping –' William told him the state of things – 'as her papa was sleeping for a time. That is what I have told Emilia. Her dear mama got very tired nursing and now it is her turn to sleep. She will soon be well enough to make us a whole family again, perhaps.'

'Could Lily help her?' Marlowe asked.

'She might, but for now things are very delicate in my household, Christopher, and perhaps we can leave the miracles to come once in a while, rather than all together. The children must not be allowed to think, the *people* must not be allowed to think that if there is a problem it can be mended with some muttered rubric and some stones.'

'But, it worked for you.' Marlowe was not an Egyptian, and yet he was; he didn't like to hear Lily being denigrated by the man who she saved.

'There is gossip in the palace,' the Statholder said, 'that my wife is a witch who arranged for one of her coven to come and save me. If she is miraculously healed, then the call for her burning will not be long in coming. I will not put my Charlotte in the way of such gossip. Let her sleep. God will save her or He will not, as He wishes.'

Marlowe sighed, but bowed to the Statholder's wishes. 'In my country,' he said, 'the Egyptians are known as the children of the moon.'

The Statholder laughed. 'The children of the moon,' he said. 'Such a nice name, much nicer than what my people will call my wife, should the stories take a hold. So, Christopher, we will let her sleep.' He topped up their goblets. 'But now, to practical matters. Your coming here has saved my life, by whatever means it was achieved. But you cannot be at my elbow for ever. What did this Walsingham intend when he sent you?'

'You'd have to ask him that, Highness.' He shrugged. 'I am a mere cog.'

'Ah,' the Statholder mused. 'We are all that. All part of God's plan. Tell me plainly, how do you rate my chances at the Prinsenhof?'

'I am no strategist, sir. You'd need a soldier for that.'

'I have soldiers in plenty,' William told him. 'Generals and colonels and boy drummers coming out of my ears. I trust these men in the field because I have to. But we are not in the field now, Christopher. We are in a former convent in a little Dutch town. Objectively now, what can we do?'

Marlowe thought for a moment. 'I may speak freely?' he asked.

The Statholder nodded.

'Get rid of Hans,' Marlowe said.

'Hans Neudecker? Man, he is my right arm.'

'He let Jean Jaureguy reach you with a loaded pistol,' Marlowe reminded him. 'His guards would have let me through with a dagger. All of you have allowed the Egyptians to camp within your walls and your wife laid you open to the ministrations of Lily. You are too trusting, sir. Too trusting by half.'

'So . . . I must get rid of Hans?'

Marlowe nodded. 'Secure the gates to the south and east. Double the guards at each point and bring in someone you can trust to lead the Night Watch.'

'Delft is a city, Christopher,' William explained. 'One of the many duties a Statholder has is to regard the economy of his people. If I turn the city into a fortress, we'll all starve.'

'If you don't,' Marlowe said darkly, 'you'll turn it into a dead house.'

William and his bodyguard fell silent, but the silence was full of unspoken thoughts which refused to crystallize out of the air.

Finally, Marlowe spoke. 'A compromise, then. Keep the city as it is, but check and double check each merchant on the road. Every pedlar, every cart. Nothing comes or goes without the closest security by the most reliable people. But the Prinsenhof. You have builders here? Architects?'

'Of course.'

'Then we'll turn *this* place into a fortress. Ramparts, arrow-head bastions, gun emplacements. I've seen something of that in my time.'

'So have I –' the Statholder nodded grimly – 'but my people, Christopher; I must see – and be seen by – my people. There were rumours enough while I lay insensible. I must walk the walls and visit the squares each day or they will lose hope. If Parma comes . . . if he lays siege to us, it will be different.'

Marlowe nodded. 'If you must do these things,' he said, 'you must. I will be your eyes and ears for as long as I can. The rest . . .'

'. . . is up to God,' the Statholder said devoutly.

Kit Marlowe smiled, but didn't speak his thoughts. They were best if they joined the flocks of the unspoken words which already thronged the room.

TWELVE

'Are you the one they call Hern?' Hans Neudecker was at his most imperious when talking to the Egyptians. Hern would have liked to have answered him with a flash of lightning and a rattle of thunder, but he settled for a low flourish and a gust of plumes in the breeze of the courtyard.

'His Highness the Prince of Nassau requests your company,' Hans looked with disgust at the rag-tail camp that had turned the Prinsenhof into a common stews. 'All of you,' he said.

Hern nodded to Simon, Frederico, Ernesto and Balthasar and the five of them followed Hans up the stone stairs that led under the archway, the others following in their wake. No one quite knew what this summons meant. They had performed for the Statholder's court several times since their arrival, with fire-eating and juggling and columns of blue smoke. But they had never performed for the Statholder because he had been lying close to death in his private apartments. Only Starshine carried her tambourine; only Brackett had the snake coiling around him.

Hans led them to a landing they had not seen before, with marble floors and blue and white painted tile walls. They reached a pair of huge doors, gilded with the Nassau arms of the lion rampant and were told to wait. Hans slipped in by a side door and moments later the huge double doors swung back and the Nassau family sat in state like a court portrait, looking at them.

William the Silent himself still had his head bandaged, but it was carefully covered by a broad plumed hat and he wore silk sashes with orders glittering on his chest. Beside him, Princess Charlotte looked old and ill and pale, but she managed a smile for the Egyptian children. The Nassau girls, in order of age and height, stood on the dais around their parents, dressed like their mother, looking like them both. Little

Katharina saw Brackett's snake and her eyes lit up. But she was six and her father was the Statholder of the United Provinces; she knew how to behave and she didn't move an inch. Emilia was less demure. At half her sister's age, she didn't have her decorum and her dress was heavy with brocade and itchy. She saw Starshine, a girl not much older than she was and she saw the tambourine.

In a second she had struggled free from her mother's restraining hand and was standing in front of Starshine, pointing at the tambourine and jabbering away in Dutch. Lily gently took the instrument out of Starshine's grubby hands and gave it to the littlest princess, who gurgled with delight and shook it, at first gently, then with all the power she possessed.

Hern had not taken his eyes off the man who stood on the dais to the Statholder's right, a little behind the throne. Kit Marlowe was no longer in the ribboned rags of the Egyptians but wore a pair of Venetian breeches and a doublet and cloak of the Dutch court, a swept-hilt rapier gleaming at his hip.

'Come forward, Master Hern,' William said in his clearest English. Hern obeyed and repeated the flourish he had given to Hans in the courtyard.

'Which is the girl, Lily?' William the Silent wanted to know.

Hern clicked his fingers and she crept forward, not wanting to look at the Statholder nor at Marlowe beside him. She curtseyed low and when she tried to rise again, Hern held her still so that she ended up kneeling, bareheaded in her sack dress, like a ragged saint in the old pictures of William's youth.

'My child,' he said and beckoned her to him. She knelt in front of him on the dais and stared at his gilded shoes. He beckoned Hans who was carrying a cushion and he took from it a gold chain with the enamelled lion of Nassau and heavy pearls hanging from it. The Statholder laid it around Lily's neck and she gasped with the cold on her bare skin and the weight of it. 'That,' said William softly, 'is for saving the life of the Statholder. For saving the life of the Netherlands.'

He glanced up at Hern who had not moved, except for his jaw hanging a little further open. 'It would buy me a warship,' the Statholder told him, 'or a regiment of pikemen. It will keep you and your band for life.' The Egyptians looked at each other, amazed and then their disbelief turned to an excited jabbering that the Nassaus could not understand. Only Hern remained silent; only Emilia was still tinkling her tambourine.

Suddenly, Hern clapped his hands and all was still. He unhooked the chain of office from Lily's neck. 'We cannot accept this, sir,' he said. There was an inrush of air from almost everybody. Protocol had floated out of the window into the courtyard below. Only the Spaniards treated William the Silent with such contempt. Hans was appalled and spun on his heel, leaving the chamber.

'My Lord,' Hern said to the Statholder, 'your fires have warmed us for these past weeks. Your kitchens have fed us. We are not used to company like this. In England –' he grinned at Marlowe – 'for a prince to entertain an Egyptian is unheard of. Descended as we are from the Ptolemies of old, there is no precedence for this. Lily did what she did because she can. Let that be enough.' And he clapped his hands again, laying down the gold chain on the dark blue carpet as he did so. Instantly, the Egyptians all bowed or curtsied and filed out, Starshine seizing the moment, as little girls will, to snatch back her tambourine.

Lily had not moved. Heaven had been offered to her with that chain and Hern had snatched it away. Balthasar read her thoughts and hung back to lift her to her feet. The royal family had not moved.

'Gunpowder!' It was Balthasar's voice echoing through the vast hall, bouncing off the vaulted ceiling and bringing armed guards at the double. The soothsayer darted across to the corner where a bright line of sparks was hissing across the floor, making for the dais. Marlowe was only a second behind him and the two men threw themselves on the crackling black line, billowing puffs of smoke now as it neared the throne.

The Statholder had the presence of mind to gather his family to him, but little Emilia was still standing in the line of fire, bereft of her tambourine, scarlet-faced and wailing. Marlowe dashed forwards and lifted the girl up under one arm and shepherded the others to the far corner.

Balthasar stood up, his face and clothes singed and black-ened. Hans clattered into the chamber with yet more guards and the halberds clashed together against all exits, penning the Egyptians and the royal family in. Marlowe checked there was no more danger. No cocked pistols, no murderous flashing knives. Then he followed the line of powder that nobody had noticed, on past the dais to a recess in a wall. Here the unburned fuse dangled from a wooden tinderbox, half hidden by a carpet. Balthasar was with him.

'*Wat heb je daar*?' William asked, in Dutch because he was so shaken.

'What is it?' Hans asked in English, only now venturing a little nearer.

'A bomb,' Marlowe told him, 'and a clever one. Balthasar, have you ever seen anything like this?'

The soothsayer shook his head. 'Never,' he said. 'My tricks are of the less earthly kind. I leave the flashes and bangs to others.'

Marlowe looked across at the Egyptians, cowering silently in the corner. Only Hern stood upright, defiant, proud, unmoved by the near miss of the last few seconds. Simon stood blinking with the speed and terror of it all, crossing himself repeatedly in minuscule movements which Marlowe only noticed because he knew who he was and what he would need at this moment. Simon the Jesuit. The man in the room who would most want the Statholder dead.

'Why wasn't the thing hidden here?' Hans asked, peering into the box full of black powder, 'under the throne? Assuming as we must that His Highness was the intended victim.'

'Because I checked there,' Marlowe told him, 'every inch of the dais, the throne, the carpet.' He looked up at the stone column against which the makeshift bomb lay. 'And this –' he patted the cold stone – 'would have been just as effective.' He pointed to the Gothic ribs of stone that radiated to the boss in the centre. 'One explosion here and the entire roof would have caved in.' He looked solemnly at the Statholder. 'Your entire family would have gone, Highness,' he said.

Hern crossed to Balthasar and Marlowe. 'You have left us, Master Marlowe,' he said, gesturing to the man's clothes.

'Nothing is forever,' Marlowe said. 'What do you know about this?'

'Saltpetre, sulphur and charcoal.' Hern shrugged. 'Black powder; deadly if you know how to use it.'

'And you do,' Marlowe told him. 'You use it in your act all the time.'

'Tut, tut, Master Marlowe.' Hern smiled. 'And here was I thinking you believed in our magic.'

'There's nothing magic about murder,' Marlowe said, staring the man down. 'Balthasar, have you been in this room before?'

'Never.' The man shook his head.

'Hern?'

The leader of the Egyptians shook his.

'Which leaves . . .' Marlowe looked at the others across the hall, huddled together, Simon comforting the children and looking anxious, Frederico not understanding any of it.

'. . . Hans,' he said softly.

Hern was too old a hand to turn to stare at the chamberlain but Balthasar could not resist it. Hans was in earnest conversation with the Statholder as each man took stock of what had just happened.

'No,' Balthasar said. 'That's impossible.'

Marlowe stood in front of him. 'Who's talking now?' he asked. 'The country bumpkin who just happened to know Edward Kelly or the seer of souls who prophecies men's deaths?'

Balthasar blinked. He'd come to like Kit Marlowe over their weeks together, but there was something about him that was dangerous. 'He's the Statholder's right-hand man,' he said. 'We've all seen that.'

'And you've seen more of it than the rest of us,' Hern reminded Marlowe. 'You tell us, Judas.'

Before Marlowe could answer, Hans had thudded the floor with his staff of office and the guards began to shepherd the Egyptians, Hern and Balthasar with them, out of the doors and along the corridor. The chamberlain bowed low to the Statholder before taking his leave and followed them out, just to make sure they'd really gone. He'd double the guard on their courtyard camp tonight; you couldn't take chances with the children of the moon. On his way, he noticed a piece of parchment flutter to the ground and swept it up in one fluid movement.

William the Statholder stroked his wife's pale cheek and kissed her, nodding to the remaining guards to take his family to their quarters. 'Check every room,' he barked at them. 'Under the beds, in the cupboards, everywhere. I'll personally see to it that any man failing in his duty has his tongue cut out.'

They saluted with heels and halberds and led the family away, the children babbling excitedly and little Emilia still lamenting the loss of the tambourine.

'Can you tell me why?' the Statholder said to Marlowe as he picked up the golden chain from where Hern had placed it. 'Why people to whom this represents a lifetime's wages would turn it down.'

Marlowe shook his head. 'I long ago gave up trying to understand the Egyptians,' he said, 'but we have more pressing problems, Highness . . .'

The Statholder held up his hand. 'My life has been saved twice,' he said, 'and by an Egyptian each time. But I thank you for your speed and quick thinking, Master Marlowe. Sir Francis Walsingham has chosen wisely.'

'It's not about the Egyptians we need to talk, Highness,' Marlowe said.

In the low-vaulted chamber below the courtyard, beyond a door through which only one person walked, the chamberlain to the House of Nassau kissed the crucifix on the altar and knelt in silent prayer. Then he opened the piece of paper he had just picked up from the floor in the passageway above and read the two words, 'Marlowe knows.'

He crossed himself and made for the light.

The Statholder was sitting at his dining table as darkness fell on that short winter's day. Around him servants drew the heavy velvet curtains and lit the candles. The logs crackled and spat in the huge ornate fireplace, cursing the world as they died in the flames. Kit Marlowe looked up from a chair next to the

Statholder as Hans swept in. For an instant, he faltered in his stride, then stood at the far end of the great table, bowing low before his master.

'Hans . . .' the Statholder's voice tailed away, 'Master Marlowe has something to say to you.'

The chamberlain raised an eyebrow and barely acknowledged the Johannes-come-lately at his master's elbow. For all his bravado and his devil-deep eyes, the man was no better than a common thug and here was the most powerful man in the Low Countries giving him house room.

'How long have you served the Statholder, Hans?' Marlowe asked.

The man blinked. 'All my adult life,' he said. 'As my father served his father.'

'And when did you break with Rome?'

'I don't understand,' Hans said.

'It's simple enough.' Marlowe got to his feet and switched to Flemish to make it easier for the man. 'When did you forsake his Holiness the Pope, whom we in England call the Bishop of Rome? When did you take the sacrament of the Calvinist church?'

Hans blinked again. 'Some years ago,' he said.

'Precisely when?' Marlowe badgered him.

'Highness . . .' Hans began, but Marlowe interrupted.

'Look at me, sir,' he growled. '*I* am your worst nightmare. When did you convert to the Protestant faith?'

'I cannot remember,' Hans shouted back, 'precisely.'

'Very well.' Marlowe was calmer now and turned to the only window still undraped. The servants had gone and William liked to leave one light at a window and to see the darkening world beyond it. 'You know the Prinsenhof well?'

'Of course,' Hans said, relaxing a little. 'I have been with His Highness since we moved from Antwerp.'

'You know all its little corridors and recesses? Its secrets, if you will?'

'The place was a convent once,' Hans told him. 'I imagine it has many secrets. If we believe half of what we're told about these nuns . . .' Hans suddenly remembered Princess Charlotte's former calling and apologized at once. 'Oh, forgive me, Highness.'

The Statholder waved it aside. He was long past caring about slips of the tongue. 'Get to the point, Master Marlowe.' He sighed.

'The point.' Marlowe folded his arms, staring at his bobbing reflection in the window panes, the scholar gypsy framed by six haloes of candlelight. 'When did you renounce the Protestant faith?' His voice was only a little above a whisper now. 'When did you rejoin the Church of Rome and kiss the arses of the Duke of Parma and King Philip of Spain?'

Hans stood speechless.

'You see, Master Chamberlain, only you could have known where to place that powder box so that the roof would cave in. Only you had access to that amount of gunpowder. You left the room in outrage because poor frightened Lily, the Egyptian girl, was told to turn down the Statholder's gold. In reality, you went to light the fuse in the corridor outside. Because you didn't give a damn, did you? Statholder, wives, children, Egyptians, it didn't matter to you. In fact, it was a bonus – Nassau and the heirs of Nassau under one collapsed, bloody roof. King Philip would give you one of his New World colonies in his sheer delight.'

The silence was almost audible. Even the logs in the grate were listening.

'Hans,' the Statholder whispered. 'How could you?'

The chamberlain leapt forward, his rapier in his hand, over-turning the table with a powerful kick and lungeing at the Statholder's head. The blade bit deep into the wood as William ducked aside and Marlowe turned like a spinning top and threw his dagger which thudded into Hans' back. He staggered, the sword gone from his grasp, trying weakly to pull the Englishman's blade out. Marlowe caught him as he fell, blood trickling from his nose and mouth.

'May your soul rot in Hell, Englishman,' Hans hissed and shuddered to a convulsing heap on the floor.

The Statholder stood up and tugged the sword free as guards, alarmed by the crash of overturning furniture, clattered into the room with servants behind them. 'I had hoped,' he muttered to Marlowe, 'it was merely the man's incompetence. Now I see it all.' He looked along the length of the chamberlain's blade, the one that had so nearly bisected his head. 'Three or four inches to the right,' he said, 'and it would have gone through my eye socket. Master Marlowe, I owe you my life or I owe it to the Egyptians. Can I ever repay that debt?'

'This man,' Marlowe said, 'was he once your faithful servant?'

William looked at the chamberlain's body as Marlowe pulled out his knife blade. 'I believed so,' he nodded sadly. 'I will always believe so.'

'Then send for the Egyptian they call Simon,' Marlowe said.

'Why?' the Statholder was curious.

'He has his own ways of comforting the dead,' he said.

The flames guttered that night in the Egyptian camp. All around the walls of the Prinsenhof rose sheer and black, the guards patrolling the walks grunting to each other in the cold routine of their march, cloaks wrapped around their leather jacks and gleaming steel.

Kit Marlowe sat by the fire with the others, but his eyes never strayed far from the windows of the prince's private apartments across the courtyard. Now that Hans Neudecker was dead, perhaps . . .

'I was wrong.' Hern's voice was strong and commanding in the firelight. 'You weren't running *away* from anything, Master Marlowe, were you? You were running *towards* it. To the court of William the Silent. To a date with destiny. That was your mission.'

Marlowe looked up at him under his brows. Is that what it was? Destiny? There had already been two attempts on the life of the Statholder – Jean Jaureguy, Hans Neudecker. But there would be others. As long as William of Nassau was there, as long as he *was* the Netherlands, there had to be others. And would this be Marlowe's life, then? A permanent exile from his own land, like Minshull at the Hook, with his Dutch pantaloons and Dutch clogs and Dutch cheese? Marlowe had missed Canterbury from time to time while he was at Cambridge. Now, in that strange, bitter night, he missed Cambridge too. The kind voice of Michael Johns, the prattling of Matty Parker and the good friendship of Tom Colwell; the cockroaches crawling in the Buttery; even the endless sniping of Gabriel Harvey; he missed all that. And he didn't answer Hern.

'Time for a story, Kit,' Frederico said, crossing his legs over a saddle and draping an arm around Lily. Perhaps their child would have a brother or sister again one day, after all.

There was a babble of excitement from the children, who left whatever they were doing and formed a half circle around the teller of takes.

'Give us the one about the piper and the rats,' Brackett shouted.

'No, no,' Lukas sprayed. 'The fox and the grapes.'

'A love story,' Lily said, looking hard at Frederico. 'Something to warm us up on a cold night.'

'No, no,' Marlowe said, shaking his head. He was looking directly at Balthasar. 'I have a new tale tonight.'

There was a chorus of oohs and aahs, real from the children, ironic from Hern and Balthasar, worried from Simon.

Marlowe waited until their noise had died down and then looked at all of them in turn, with their grubby faces and bright eyes in the flicker of the flames. 'You may scoff –' he smiled – 'but I think you will enjoy it. It is a love story, a story of a journey and a cautionary tale, all rolled into one. So, lie back, my best beloved, curl up somewhere warm and soft where you can close your eyes and listen to my tale.'

He waited in the firelight until the rustling had stopped. Everyone had found their best positions and were comfortable after a good meal from the Statholder's kitchen. The guards stepped more quietly as they passed, to catch a little of the story. Mothers clasped children in their laps, lovers clasped each other. Maria was tenderly propped on some sacks until her poor, tired back was relieved of the burden of Hern's child in her belly, just for a while, just while she listened to the story.

'My story begins,' Marlowe said, in low tones which never-theless could be heard in every corner of the courtyard, 'both many years ago and yesterday. My story was old when Adam first walked in Eden and is as new as a new-laid egg still warm from the hen. My story is of a man who loved a woman, so much that he hardly dare look at her, let alone touch her.'

There was a sigh and a snuggling noise as Lily nestled closer under Frederico's arm.

'This woman was as beautiful as the day. Her hair was like the sun and her eyes were like two pools of molten sky. Her ears were like shells, pink and convoluted and when she stood in the window of the great house the man had given her to live in, the light shone through, just a little, at the tips and made them into lambent gold. Her form was as a fallow deer, spring was in her step and where she walked, flowers bloomed.'

'There was never a woman like that,' a voice called from the darkness. It sounded like Simon, and Marlowe thought it amusing that he alone knew; of all present, Simon was the one who should know that the least. But perhaps even priests were men, underneath.

'No, there was not,' Marlowe said. 'The woman, to everyone else, had yellow hair, bluish eyes, sticking out ears and she was a bit heavy in the beam, a bit lacking up top here.' And he sketched a shape with his hands. The men guffawed and the women sniffed their disapproval. The children, knowing a joke had been made, but not really understanding it, laughed as well.

'But to the man who loved her, there was never one such in the world. He feared that another man would see her and win her away from him, so he kept her shut away in his great house, where she was quite tolerably happy. She had had a life before which had not been so comfortable and so she liked the feather beds, the big fires lit and tended by someone else and the food at regular times, with not too many burned bits and nothing that still had the fur on it.'

There was a dutiful chorus of various sounds of disgust and he let it settle down before continuing.

'The woman had never thought herself beautiful, but when she saw herself reflected in the man's eyes, she could see what he saw and this made her happy. They spent many hours gazing at each other, he drinking in her loveliness, she seeing a self that she had not known existed. Because what the man could see was the beauty within.'

Marlowe sought out where Lily lay in the darkness and knew she was looking at him from the reflected firelight in her eyes.

'Then, one day, into their great house there came a pestilence that had no name and although it touched all there with a cold, cold finger, only the woman was really chilled by it. She fell into a deep sleep and nothing that could be done would warm or wake her. The man was by way of being a bit of a wizard, which perhaps I should have told you before. But he had not used his magic since he had met the woman, because she didn't like it. The servants begged him to use it now, to bring their mistress back to life.'

There was a sob from far back in the courtyard and Marlowe could just see the dull shine of a guard's helmet, bobbing as he wiped his nose on his sleeve.

'For a long time he refused, but when it was clear that she would not wake up, he promised that he would do his best to work his magic, as he had so often for so many people before. So he told his servants to keep their mistress safe, to keep her warm and to wet her lips every hour with honey, so that she should not starve, and every half an hour with clear spring water, so that she should not die through thirst.'

'Did they do it?' Starshine leaned forward and touched him on the knee. 'She didn't die, did she, Kit?'

Hern leaned forward and cuffed her lightly round the head. 'Master Marlowe to you, miss,' he said.

'She didn't die, did she, Master Marlowe?' she repeated.

'Wait and see,' he whispered and opened his arms for her to sit on his lap. He didn't ever see himself as a father, but any father could do far worse than Starshine. She jumped up and turned sideways in his lap, her ear against his heart, sucking her fingers for comfort.

'Every day, the servants did as he told them and every day the beautiful woman lay as the dead, except that she was just slightly warmer than the air in the room and she breathed slowly, so slowly that it could hardly be seen. A flutter at the side of her neck told them that the blood was still in her body, but she was as pale as ice, and so still. While she lay there, the man travelled the world. He needed certain things and they were not to be found in the grounds of his great house.'

'What did he need?' Maria said, completely ravelled up in the story, her back forgotten.

'He needed ten things,' Marlowe said. 'He needed a kiss from a girl with flaxen hair, given freely as the moon turned blue. He needed a thread from the robe which Christ had worn when he took his last supper. He needed an eyelash from a frog, a feather from the wing of a wandering albatross, the last breath of a man who had never spoken a blasphemy, the spittle of an albino bat.' He looked at Brackett, still wound round by his snake, both of them basking in the heat of the fire. 'How many is that?'

'Six,' Brackett said. 'You need four more.'

'Not *I*,' Marlowe said. 'This man, the wizard needs four more. He needed a stone from the head of a toad, he needed the first catkin of spring and the last leaf of autumn from the hazel tree that grows out of the wall of the innermost temple in the Hagia Sofia in Constantinople. And finally, he needed the blessing of his mother, in her grave the last forty years.'

'Impossible,' grunted Ernesto in the dark.

'Impossible you say and you would be right. He knew that only one of these things was the magic one, but he didn't know which one. So he travelled the world and time to get them all and after many adventures was back at the bedside of his beloved, his beautiful wife.'

He paused to listen to the clicking silence of the courtyard and felt the thrill of having an audience in the very palm of his hand. Eventually, as he had intended, someone could no longer bear it.

'And did she come back to life?' Eloise said.

'Oh, yes,' Marlowe said, with a cold smile. 'She came back to life and told him all he ever needed to know, about how the dead live and what it was that sent them to the dead place where she had been. She knew everything and told it to the magician, the wizard, her husband.' He finished with a flourish and said, 'There. Did you enjoy that story?'

'It has an odd ending,' Maria said. 'Does it have a moral?'

'Oh, yes,' Marlowe said. 'It has several. One is that you shouldn't believe the opinion of your own eyes. Just because it looks like a duck and sounds like a duck it still might not be a duck when the wizard gets to work on it. And the other is . . . it's late and we should all be in bed.' He stood up, with Starshine in his arms. 'Whose is she, exactly?' he asked, holding her out to the assembled Egyptians.

'I'll take her,' Lily said. 'Thank you for the story, Master Marlowe.'

'You're welcome, Lily,' he said. 'Beauty is in the eye of the beholder. But you don't need to know that – you are beautiful right through.' He touched her cheek and Frederico pulled her to him, jealously. If there was one thing Christopher Marlowe was good at, it was making men jealous.

THIRTEEN

To prepare a trap was one thing. To see it work was another. Kit Marlowe didn't sleep that night. He was taking a gamble, but then, all his life had been a gamble. He was staking it all on the reputation of John Dee, on the man's ability to raise the dead. He heard the old convent clock strike one, echoed by the chimes of the Nieu Kirke and the Old Kirke moments later. Time, like everything else in South Holland, was only approximate.

He would have heard the clocks strike two but there was a sudden alarm from the south walls, harsh shouts and the crash of an arquebus, its smoke drifting along the ramparts.

'Where?' he heard the shouted question in Flemish.

'South-west,' came the reply. 'One figure. Running.'

'Where to?' the question was peppered with the rattle of boot studs on cobbles and the clicking of matchlocks.

'Ely,' Marlowe muttered to himself.

'Who is it?' one guard asked another.

'The murderer of Helene Dee,' Marlowe smiled quietly. It was time he was gone too.

The moon was silver on the *vennen*, a lace of water like a vast spider's web on the blackness of the night. Marlowe had slipped over the wall of the Prinsenhof in the confusion of whoever had gone before him and crept along the alleyways where the Night Watch rarely watched or even thought of going. Even so, there had been the odd moment. At the Milk Cross he had stumbled over a sleeping vagrant and the dogs had barked at him as he ran for the Malt Market and the Customs House. In daylight, he would have found the Wasp or, failing that, stolen a horse and ridden for the coast – it was the fastest way to go. But at night, it was different. All Holland lay on the rim of the sea, flat and vulnerable and one false step could see a man drown in the choking weed of the fenlands, the cold and lonely *vennen*. Men had gone that way in Cambridgeshire and Marlowe had no time to swim his way out of trouble. Not that swimming would come into it. In the freezing temperatures of the Low Countries on the eve of Christmas, the water would freeze a man's marrow long before he could even try to strike out for dry land.

So he had hired a boat and a boatman. He gave the startled sleeper a choice. He could accept his gelder or he could accept the point of Marlowe's dagger. It was a better choice than old Hobson ever gave anybody and the man was soon bending his back against the oars with Marlowe roaring him on in his best Flemish.

It was nearly dawn as the pair reached the Hook. All the way there, along the canals and dykes that all looked identical in the dark, Marlowe cursed himself that he had not checked the beds of the Egyptians before he left. His tale had pricked the conscience of one of them, that was certain and his killer had to be a man. No woman, not even the mercurial Lily and certainly not the encumbered Maria, could climb the walls of the Prinsenhof and drop safely to the other side wearing the heavy skirts that all the Egyptian women did. But which man? Frederico the fire-eater, who seemed so simple and yet was not? Simon the strong man, the secret Papist who brought the Mass to the desperate and abandoned? Balthasar the sooth-sayer, who knew Edward Kelly and had loved Rose but not saved her and saw things that other men could not? Or was it Hern, the lord of the Egyptians, who led them all across a wilderness of fear and mistrust on their journeying through the wild?

Marlowe threw his coin to the boatman who would go home grumbling, telling everyone how he was set upon by five, no, six big ruffians and how he had fought them all off in defence of his little boat. Holland was full of heroes. Marlowe hoisted his sword over his shoulder and ran through the streets, lighter now in the frosty dawn, the cobbles like glass with ice which melted as his boots struck sparks from them. The wharfs were already flickering into life as surly men were hurling barrels into place and lighting their braziers against the cold of another bitter December dawn. He reached the Customs House as the town clock clanged six. Damn. The place was bolted and barred and he rattled the locks pointlessly.

'What's your hurry?' a voice croaked under an awning to his left.

'I want a ship,' Marlowe said. 'To England.'

A solid-looking man in the flannels of a seafarer emerged with a pewter pot in his hand and blinked at him.

'Is the tide right?' Marlowe asked, hoping his Flemish was making sense.

'Oh, yes,' the man said. 'The tide's right, all right.'

'Well, then . . .'

'Well, then you've missed her.' The man spat volubly on to the cobbles. 'The *Antelope*. She's just left.' He pointed out to the flat darkness of the sea where a single streak of light slashed through the fleeing night clouds and showed, for an instant, the spars and sails of the *Antelope* making nor'-nor'-west for the Wash.

'Was there an Egyptian on board?' Marlowe asked.

'A what?' the man frowned. For the first time, he took in the foreigner in front of him. He wore Dutch clothes, expensive. And he was armed to the teeth. But there was no retinue, no man, no horse. And there were such strange people abroad in the fens these days.

'Never mind,' said Marlowe, absently, already planning what to do next.

'There was only one passenger, though.' The man spat again, clearly having his old lung trouble in the winter morning.

'What did he look like?' Marlowe asked.

'Didn't see him,' the man croaked. 'It being dark and all. But he was in a hurry. Had to get to England fast, he told the Master. Matter of life and death, he said it was.'

'Death, anyway,' Marlowe muttered. Then, 'Do you have a boat, sir?'

The man frowned, then looked horrified, then retreated into the shadows.

The man did have a boat. He often took it out into the shallows of the Hook, catching herring. But cross to England? Never. It wasn't built for that and he wouldn't do it for ready money. What he would do it for was Kit Marlowe, especially when the man was pricking his epiglottis with the tip of his dagger. But he wouldn't be held responsible – he'd known seas like mountains at this time of year and then there were the sea beggars.

'Mother of God!' the man crossed himself as he saw their oars slide out of the mist like a ghost ship. '*Waterguizen!*'

'What?' Marlowe wasn't sure he had heard right.

'Sea beggars.' The man pointed, a terrified look on his face. 'See, the wallet and the pot. I told you. I warned you. But you wouldn't listen, no, not you as would.'

The strangest craft Marlowe had ever seen was heading on a course straight for them. It was a galliass, but small and low in the water, its single sail a livid scarlet in the grey morning and it rattled with rows of copper pots bumping and clanging along its hull. At its prow stood a man in a Spanish morion and breastplate roaring commands in northern Dutch, which Marlowe didn't understand at all.

'What does he want?' the Englishman asked the Dutchman, who was already hauling in his sail with both hands.

'Us!' the man screamed at him. 'Are you simple or something?'

'Can't we outrun him?'

The Dutchman stopped in his frantic work in disbelief and pointed to the galliass. 'You don't know much about the sea, do you, mate?' he snarled. 'How many oars do you count?'

'Er . . . fifteen.' Marlowe peered through the mist.

'That's just on the one side,' the fisherman said. 'So make that thirty. Thirty oarsmen against me. Oh, and you, I suppose, for all the good you are.' He spat over the side with all the contempt he could muster.

'We've got the wind,' Marlowe said, grasping at straws. He had always been strictly land-based. Although his mother came from Dover, his father was a cobbler, not a noticeably seagoing profession.

'So have they,' the fisherman told him. 'See that sail? That big red thing? It's like this one, isn't it? Only bigger.' He was screaming at Marlowe now and waving a piece of white cloth frantically.

As the galliass came alongside, it nudged the little fishing boat amidships and both its owner and Marlowe were sent sprawling in the bilge water sloshing around in the keel. When they got to their feet again, a dozen arquebuses were trained on them.

The fisherman scrambled upright then dropped to his knees. 'He made me do it, sir,' he gabbled in a northern dialect Marlowe couldn't follow. 'This mad Englishman. I wouldn't have sailed out of my own accord, not in your waters. Not today.'

The man at the helm of the pirate looked at Marlowe, an odd expression on his face. Then he nodded at someone to his left and a metal pot hissed through the air as the grappling irons held the fishing boat fast. It caught Marlowe a nice one on the side of the head and he dropped to the deck like a stone.

Even when his eyes opened, Kit Marlowe's world was rocking. He was on a hard wooden bed, shackles at his wrists. His sword, dagger and doublet had gone and something was shining in his vision. At first he couldn't make it out. It was like a star, bright in the firmament, a jewel against a field of dark velvet. Then, when he could focus, he realized it was a silver crescent with a cruel, smiling face in the curve. And around the rim ran the legend 'en Despit de La Mes'.

'It means "despite the Mass",' a voice told him in broken English. 'It's a sort of . . . letter of introduction, I suppose you'd say.'

'Introduction to what?' Marlowe asked, keeping to English to see how far the holder of the talisman could follow him. The man holding the crescent on the point of Marlowe's dagger had been at the bow of the galliass . . . how long before?

'The beggars of the sea.' The man half bowed, smiling. 'I am Adam van Haren, by the way.' And he held out a hand.

Marlowe rattled his chains to remind the pirate that he was hardly in a position to reciprocate.

'I am sorry about those,' Van Haren chuckled. 'These days, you can't be too careful.'

'Nice doublet,' Marlowe murmured, recognizing the good Flemish leather that used to be his.

'Well, that's why I had you hit with that pot,' van Haren explained. 'I could have shot you but I didn't want to risk damaging the leather. Apart from the hole, blood is such a difficult stain to get out. Where did you get it?' Without taking his eyes of Marlowe, he stroked the doublet appreciatively. 'It is the very best quality, and I think you can probably tell that I am a man who can tell a good thing when he sees it.'

'Clearly you are a man of taste and discernment,' Marlowe said, bitterly. 'I got it from the Statholder, the Prince of Nassau.'

There was a silence, then van Haren roared with laughter. 'Oh, that's good,' he said, slipping the crescent into a purse on his hip. 'That's very good.' He suddenly frowned and peered more closely at his prisoner. 'You know,' he said quietly, 'I've been here for quite a while, looking at you.'

'Oh?' Marlowe raised an eyebrow. He'd heard much of the sea beggars during his time in this country, but nothing like that.

'Your name wouldn't be Arthur, would it, by any chance?'

'Not by any chance,' said Marlowe; then, 'Do you mean surname or God-given name?'

The Dutchman's eyelid flickered for a moment while he translated in his head. 'Surname,' he said.

'No,' said the prisoner. 'My name is Marlowe.'

'Ah,' said the captain of the sea beggars, looking disappointed.

'But my mother was an Arthur,' Marlowe went on. 'From Dover.'

'I knew it!' van Haren thumped his knee in his enthusiasm. 'Katherine, yes?'

Marlowe nodded.

'Lovely girl. You've got her eyes and mouth.'

'Have I?' said Marlowe. 'I'd better give them back.'

'Give them . . .' and van Haren guffawed again. 'Ah, your English sense of humour, yes? Very good, very good. What have you to do with the Statholder?'

'That's my business,' Marlowe told him. 'What had you to do with my mother?'

Van Haren paused, a smile playing around his lips. 'It was all a long time ago,' he said softly, 'and perhaps there are some things a young man should not know about his mother. How old are you, Master Marlowe?'

'I am twenty,' Marlowe said.

Van Haren seemed to be doing a little mental arithmetic. 'Does your mother live?' he asked, suddenly serious.

'She does,' Marlowe said.

'Good.' The sea beggar smiled. 'I am happy. So –' he stood up and began to prowl the cramped space under his own deck – 'William the Silent?'

'My mother,' Marlowe continued.

Van Haren paused and looked at him. 'A long time ago, I came to Dover,' he said. 'You know, we sea beggars have a base there?'

'I didn't know,' Marlowe admitted.

'An arrangement with your Queen Elizabeth,' the pirate said. 'I don't understand politics.'

'No,' Marlowe said, 'but you do understand robbery on the Queen's seas.'

'The Statholder's seas!' The sea beggar was suddenly, defiantly Dutch.

It was Marlowe's turn to pause. 'I believe we are both deluding ourselves, Captain van Haren,' he said. 'They are actually Philip of Spain's seas.'

Van Haren spat on to the timbers at his feet. 'Spaniards,' he snarled.

'You don't object to wearing their armour,' Marlowe observed. 'Up on deck . . .'

'Let's just say the gentleman who owned it no longer had need of it.' Van Haren smiled. 'Not after . . . Well, these things happen in war.'

'My mother,' Marlowe said, trying to keep his voice level.

'A fling,' the captain said dismissively. 'Oh, there was a time. Your mother . . . those eyes, those lips, those breasts . . .' He caught the look on Marlowe's face and changed tack. 'She had a lovely personality. I like to think there was something between us. Some spark. I think she shed a tear when I left.'

'You left her?' Marlowe wanted to know.

The pirate muttered something in Dutch as if tasting the words. 'No, not put like that. It sounds different in my language. We were both very young, with our lives before us. Tell me, er . . . your father?'

'A tanner and bootmaker,' Marlowe told him.

Van Haren shook his head sadly. Katherine Arthur could so easily have been a sea beggar's wife instead. Or at least, a sea beggar's wife in Dover – there were many other ports in the world, after all.

'They are very happy,' Marlowe said.

'I'm glad,' said his captor after a while. 'Now, the Statholder.'

And Marlowe told the man who could have been his father the story of a little part of his life.

The proctors, Lomas and Darryl, stood at each side of the gateway to Corpus Christi as the Buttery bell sounded for luncheon. Their hands were clasped in front of them and their faces were grim as they counted the scholars hurtling in from various errands in the town. They checked their passes one by one, familiar with forgeries as they were. They could recognize a fake Lyler or a fraudulent Harvey at twenty paces and it took an ingenious scholar indeed to get one over on them. It would take someone of the mettle of Kit Marlowe and Kit Marlowe was a graduate now, infuriatingly beyond their grasp.

Many was the time the roisterer had slipped in through St Bene't's sleeping churchyard or rung the fire bell or used the old ghost of Corpus ploy; though they'd die rather than admit it, he got them every time.

They were just about to call it a day and grab their own midday fare when a lady and her servant swept along the cobbles of Trumpington Street towards them. Females in the colleges were a rarity and this one was beautiful, with a cloak and hood of rich burgundy and a French cap crowning her high forehead.

Lomas, as the senior man, held up his hand. 'Good afternoon, madam,' he said. 'May I help you?'

She looked him up and down. He was an oaf of a man, thickset and bull-necked. His colleague looked like a weasel.

But they both wore the pelican and lily badges of the college, so she knew she had to deal with them. 'Is this Corpus Christi?' she asked.

'It is, madam,' Lomas told her. 'Do you have business here?'

'Proctor Lomas.' Professor Johns was suddenly at the man's elbow and Lomas doffed his cap. 'I think you can leave this to me.' He smiled, removed his cap and turned to the lady. 'Madam.' He bowed. 'I am Michael Johns, Professor of Rhetoric at this college. May I be of assistance?'

'I am Catherine Shelley.' She curtsied to him. 'I was looking for . . .'

Johns held a finger to his lips. 'Lomas,' he said, 'Mistress Shelley and I will be in the library. Madam, will you take some luncheon?'

'That is very kind, sir,' she said. 'My man . . .' She indicated the silent servant behind her.

'. . . is welcome to join us,' Johns said. 'Luncheon for three, Lomas. My Buttery account will cover it. Will you take some college wine, madam? I fear it will not be what you are used to.'

'I have become used to Yorkshire ale, sir, in recent weeks. Thank you.'

Johns led the way from Golden Gate across the court with its Cherry Hinton chalk and its solid buttresses towards the front door. On the apex of the roof overhead, the little stone dog of the Talbots watched the trio go, the scholar in his grey, the lady in her crimson and the servant carrying a large square something, wrapped in sacking.

As Johns had guessed, the library was empty at this time of day, everybody tucking in to the best the most expensive Buttery in Cambridge could offer. Catherine Shelley wandered the panelled hall with its gilded ceiling and its leather-bound volumes, before she gasped at the large volume open on the lectern.

'What is this?' she asked.

'A *mappa mundi*, madam,' Johns told her. 'A map of the world. We are –' He pointed to a pinprick near the centre – 'here. Though I fear, this map is a little out of date. Masters

Drake, Hawkins and Frobisher have changed the world rather
since this map was made.'

She looked at him. 'And where in the world is Christopher
Marlowe?' she asked.

Johns glanced at the servant.

'Richard has my full confidence,' she said. 'I was about to
mention Master Marlowe's name at the gate, but you stopped
me. Why was that?'

Johns walked her to a padded seat by the window and the
servant, gratefully, put his parcel on its edge on the floor and
rested it against his knees. 'May I ask your business with
Dominus Marlowe?'

'That is between us, sir,' she said, frostily.

Johns took in the woman's dress, her clear eyes, the sweep
of her hair under the lace. She was in half-mourning. That
meant that she had recently lost a loved one. An educated
man, he took an educated guess. 'Accept my condolences at
your loss, Mistress Shelley,' he said, sitting opposite her. 'Your
husband?'

Her eyelids flickered. 'The intelligences will have reached
you by now,' she said. 'You will know that my husband suffered
a traitor's death at the hands of the headsman. Not two months
since. On Tower Hill.'

'Madam,' Johns said. 'Look about you. Over there is a copy
of the Anglo-Saxon Chronicle. Behind that partition is St
Augustine's Gospel Book. It is the one the saint brought to
England in the year of Our Lord 597. It may well be the oldest
and the most important book in England. This is my world. I
know nothing of what happens beyond these walls.'

'You knew I had come to see Master Marlowe,' she said,
'before I had spoken his name. Can you read women's minds,
Professor Johns?'

The scholar laughed. Women were as much of a mystery
to him as the planets that, some men said, revolved around
the sun. 'No mind-reading, I assure you. Just our little
Cambridge winds. One of them lifted a corner of your servant's sacking. He is carrying a portrait. And it is of Christopher
Marlowe, to the life. The good proctors didn't see it because
they have between them the intelligence of this chair. Almost.

Suffice it to say there are reasons to whisper the name of Marlowe in this university.'

'And in Sussex,' she added.

'May I see?' Johns asked.

Catherine nodded to the servant, who untied the cord that held the sacking and let it fall. He turned the framed canvas so that the subject faced them all. Kit Marlowe in paint half-smiled at them, his arms folded, his hair swept back from his face. Incised gilt buttons glittered on his slashed doublet and his double collar was edged white.

They looked at it for a long moment. There was something about the glint in the eye and the expression on the face that made Johns feel it was about to speak to him. There was an air of a breath just taken, in readiness.

'I'm not sure that the mouth is right,' Catherine said. 'And I know I've made the chin too weak.'

'*You* painted this, Mistress Shelley?' Johns was impressed.

'No,' she said, half laughing. 'My uncle George. George Gower. He worked from sketches I made.'

'In Sussex?'

'Is Kit here?' she asked in answer to him.

'No,' he told her. 'In truth, madam, I have no idea where he is.'

'I promised him this,' she said. 'I told him that I would have a likeness made of him.'

'I'm sure he will be suitably flattered,' Johns said. Then he pointed to the top corner of the portrait. 'This motto, here . . . ?'

'It means that which feeds me destroys me.' She blushed and looked down, remembering where she was. 'I'm sorry. You know that already, of course. I didn't mean to imply . . .'

Johns laughed. 'Yes, you're right. I learned Latin almost before I learned English. No,' he said, 'I mean why is it written there?'

'It was something I found,' she said, 'shortly after I left Sussex. It was written in the margin of a poem. A poem written by Kit. A poem addressed to me.'

'I had no idea that Kit was in Sussex,' Johns said.

'Neither did a lot of Catholic traitors.' Her voice was

suddenly harsh, different, cold. 'Do you really know nothing of politics, Professor Johns?'

'It is sometimes safer in these troubled times,' he said, 'to know nothing of politics. I prefer the safer way.'

She nodded, looking at Marlowe's portrait. 'My husband hired Kit as a tutor for our daughters. He told them stories too and sang to them. But he was really an intelligencer, an agent for Sir Francis Walsingham.'

'Kit? The Queen's spymaster?' Johns mouthed.

Catherine smiled. 'So you do know something of politics?' she said.

'This is Cambridge, Mistress Shelley,' Johns reminded her, 'not the far side of the moon. Let me see if I understand this? Kit Marlowe worked in your household in order to entrap your husband?'

She nodded. 'Who was in league with Francis Throckmorton, the Spanish ambassador, the Queen of Scots and God knows who else. Their purpose was to overthrow Elizabeth and place the Scots woman on the throne. Treason and sacrilege.'

'But . . . your husband . . .' Johns was at a loss.

'Was living a lie, Professor,' she said. 'All our life together, I had no idea. While I attended the Anglican Church and took the sacrament, he was taking the Mass, in Latin, usually in Lord Howard's private chapel in Arundel Castle. He was plotting with renegades and fanatics and murderers . . .' She caught the look on his face and stopped. 'Understand this, Professor Johns,' she said. 'Like you, I don't care a fig for politics, whose prayer book we use, who sits on the throne. But what I do care for is my family – my girls – and, once upon a time, my husband. He lied to me, lied to us all and put my girls in terrible danger. Kit Marlowe did not betray him, he saved us. We are safe in Yorkshire now, because of him.'

There was a silence, then she stood up. 'Professor, I thank you for your offer of luncheon, but Richard and I must be away. If ever Kit Marlowe returns to Cambridge, you will see that he gets this, won't you?'

'Of course.' He stood up with her and bowed to kiss her hand before seeing them both out.

At the gate she stopped and looked at Johns. 'Tell Kit I'll always remember him,' she said, 'and especially the last lines of the sonnet he wrote. "And this I leave you; this, a single thought – A love; a fond old age; a silent court." I know what that means now.'

The watery sun was filtering through the clouds as Kit Marlowe stepped ashore on the flat beaches of Norfolk. The sea beggars didn't usually bother with fishing boats, but they'd lost the *Antelope* in the fog and van Haren's men were determined to have *something* for their trouble. And van Haren, for all his rough, light-fingered ways had a great respect for the Statholder. He'd willingly signed the Articles of War at William's insistence and even, in accordance with that, had a minister on board his ship (at least he would once he'd sprung the man from gaol in Altmark) and he allowed, still in accordance with that, no one on board his ship except those of good fame and good name – which is why he'd taken Marlowe on board in the first place.

Van Haren was happy to take Marlowe to England, but not exactly into the port of King's Lynn, for obvious reasons. The Queen's writ extended to Dover but nowhere else and van Haren was not a man to take too many chances. The prospect of years in an English prison had almost no appeal for him whatsoever.

On the beach, the North Sea rippling around his boots and wearing the doublet van Haren had graciously returned to him 'for old time's sake', Marlowe took his leave of the beggars of the sea. He handed his former gaoler a purse of coin which van Haren had handed back to him only minutes earlier.

'That's for the journey.' He smiled.

Van Haren smiled too but he wasn't ready for what happened next. Marlowe's right arm swung back and his fist crashed into the Dutchman's mouth. He sprawled on to the wet sand, a large gap where his front teeth used to be.

'And that's for bedding my mother.' Marlowe smiled again, turning away. 'Look after yourself, sea beggar.'

'I knew you weren't mine!' van Haren called after him,

trying to cope without his teeth. 'Any son of mine would have ducked before the pot struck home.'

'Well, I'm looking for Master Dee, too!' Gregory Leslie was not best pleased with the young idiot who had come galloping through his knot garden that morning, spraying plants and clods of earth in all directions.

'Who are you, sir?' the young idiot asked him.

Leslie turned a vicious shade of purple and toyed for a moment with dashing to find his sword. But scurrying away at one's own front door rather than answer a simple question from a whippersnapper dressed as a Dutchman, albeit rather a salt-stained one, seemed rather beneath his dignity.

'I *own* this house, sir.' He spat as his womenfolk and a clutch of servants looked on. 'My grandfather built it and I shall probably die in it. That is if Master Dee has left one stone safely upon another. What do you want him for?'

'That's my business.' Marlowe caught up the reins again. It was clear that Leslie was not hiding the man anywhere.

'Who did you say you were, again?' Leslie demanded.

'Christopher Marlowe.' And when that achieved no response at all, he leaned forward in the saddle. 'I work for Sir Francis Walsingham.'

Leslie paused, but he would not be rattled by a whipper-snapper on his own doorstep. It had been his father's stance at times of trouble and it would be good enough for him and for his sons. Things didn't change fast in the world of Gregory Leslie. 'So, you work for Sir Francis, do you?' The use of the more familiar title should have made the youth blench. Youths used to blench in Gregory Leslie's young days; what was the world coming to? But there wasn't the slightest sign that he was at all discomfited. 'Do you work for Dee too?'

'No,' Marlowe said. 'I work *with* him.'

'In that case,' Leslie drew himself up to his full height, 'I shall send my bill to Walsingham. Do you *know* what Dee has done to my Great Hall? Rings of fire damage all over my three-hundred-year-old table. Two tapestries burned beyond repair. And all manner of stuffed creatures hidden all over the house are still giving my wife the vapours. She may never recover.'

'Do you know where Dr Dee went?' Marlowe had to ask.

'If I knew that I'd have sent my bailiffs after him. The man, apart from everything else, owes me three months' rent. Bailiffs?' He had just realized what he had said. 'Damn it, sir, I'd send my hounds!' And he turned and marched indoors, his family and servants clucking around him.

Marlowe took the reins more firmly in his hands. Then he noticed a servant in Leslie's livery hovering by the hedgerow that led to the stables. The man was winking at him, beckoning him as subtly as he could. He turned the bay into the shadow of the east wing and leaned low in the saddle.

'I know where's gone, sir,' the man hissed.

'Where?' Marlowe asked.

The footman dithered, hopping from foot to foot with the cold and the hope of his time not being wasted. Marlowe threw him a groat from his purse. For all van Haren had returned it to him intact, it was considerably emptier than when he had left Cambridge.

'He was going back to his Alma Mater, sir.' The man nodded wisely. 'Perhaps you know where Master Dee's mother lives, sir, but I can't help you any further, because I don't. I was just surprised to hear the old besom was still alive, but there you are . . .'

Marlowe snatched at the snaffle and the bay wheeled round.

'There's been another man here today,' the servant said, still hissing in case his master heard. Marlowe reined in.

'Who?' he asked.

'An Egyptian,' the servant said. 'One of them as was here while Master Dee was here. You was here as well, sir.'

Leslie had not left his staff to run the house in his absence. Dee would not pay the going rate plus a perfectly reasonable fifty per cent for out of pocket expenses and other considerations, so he had housed them in the lodge and halved their wages. They were now having to pay the price of having allowed Dee to play havoc inside a house they were no longer living in. Leslie was a hard master and a hard man. The footman was only sorry that his information was not to his master's detriment; he had heard that the country was lousy with spies anxious to find out all they could about nobs who were no better than they should be. But never mind, he would know a spy when he saw one, and then old skinflint Leslie had better watch out.

'Yes, I was,' Marlowe said. 'So tell me, man, which one of the others was here? Who was it?' He was leaning down so far that he was eyeball to eyeball with the man. 'Who?'

'I dunno their names, sir,' the man said. ''Cept Lily. I learned her name all right. Got lovely healing hands, ain't she, that Lily?'

'Indeed she has.' Marlowe nodded. The man's information had been helpful, but how he could not tell the difference between the men of the Egyptian band, Marlowe could not imagine. Balthasar with his crop of blond curls was as different from the saturnine Frederico as it was possible to be. And, taking the eldest to the youngest, there must be forty years between them. But, forewarned was forearmed, even if he didn't know who the warning was about and he spurred away into the morning.

FOURTEEN

He took the road south across the fens that marked the Bedford Level, his cloak flying out behind him and his face low over the bay's neck. The animal was not as fast as the Wasp, left behind in Delft, but she was steadier and by cock-shut time Kit Marlowe was clattering over Magdalene Bridge past the twinkling lights of the colleges and the skiffs bobbing on the river.

Leslie's man had told Marlowe where John Dee had gone. And he was under no illusion that he would not have also told the Egyptian. Any man's coin was the same as far as the footman was concerned. Marlowe's only hope was that the Egyptian would not know Cambridge like he did. Despite the tides in the North Sea, despite the false start with the sea beggars, despite the Mass, he might yet make it in time.

He clattered into the gateway of St John's College where the Yales of Beaufort battled for the king's shield in the gilded stone over the arch.

'Whoa!' A startled Proctor Boddington scuttled out of his lodge door and grabbed his bridle. 'What brings you so late to college, sir?'

'Dr Dee . . .' Marlowe was as out of breath as his horse. 'Where is he?'

'Who's asking?' Boddington refused to be impressed by good horses and flashy clothes. This was St John's College, the finest place of learning in all the fens and probably beyond.

'Christopher Marlowe,' the rider told him, springing out of the saddle.

The proctor was even less impressed now that the man stood at his eye level. 'Christopher Marlowe of Corpus Christi?' Boddington's words dripped with contempt.

'The same.' Marlowe nodded.

'The one they call Machiavel?' Boddington said slowly, images of Hell creeping into his mind.

'It doesn't matter what they call me, Master Proctor,' Marlowe said. 'Now, do I have to smash down every door in your God-forsaken college to find Dr Dee or are you going to tell me?'

'Kit?' a voice made him turn.

It was Robert Greene, swallowing carefully because Kit Marlowe's dagger point was already poking a new hole in his ruff.

'Er . . . hello, Kit. What a surprise.' Greene managed with his head seriously at an angle.

'Still writing bad poetry, Robyn?' Marlowe asked.

'Well, we try, you know. Do I understand that you're looking for Dr Dee?'

'Robyn.' Marlowe shipped the dagger away. 'You and I both know that you've been listening to this conversation ever since I arrived, so let's drop the all-innocence bit, shall we? What do you know?'

Robert Greene knew – or thought he did – that Kit Marlowe had sold his soul to the Devil and he knew a good deal more besides, but he realized that that was not what Marlowe meant.

'You're looking for the Queen's magus?' he checked.

Marlowe nodded. 'And unless you want his blood on your conscience and Master Topcliffe's rack under your arse cheeks, I suggest you tell me where I can find him.'

'Topcliffe?' Boddington repeated. He didn't get out much.

'The Queen's rackmaster,' Greene explained. 'Well, if you must know, he's in the rooms that should rightfully be mine. Off the court, in the north-west corner. You can't miss it – there'll be goose shit on the staircase. Dr Dee has brought his own Christmas dinner with him.'

'Dominus Greene . . .' The proctor was outraged at betrayal on this scale.

'Go hang yourself, Master Proctor,' Greene snapped and ran off into the Cambridge night to find Gabriel Harvey.

Two or three sizars were crossing the Court behind a college professor, struggling under the weight of his books. There were candles burning at some windows as Marlowe reached the far corner. A solitary torch guttered on the turn of the stairs and he trod as soundlessly as a cat until he reached the landing.

If Dee had brought a goose, he had also brought his cook and that meant Sam Bowes too. Three rooms – two at a pinch. Unless, of course, Dee had insisted on one for the goose. He paused by the first door and pressed his ear to the black and knotted oak. Nothing. Nothing either from the second. But at the third, he heard voices – or was it one? – muffled and secret, gabbling fast and low.

The next thing he knew his head was yanked backwards by the hair and rammed forward so that the bruise raised by van Haren's man's thrown pot was purpled again and he was kicked forward into the room. When he scrabbled to his feet, the door had been slammed shut and he found himself staring down the bores of two wheel-lock pistols, wound and ready, one in each of the hands of Hern, the lord of the Egyptians, father of the children of the moon.

'You will unhook your pickle stabber, Master Marlowe.' Hern indicated the rapier. Marlowe looked across at John Dee. The man was crouching near the bed, already in his night cap and he had quill and parchment in his hand.

'Good evening, Christopher,' he said quietly.

'Dr Dee.' Marlowe nodded.

'Now!' Hern snapped and Marlowe unhooked the sword from its hanger and threw it on the bed.

'And now the dagger,' Hern said.

Marlowe held out both arms and shrugged.

'Don't play games with me, *Christopher*,' Hern snarled. 'I've forgotten more than you'll ever know. And I've known all about you since I looked at your papers from Sir Francis Walsingham. I should have disposed of you much earlier. But the women liked you and you kept the children amused, so I let you live. But now, with your left hand and slowly.' He raised his own left hand. 'Do it, or the first ball goes through Dee's left eye. And I'm no Jean Jaureguy; I won't miss.'

Marlowe reached round behind him, his right hand still in the air. He caught the hilt and just for a moment toyed with sending the blade hissing through the air, as he had back in Delft what seemed like an eternity ago. But now was not the time to test which was faster – the pistol ball or the steel; not with John Dee's life in the balance. He threw it, sheath and all, to join the sword on the bed.

'Where is she?' Hern asked.

'Who?' asked Dee.

'More games, magus?' Hern chuckled. 'After tonight, the Queen will be looking for a new fortune teller. Strange, isn't it? Your skills and those of my people are so alike, yet you are fêted and lauded wherever you go, sitting at the Queen's right hand and whispering in her ear. While the children of the moon are shunned and spat at and hounded out of the civilization of men. Now –' he held the pistol level again – 'for the last time, Dr Dee, where is your wife?'

Dee blinked, then frowned, then looked at Marlowe. Had this mad Egyptian come back from God-knew-where to pose imponderables; to debate philosophy? And what did Hern expect to hear? That Helene was with the angels, or wandering in purgatory or stoking the fires of Hell? And why should it matter to him?

'You see,' Hern went on, 'Master Marlowe here tells me you can raise the dead. All I saw at Ely was smoke and mirrors, the sort of gimcrackery my people do at fairs up and down any country you'd like to name.'

'But you couldn't risk it, could you?' Marlowe asked him. 'Just in case my story was right and Dr Dee does indeed have powers . . .'

'Powers!' Hern spat on to the straw-strewn boards at his feet. 'A pox on those. You are a bigger fraud than any of us,' he growled at Dee. 'You on the other hand –' he pointed his other pistol at Marlowe's head – 'can indeed turn a tale. Your death will deprive the world of that and I am truly sorry to be the instrument of such a loss. The world needs stories, Master Marlowe.'

'I thought you didn't believe in Dee's powers,' Marlowe said.

'Oh, I don't,' Hern assured them both. 'But my own are limited too. What if Dr Dee didn't have to bring his wife back from the dead because she wasn't dead? Because my poison hadn't worked? People have woken up from worse sleeps than hers; look at the Statholder, for example. Lily roused him and all had thought him dead to all intents and purposes. So . . . it might have been so with Helene. So, I came back to finish the job.'

'Why?' Dee croaked. 'Why did you have to kill my Helene, the reason for my existence, half of my soul . . . ?'

'Spare us the platitudes, old man,' Hern sneered. 'The reason for my existence is this.' He used his elbow to jingle the coins in his purse. 'We children of the moon put our heads in a noose every day of our lives because of your narrow laws and Puritan small-mindedness. All that makes it worth the risk is cold cash – the only God I need.'

'I still don't see . . .' Marlowe began.

'Helene Dee may have been this old fool's reason for living, but she was actually a nosy busybody. I caught her listening at the foot of her stairs to our casual chat. She overheard a secret Mass being planned by that religious maniac Simon. She had identified him from the first; she was looking at him all night. She had the look of a hedge witch, I knew it from the start and when Rose told Balthasar she knew her in her old life, I knew for certain. She had a lot to lose. She'd have told you, Dee. And you would have told the world, if only so that no one could accuse you of being a secret Catholic yourself. I make my living secreting Catholic priests around this country and the Church pays me well for it. I wasn't going to have all that jeopardized by a careless word. Helene Dee isn't the first I've had to silence and I doubt she'll be the last. Rose, for example, will probably end her days shivering with gaol fever in some stinking cell.'

'Is that it?' Dee blinked in disbelief. 'You would snuff out a life to save your purse?'

'Life is cheap, Dr Dee,' Hern reminded him. 'But a good paying proposition – how many of those come along in the average lifetime? Not many, I can tell you. I have had too many years of starvation and privation to want to have them again. A well-lined purse can keep you very warm at night.'

'What about Maria?' Marlowe asked. 'She is having your child any day now. I was sure when you ran that it was any one of the Egyptians but you. You seemed to love her. I couldn't believe you would go.'

Hern shrugged. 'What's love got to do with it?' he asked. 'Maria and I have been together a long time. She has borne me a lot of children, some dead because of the lean years, some left us, some still with the troupe. She will understand.'

Marlowe, remembering the woman, struggling with her aching back, wondering what this last child bed might bring, wasn't so sure.

Hern levelled the wheel lock at Dee and took aim. 'I really don't give so much as a flying fart for anyone but myself, please believe this. I will kill anyone who gets in my way. The nights are too cold as my bones get older, Master Marlowe, and if you have no wish to find out how old bones feel, then please, step in front of me and we will see how a young man dies.'

Dee looked up at Marlowe. 'Christopher,' he said. 'My life is a burden to me without Helene. Let him kill me. He can't kill us both at one moment. Use my death to get away. Find the proctor. Get the constables. Don't let Helene be unavenged.'

'She needs no avenging, Dee,' Hern snapped. 'I know she lives yet. For the last time, Doctor – *where is your wife?*'

'Behind you!' Marlowe hissed.

It was the oldest trick in the book, but Hern didn't know the Cambridge winds on college stairways and Marlowe did. The creak of the timbers made Hern turn, just for a second and Marlowe threw himself forward. A wheel lock crashed in the half darkness and Dee's desk and Dee's candles went flying. Two men struggled on the floor, wrestling desperately for the remaining gun with its single shot. Each time the muzzle moved in the grappling hands, Dee threw himself sideways, first left, then right. Then the muzzle disappeared as Marlowe forced Hern's fist down to his chest. Locked together as they were, the explosion made them both jump and lie still.

Blood trickled out from the lifeless figure and crept over the straw.

Professor Michael Johns looked at his reflection in his window pane. In the glass it looked for all the world as though Kit

Marlowe was at his shoulder, his portrait misty in the shadows across the room. He had hung the picture up to keep it safe, or so the story would go should anyone ask him, but it was already both a comfort and an irritant to his soul. The chapel bell at Corpus Christi was tolling the faithful and the not-so-faithful to prayer, but he wouldn't be going to the morning service today. And probably no other day. Not in this chapel. He checked the leather on the beautiful volume of Bale's Acts of the English Votaries. Michael Johns didn't approve of bribes, although he acknowledged that they were how the world turned. He was due that morning to explain to Dr Norgate why he had not mentioned the sudden disappearance of Kit Marlowe, Quartus Convictus of Corpus Christi College in the University of Cambridge. So either Bale's hideously expensive book would buy Johns a second chance to keep the post he loved or it would be a magnanimous farewell present for the Master. He hefted the thick volume up under his arm a little more securely as he reached for the rail of the stairs with his other hand.

The feel of the worn wood under his palm, the touch of the stair under his foot, the smell of the cool stone, the leather book, the paper, the humanity; the slow peal of the bell, the sound of the scurrying feet of the scholars, the whisper of their fustian gowns; the sudden shaft of thin sunlight through a small and dusty window of the stairs, the dead fly caught in a cobweb which had been there, unreachable high up in the rafters since he had been a scholar himself – all of this moved him so much suddenly that tears smeared his eyes and he could hardly go on. To lose all this, even the dead fly, would surely break his heart.

He shook his head to clear away the tears. 'Kit, Kit, Kit,' he muttered, and continued up the stairs.

'What did you say your name was again?' Dr Norgate peered over his spectacles at the sorry-looking huddle in front of him.

'Kelly,' the man said. 'Edward Kelly. Personal friend and private secretary to Dr John Dee, late of this college and the Queen's magus.'

Norgate frowned and swept off his glasses. 'I have no doubt

that Dr Dee is the Queen's magus,' he said. 'But he is not, not has he ever been, to my knowledge, a member of this college.'

Kelly blinked. Since Ely and the disastrous night when Helene Dee died, he had been living on his wits. Nothing amiss there – it was what the man had done all his life – but Edward Kelly was staring forty in the face and perhaps, just perhaps, his old touch wasn't quite what it was. He'd been run out of Ely by the Constable and his dogs. He had been set upon by angry fishermen at King's Lynn who had accused him of cheating at cards. *Him*. Edward Kelly. Personal and private secretary to the Queen's magus. Just because a man had clipped ears, it didn't mean he was a bad person, but for some reason everyone seemed to think that he was some sort of confidence trickster. What ever had happened to Christian charity? That's what he wanted to know.

'Are you trying to tell me that John Dee lied to me? That he was never a member of St John's College?' Kelly was outraged. He hated it when people lied to him.

'No, indeed I am not,' Norgate said, winding his spectacles over his ears again with the intention of continuing his inter-rupted studies. 'I believe that Dr Dee is a very well-respected member of that institution.'

Kelly thought for a moment. What was the man saying? Then he worked it out. 'Tell me the truth, you old fool!' Kelly snapped at the man sitting in front of him, so smug in his gold tassels, surrounded by his parchment and his inkwells. 'Is this or is this not St John's College?'

'Heaven forfend!' Norgate mouthed, deeply affronted. In the good old days, he would have crossed himself, but the world had turned.

Kelly's knife was suddenly in his hand and he grabbed the Master by his ruff, hauling him upright. 'Tell me the truth, you lying old shit!'

It was the last thing he said for a while, because a large leather-bound volume of Bale's Acts of the English Votaries knocked him into the middle of next week. The book had Professor Michael Johns on the other end of it.

'Are you all right, Master?' he asked Norgate, stepping over Kelly's recumbent form.

'I believe I am.' Norgate had turned several shades greyer in the past minutes and had aged by several centuries. 'Thanks to you, Michael.' He suddenly smiled and gripped Johns with both hands. 'You've saved my life.'

'Oh, I doubt that, Master,' Johns said. 'Who is this?' He knelt by the fallen man.

'Er . . . I can't quite remember,' Norgate said. 'I didn't catch the name, I'm afraid. He did have a tendency to mumble, as so many people do nowadays. But I believe he said he was looking for Dr John Dee, of St John's. Wandering lunatic, I expect.'

Michael Johns wasn't quite sure to whom the Master was referring, but chose to believe it was the man now groaning slightly on the floor. 'He's a convicted felon, I can tell that much at least,' he said. 'Look – clipped ears.'

'Oh, yes.' Norgate peered closer with some distaste. 'I thought perhaps he'd been out in the cold; frostbite, perhaps. Something of that nature.' He shook his head. 'I really should try to get out more.'

Johns stood up, having removed Kelly's knife for health and safety reasons. 'About the other matter, Master,' he said.

'Other matter?' Norgate blinked.

'Christopher Marlowe,' Johns reminded him.

Norgate frowned, then he smiled and clapped an arm around his protégé's shoulder. 'My dear fellow,' he said softly. 'I think we can let those particular sleeping dogs lie, can't we? In light of my gratitude . . .' And he nodded at Kelly, who had stopped groaning, but was breathing loudly and jumping slightly in his book-induced sleep.

Johns smiled and picked up the book that had felled him and handed it to Norgate. 'For you, Master,' he said. 'For your collection.'

'Bale!' Norgate read the spine. 'A particularly useful volume, eh, Michael? Thank you very much. I shall treasure it. Especially this dent in the back board.' He smiled at the professor. 'Yes, thank you very much.'

They were standing in silent companionship when the door

of the study suddenly crashed back and Gabriel Harvey stood there, fuming as usual, his gown still billowing from the speed at which he had taken the stairs. He checked himself as he noticed Kelly sprawled on the Master's carpet, where he had hoped, metaphorically, to find Johns.

'Sorry, Master,' he said. 'Is this a bad time? I just thought you ought to know about Christopher Marlowe . . .'

'I know about Morley,' Norgate assured him. 'One of the finest graduates of Corpus Christi. He has been at the College for a while now, Gabriel.' He gave a mirthless smile at Harvey's discomfiture. 'Do try to keep up.'

'But last night, sir.' Gabriel Harvey tried to reason with the senile old fool. 'At St John's. You clearly haven't heard.'

'St John's,' Norgate thundered. 'That's twice this morning I've heard mention of St John's.' He pulled himself up to his full height. 'This is Corpus Christi, sir. And I wish you a good morning.'

Dr John Dee stretched out his hands to the fire, which Sam Bowes had built up with what looked like half the winter store of the whole college. The heat was browning the paper of the book on the floor at the side of Dee's chair and the room smelled pleasantly of warm wool, warm paper, warm people and cooked goose.

On this Christmas Day, Dee had set aside sad thoughts, as far as he ever could, these days. Helene had been a clever present-buyer and he had never had to worry about what to give anyone, from Bowes and the cook to the Queen herself. Helene even bought her own gift from him and was always charmingly astounded and delighted when she opened it on Christmas Day, as though she had never seen it before in her life. The book on the floor had been her gift to him, bought in plenty of time and hidden in her linen press, to be found later by the cook. She and Bowes had spent many anxious huddled minutes trying to decide whether to give it to him, but it had pleased him exceedingly. As neither of them could read, it had been a real gamble, but he had had his nose in it ever since breakfast, breaking off only to eat the goose.

'I can't believe he isn't here with us,' the cook suddenly

said, from the corner of the room, where she was tidying up the remains of the meal.

'Nothing's forever,' Bowes said, gruffly, scratching at the dripping glazed to the pan. 'It's not as if you knew him all that long.'

'You get used to it, though,' the cook said. 'Having him around all the time. I thought . . . well, I thought he would be here today.'

'He's dead,' Bowes said, brutally. Then, seeing the bent back of his master by the fire, tried to change what he had said. 'I . . . I don't mean dead, of course . . . I mean . . .'

Dee turned round. 'Sam,' he said, kindly. 'We can't go the rest of our lives not saying "dead", can we? It will make conversation very difficult, especially in my line of business. Helene will always live while we remember her. And as for you –' he twisted round further to address the cook – 'I seem to remember that you ate more of your lamented friend than Sam and I put together, so please don't waste your tears on him. Did you put some aside for Master Marlowe?'

The door opened and the scholar put his head around it. 'Taking my name in vain, doctor?' he said. 'Is that goose I see? I hope you have saved me some.'

The cook, wreathed in smiles now that nice Master Marlowe was here, pushed a plate across the table. 'They're the crispy bits,' she mouthed to him.

'My favourite.' He smiled at her. 'What's that you're reading?' He reached across and took the book from Dee's hand. '"Even such as by Aurora hath the sky or maids that their betrothed husbands spy, such as a rose mixed with a lily breeds or when the moon travails with charmed steeds; or such, at least long years should turn the die, Arachne stains Assyrian ivory. To these, or some of these like was her colour, by chance her beauty never shined fuller. She viewed the earth; the earth to view beseemed her. She looked sad; sad, comely I esteemed her."' He raised an eyebrow. 'What do you think, doctor? I sometimes think I forced a few lines there, to make it scan.'

'It was a gift from Helene,' he said. 'Bought for me before she . . . died.'

Marlowe raised a crispy bit of goose in the air as a toast. 'Then it is perfect,' he said. 'She had good taste, your wife. May she rest in peace.'

'Amen.'

The new Chamberlain, Willem de Groot, hated disturbing the Statholder at dinner. The children had kissed the royal guest, Rombertus van Uylenburgh, who they knew as Uncle Rom, and had scuttled away with their nurses, babbling over the presents he had bought them. Charlotte had chosen her moment, too, to leave the men to their talk. She was very tired these days and had never really recovered from her nightly vigils as her husband had slept like the dead.

William was pouring more claret for his guest when de Groot bobbed into view.

'Apologies, Highness –' he bowed – 'but the Egyptian Balthasar is at the door. I told him you were dining.'

'Nonsense.' The Statholder dropped his napkin on the table and scraped back his chair. 'One of the company of travellers I told you about, Rom, the ones who saved my life. I think I owe the man a few moments.'

'Of course.' Van Uylenburgh raised a glass to his host.

'Where is he, Willem?'

'By the stairs, Highness; he says he won't keep you waiting.'

The Statholder swept out of the room and saw Balthasar Gerard standing at the foot of the stairs, still in his multicoloured Egyptian rags, bareheaded.

'Balthasar,' William boomed. 'You are well?'

'Very, sir, thank you.' Balthasar bowed.

The Statholder was disappointed to see the man in tatters. He had sent clothes and money to the Egyptians, drip-feeding the gifts over the weeks that had passed since Lily had saved his life. He knew how proud they were, for all their thieving ways and everyone at court had instructions to turn a blind eye to that.

'Are your quarters comfortable?' the Statholder asked.

'Perfectly, Highness,' Balthasar said.

'Tell me –' William walked down the steps towards his man – 'any news of Hern?'

'None.' Balthasar shook his head. 'Any news of Kit Marlowe?'

'Likewise.' The Statholder sighed. 'Odd that, both of them vanishing like will o' the wisps. Now, what can I do for you?'

Balthasar straightened. 'Unfinished business, I'm afraid, Highness. You have been so kind to us all, but I have a greater allegiance to others.'

'Oh?' The Statholder didn't understand.

'His Majesty King Philip of Spain.' Balthasar wrenched a wheel-lock pistol from under his rags, then a second. 'Not to mention –' he fired point blank at the Statholder's chest – 'His Holiness the Pope.' And he squeezed the trigger of the second gun. 'Not to mention God. Not that there's any chance of your meeting Him.'

William the Silent thudded back against the wall with the impact of both bullets. The blood trickled from his doublet, nose and mouth as his eyes glazed and he pitched forward to roll at Balthasar's feet. It was something they argued about in the years ahead, whether it was Rombertus van Uylenburgh or Willem de Groot or the nameless guard on duty in the Hall that night who grabbed Balthasar Gerard first. Perhaps they all did. And certainly they all drove their boots into his body and head before dragging him off to a cell.

Van Uylenburgh turned the Statholder over, cradling the dying man's head, the one still carrying the lead fragment of Jean Jaureguy's attack. William clutched convulsively at his friend's sleeve.

'My God,' he muttered through the coughing and the blood, 'have pity on my soul.' Then he raised himself up on one elbow, trying to focus on the far wall and the desperate, forlorn land that lay beyond it. 'My God, have pity on this poor people. Where's Kit? Where's Kit Marlowe?'

Charlotte reached the head of the stairs. She was already in her nightdress and her braided hair was wild and flying. She saw two holes in the plaster above the steps from which blood trickled to the stone. She saw van Uylenburgh holding half her life in his arms. And from that moment, Charlotte Bourbon-Montpensier began to die too.

The Parker scholars sat around a table at the Brazen George that night. They'd drunk, they'd talked, until long into the spring darkness and the town of Cambridge had fallen silent around them. The stallholders had locked up for the night and Joe Fludd's men wandered the night with their horn lanterns and tipstaffs, keeping a careful eye open for the children of the moon.

Kit Marlowe got up and threw his coins on to the mug-littered surface.

'Are you sure about this, Kit?' Tom Colwell asked. Whatever they had talked about that evening, the conversation kept coming back to it. 'London?'

'That place'll kill you, Kit,' Matthew Parker prophesied.

Marlowe clapped a hand on his friend's shoulder. 'Not if I can help it.' He smiled. 'And if things don't work out on the stage, I can always try to charm old Norgate again. He took me back once; he'll do it again.'

He hugged them both, squeezing them tight and patting their backs, to comfort both himself and them. They had been part of his life for so long and he hoped this was not goodbye. It wasn't as though they had not been in this very situation before, but even so it was an emotional moment and Kit Marlowe's emotions always ran near the surface.

'Look after yourselves, lads,' he managed, and was gone into the Cambridge night to pack his bags and find his horse. The proctors, Darryl and Lomas, had long ago collapsed into their truckle beds and Corpus Christi stood black and silent in the watches of the night. He stood for a moment, savouring the quiet dignity of the place, the only sound the jingle of his horse's bridle and the gentle scrape of a shod hoof on the cobbles.

'Kit.'

He spun round at the whisper of his name, knife blade glinting in the flicker of torchlight on his stair. There was a quiet laugh in the darkness. Then the blackness resolved itself into a man, wrapped in a dark cloak with a hat pulled over his eyes. 'Not lost your touch, I see.' He raised his face to the dim light.

'Nicholas Faunt.' Marlowe relaxed slowly, sheathing the dagger. 'To what do I owe the pleasure?'

'News from Delft,' Faunt said, his face grim, his mouth tight. 'The Statholder is dead.'

Marlowe's jaw dropped a little and his eyes widened. 'How?' he asked.

'Shot twice, through the chest, or so the report goes.'

'You heard this from Minshull?'

'And others,' Faunt told him. 'You never trust just one version of anything in our business.'

'Who?' Marlowe dare not ask, but he had to.

'A Frenchman from Franche-Compté. We don't know what his real name was, but he called himself . . .'

'. . . Balthasar Gerard,' Marlowe finished the sentence for him.

'You know?' Faunt's voice was cold.

'When I told the last of my stories to the Egyptians at William's court, I calculated that a murderer would run. It could have been anyone. My mistake was in thinking that the murderer of Helene Dee was also the murderer – or potential murderer – of the Statholder. I didn't think for a moment that there might be two men with murder in their hearts so close together . . . Do you think either of them knew? I . . .' Marlowe was unable to go on. Words were his lifeline, but they had deserted him.

Faunt raised his gloved hand. 'Don't be too hard on yourself, Kit,' he said. 'You saved the Statholder's life twice. As for the third time? Well, it was not to be. These things happen in our business.'

'To Hell with your business!' Marlowe yelled at him. 'You and Minshull and Walsingham. I'm sick of your business. Don't come to me again, Nicholas. I don't want to know.'

Faunt looked him up and down, noting the cloak, the gloves, the boots. 'You're dressed for the road, Kit,' he said. 'Where are you going?'

Marlowe had half turned to take the stairs, to begin his life all over again. He turned back. 'To London,' he said. 'To see if, indeed, the streets are paved with gold.'

'How will you live?' Faunt asked.

Marlowe smiled and tapped his forehead. 'By this,' he said. 'As always.' And he clattered up the risers.

Faunt turned to the moonless Court. 'Take care, then, Kit Marlowe,' he said, half to himself. He walked out into the spring air and sniffed the breeze. There was always something new for Nicholas Faunt and his kind, and there was a hint of it now, blowing from the south. He looked up to where a candle was glowing in Marlowe's rooms, clearly just a final stub in a chamber stick for him to see his way for one final time. He laughed quietly and turned on his heel. 'Keep in touch, won't you, Kit?'